Counterfeit

by

Lee Carver

ISBN-13: 978-1539041849

ISBN-10: 1539041840

Graphic Designer: Laura Dubroc

Chapter 1

Richard eased his cell phone from his pocket and snapped a photo of the young woman from the back, recording little more than her clothing and height. And her slender frame. She had stood in front of the Vermeer for a good twenty minutes, sometimes taking a step left or right, backward or forward. At times she slipped a small camera out of her jeans to snap a specific area of the canvas, which the Rijks Museum allowed without flash, her attention focused on each element of *The Milkmaid*.

Sure, the painting was beautiful. Exquisite even. But for detail and complexity, it didn't compare with Rembrandt's *The Night Watch*, which covered most of the wall at the end of the gallery. A shifting swarm of museum visitors gaped and photographed that canvas, his personal favorite. Such intricate detail. Such masterful use of shades and focusing.

Maybe he'd finally stumbled upon a lead to the counterfeit art. He could be back on the plane in a few weeks with a feather in his professorial cap. The element of danger in this assignment had intrigued him at first, but he was way out of his element.

The woman sighed and checked her watch.

Richard smoothly moved to a painting on a different wall, turning his back to her and bending his face down to the information plaque at the right. Her steps sounded toward the double glass door. He looked up as she waltzed through the great hall as if she owned the place and was scanning it for decorating ideas about the ball she would give that weekend. Her expression, glimpsed from the side, radiated a calm pleasure. Not what he would expect from a fraud artist.

Effecting a casual but quick walk, he followed just in time to see her descend the stairs rather than take one of the two crowded, slow elevators. He did the same.

Crossing the marble exhibition hall toward the museum's in-house restaurant, she paused before the menu on a stand at the top of a short, open flight of stairs. Instead of presenting herself for seating, she turned, descended, and headed for the exit.

Outside, she flipped her chestnut brown hair in the sun, glided down the front steps to the street, and made for one of the food trailers set up along the park. Sizzling wursts slathered in mustard riding on fresh buns enticed him, but he kept his distance.

Aware that he had no spy craft lessons in how to follow a suspect, Richard hung back and found a bench with a view of his quarry. Maarten had given him a few tips on police investigation as they worked the case together, but that and watching crime shows left him insecure about how to effectively trail a criminal.

The suspect wore the clothes of a youthful tourist—old jeans, the ubiquitous Aeropostale T-shirt, and tennis shoes— which helped her blend into the crowd. She could easily be one of his art history students, but maybe a few years older. He brushed his hands along the pleat of his khaki slacks, thinking that he had dressed a level above the average traveler.

His phone buzzed with a message, Maarten asking if he was on to something. He tapped in a reply: *See the woman getting a wurst at the first stand right now? I'm following her.*

Want me to take a turn? Maarten answered.

Yes. I'll stay out of sight for a while.

Maarten ambled up to the food stand next to the one where she waited in line, bought a paper plate of hot French fries, and found a bench. He proceeded to dip the end of each one in turn into mayonnaise before eating it. How English of him, though a lot of the Dutch had picked up the custom.

Forcing himself to leave the area, Richard walked a block away to a stand-up pizza restaurant. While the slice didn't come up to the flavor of a loaded combination American pizza, it provided stomach fodder and kept him occupied when all he wanted to do was follow the woman.

Distracted, wishing Maarten would message him again, Richard chomped his lunch and washed it down with a cup of iced Coke. After a week of talking to museums and art gallery owners, his only progress had been adjusting to the time difference between Atlanta and Amsterdam.

He checked the photo he'd taken of her and decided on a new course of action, based on the good reception he'd gotten from the museum management.

He returned to the Rijks Museum and waved his pass at the guards, who recognized him by now and gave him a nod to enter. Noting the watchful cameras in every room and passageway, he went behind the busy ticket counter and tapped on the door leading to the security offices.

A bleary-eyed guard, who looked as if he walked a beat at night and stared at monitors all day, opened up. "*Ja?*"

Richard showed him the director's letter of permission to all areas of the museum and received admission. He held up his cell phone photo of the woman. "Recognize her?"

Most of these guys spoke a good bit of English. Certainly more than his budding attempts to speak Dutch. No language should have that many consonants. Richard swept across his phone's screen to another view with just a sliver of her face from the side.

The guard nodded. "She comes here every day. *Every*

day. Alone, not like bus tourists."

"She has a monthly or annual pass?" If she bought a pass, he could get a name. Maybe not her real name and address, but it was a start.

Shrugging, the guard turned to his monitors. "This week, she likes Vermeer. Last week, Rembrandt. Not like other tourists. She waits a long time at paintings."

"Yeah, like nearly a half hour. Do you have any tape that shows her face? I need a good picture. She was staring at *The Milkmaid* this morning." The guard would know the painting by its Dutch name, though. "She left the Seventeenth Century Gallery about forty-five minutes ago."

The man knew his equipment. Before his pizza had settled, Richard was looking at a video of himself watching her. When she turned to leave for lunch, the corner camera caught her full face in a great shot. Richard left with a copy of that sequence, so happy that he tipped the guard and slapped him on the back.

The man's face cracked with a smile as he unlocked the door for Richard's departure. "Glad to help. Anytime."

Richard took the tram from its stop near the museum's front door to the main Amsterdam police station. After being admitted to the building, he climbed the stairs to the desk of his police contact on the next floor.

Jakob got off the phone and greeted him with a warm handshake. "What have you found, my friend? You have good luck already?"

"You're good at reading a person, aren't you?"

"It's convenient in my profession. So tell me."

Richard handed over the jump drive with the woman's face. "I need identification of a woman. Or even who she claims to be. She may have a monthly or annual membership at the Rijks."

"We'll do our best. Does she have a record?"

"What you'll see is all I know. She looks American, dresses like a tourist. I haven't heard her voice. Maarten Alders is following her now, so we may soon know where she's staying."

The director moved around his desk and called to a young female officer. He spoke to her in Dutch, which Richard more or less understood only because he spoke German and knew what was being said.

"Oh, by the way," Richard added with a wave of his hand, "can you put a single photo from that tape segment back on the jump drive when you return it?"

"Sure. I'll ask Andries to do that."

Having called all these resources into play, Richard realized they may be chasing a red herring.

Kendra closed her eyes against the early afternoon sun and savored the salty wurst and fresh, crunchy bread. She'd been so hungry. When she opened them again, the man who followed her out of the museum had risen from the park bench and left the area. Good. Moving about the city alone, day and night, she made it a practice to observe her surroundings and be cautious.

He looked okay—attractive, in fact—but he'd been sticking pretty close to her in the gallery. So maybe they had the same taste in fine art. That would be refreshing, especially if he were straight. She'd met some real dorks in this business. She hadn't looked right at this guy, but his sandy hair was clean and well cut, tousled with curls, and he was lean and tall. Not as lean as the typical runner build. He apparently exercised in some way that developed his chest. She liked that.

She snuffed a chuckle to herself and took another bite. Pathetic to be fantasizing about a stranger in a museum. Should she return to study handiwork of the masters or go back to her room in the old residence and try to duplicate what she'd observed? She could practically smell the oil paints calling to her. Yes, go while daylight still shined. The light in her room was totally inadequate after dark.

Reaching for the water bottle in her denim shoulder pack, she scanned the crowd strolling the food area. She felt uncomfortable somehow. The good-looking guy hadn't returned, yet she still sensed she was being watched.

Not delaying after her last bite, she marched quickly toward the tram and hopped aboard as it clambered to a stop, swiping her transportation pass through the reader. A lot of people crammed in behind her, but she didn't see anyone looking directly at her. Tourists, locals, a couple of women with young children.

Taking line five to the Central Station, she went inside the subway building, downstairs on the escalator, and immediately up again. She found nothing to be worried about in the milling crowd, but her skin crawled with suspicion.

Leaving the subway building, she grabbed line thirteen of the tram to the less expensive area of Amsterdam where she'd found a room. She swung on the hand strap to the stop over two miles inland from the canals and art district. As she descended from the tram, a Dutch-looking man helped a lady get off first with her stroller. No one followed her.

"Good afternoon, Mrs. Graham." She greeted her landlady, who swept around the front door with a sturdy broom. "Your flowers look nice." A bit of fragrant mint and a couple of basil plants had sprung up among them.

"Ah, yes, they're enjoying these summer days. They know this sunny warmth won't last long."

Kendra paused, enjoying a moment with the sturdy woman whose peppered-silver hair glistened in the direct sun. In her simple print dress and leather shoes, she would be taken for Dutch. "Do you ever think of moving back to the US?"

"Not as long as my daughter and grandchildren live here, dear. You'll understand someday."

Kendra thought of how little family she had that she would travel to see, but Mrs. Graham didn't know about that. "Oh, I understand. You have to be near those you love."

After giving the street a final scoping, Kendra headed up the flight of stairs, ready to inspect her canvas with fresh eyes. She unlocked her room, trembling with excitement to return to her work. She dropped her shoulder bag on the single bed and circled the easel to view the canvas, which was still turned toward the window. Her view darted from the milkmaid's shoulder to her face, from the soft light coming in the painting's window to the shadowed background. Not bad. Really. But not Johannes Vermeer. Would she ever find that perfect combination of oil paints and brush strokes?

She shrugged into a painting smock, uncovered her oil palette, and calmed her frustration with a deep breath. Deciding to work on the subject's frock while she had good light, she carefully adjusted the color of the oils for just the right shade of royal blue in the folds of her skirt.

As she lifted her brush, her cell phone's melody indicated she had a message. She paused. Having limited her use of the phone while in Europe, it could be important.

She reached in her bag and found the phone's message from her boss at the Kimbell Museum. Mrs. Odem's request, so surprising that Kendra's head jerked back when she read it, was that she make an appointment with a local gallery owner about the purchase of a painting. The museum wanted copies of its provenance as well as her evaluation of its condition. As an art librarian, Kendra felt far out of her pay grade.

After flipping a series of texts back and forth about how valuable and cost-saving her assistance would be, she agreed to make an appointment with Stefan Appelhof, of the Appelhof

Gallery. Mrs. Odem sent the number and address.

Kendra took a deep breath to calm her jitters and thought about what she would say. Mr. Applehof's congenial voice made the call easy, and his Dutch accent proved to be interesting and understandable. "Yes, I received a call from Mrs. Odem that you were in our city and would be contacting me. How very convenient. Could we plan a time at the end of the business day? I could give my full attention to your visit."

Relieved that she wouldn't be interrupting a vacation day too much, she readily agreed.

"Then I look forward to receiving you at six tomorrow, Ms. Cooper. It will be a pleasure." He spoke the words with such warmth that she put away any dread and anticipated the meeting. She went back to her painting with a smile—until she realized what a heavy responsibility she had just accepted.

When the natural light from the window faded, Kendra turned on the weak ceiling bulb and added the small lamp she'd bought second hand. Her stomach growled, long ago unsatisfied by her quick wurst in the park. Still she placed the pigments lightly on the canvas, hoping to achieve some degree of accomplishment before quitting.

A tap at her door jerked her back to the real world and her rented room. "Kendra? It's Hattie Graham. Would you like to have a bowl of soup with me?"

She rested her brush on the palette and straightened her aching back. After hastily turning her painting around, she opened the door. "Thank you. That's so kind."

"I noticed you hadn't gone out for dinner, and…well, I've got plenty to share, if you don't mind simple food. My mother-in-law will join us."

Her stomach gave an extra squeeze at the prospect of warm stew again, as Mrs. Graham had shared once last week. She widened the door with a huge smile. "I'd love to eat with you. Give me a minute to wash my hands, and I'll be right down." Maybe she had some of that fresh brown bread to go with it like last time.

Mrs. Graham bent around her. "How's your painting going?"

Kendra remained in the doorway blocking her entrance. "I'm having fun with it. Nothing more. Going to the Rijksmuseum always inspires me. See you in a few minutes."

Later, sated with vegetable stew, brown bread, cheese, and conversation with the two Mrs. Grahams, Kendra let herself into her cooling room and pulled on a sweater. She clicked through the photos she'd taken at the museum, deleted a few, and moved the rest to the old laptop she kept locked in her suitcase. Viewing them on the monitor, she compared the colors with what she had painted. At some point, she would have to let the canvas thoroughly dry so she could roll it up and take it home.

Three weeks had seemed like such a long vacation when she planned this trip. She'd hoped to make her hard savings pay over the next couple of years by investing in an art vacation in Amsterdam. That aspiration was based on everything her graduate professor had said about copied fine art and specific comments by her boss at the Kimbell Art Museum. Speculations on the dollar value of her work kept her awake late into the night.

The Dallas/Fort Worth art market was rife with opportunity.

Chapter 2

Richard jogged up the front steps of the main police department on Saturday morning, eager to find out what the tech had discovered about the woman in the museum. Hopefully, he'd have a photo of her face that he could send to his boss at Interpol, Klaas Van Der Veen. With only a few weeks more in Amsterdam, he needed to produce something specific for Interpol on the source of all the art frauds.

The techie, Andries, had no hard information. "We think she is probably American because of the brand of her shoes and the design of her earrings." He pointed toward an enlargement of Richard's still shot, which captured part of her face from the side, and the frontal view from museum security.

"Earrings? I didn't notice—"

"A fairly simple design, gold oval shape, but if you look at this engraved pattern—"

Richard bent close and squinted. "That little curlicue?"

Andries chuckled. "Curlicue? Nice word. This exact earring comes from Jared, a jewelry store chain in the US."

"I've heard of it." In fact, he'd bought Taylor's engagement ring there, and would have returned for the wedding ring. A bitter taste came to his tongue. "So the Aeropostale T-shirt didn't indicate Europe to you?"

"Those T-shirts are on every continent." Andries gave a dismissive wave of the hand. "Tourists wear them everywhere. It means nothing."

"No face match at all?"

"We think she has no record. If she is a criminal, she is a careful one. Give us a little more. A name, a fingerprint. We can not do anything more with these pictures."

Richard nodded. He'd expected too much. "I'll try. Have a good weekend. And thanks." He retrieved his memory stick and wandered outside without speaking to the police captain. Maybe his suspect would be back at the museum today. He didn't even request copies of her photo to spread to the guards. If he couldn't prove her guilty of a crime, that might constitute harassment.

Maarten was working another angle today, so he returned to the museum alone. He wasn't above trying to pick her up—in the romantic sense—to get fingerprints. Just hearing her language and accent would give him more to go on than he had now.

He showed the photo to sales staff at the long, wooden ticket counter. "We think she may be American and have a monthly pass or annual membership."

"Sir, this museum has a million visitors a year. A lot of them are American tourists. We don't remember their faces." The irritation in his voice indicated that he didn't have time to waste. Even with five people selling tickets, the slow-moving line strung out ten yards long, and the day had hardly begun.

Richard climbed a long flight of stairs and scanned the Asian collection on the first floor—second floor to Americans. He didn't expect to see her and therefore wasn't disappointed. Continuing up, he rose to the Great Hall and admired its regal details, including enormous paintings directly on the walls. Turning right into the Gallery of Honor, he cruised the whole room before taking a position within sight of the Rembrandts, Vermeers, and others of that school.

Eventually he tried to chat with the guards. Showing her

picture, he found two who thought they remembered her but had no information.

The weekend crowd swarmed in the afternoon. If he had not been so impressed to be in the presence of the great masters, he might have dozed on his feet and bonked his head on the marble floor. He'd read every little information plaque twice and mentally worded a message to Van Der Veen fifteen different ways that essentially said he had nothing.

Kendra needed a day outside. The weather was gloriously beautiful, with rain predicted Monday. The Rijksmuseum was open every day of the year—even Mondays and Christmas Day—but she planned to stay home and paint through the rain.

She'd spent all Wednesday trying to perfect *The Milkmaid* before deciding only a masterful painter could copy a master painter. She should have tackled another Van Gogh project. After all, he completed more than a painting a day for the last hundred and fifty days of his life. Yes, and then killed himself.

She needed a break. Strolling a few blocks of her neighborhood, she enjoyed the tall, slender houses planted right against the cobblestone streets. Situated on small plots, the three-story dwellings took advantage of bits of land and the fact that heat traveled upward.

Maybe she would rent a bicycle Sunday and join the throngs of locals who pedaled everywhere. She could take a picnic lunch and a good map and see the outlying areas of the city. A rather adventuresome idea for a woman alone, but this whole trip had been. Her friends were blown away that she came by herself. Traveling alone sure beat staying home alone.

Van Gogh hung in her mind until she took the tram back

into the art district. The Van Gogh Museum also had some Gauguins, too, and a great running discussion of how the painters in that group developed their techniques. The bright colors and vibrant strokes of paint had to be easier to copy than Vermeer's subtle tones and perfectly lighted objects.

Her dad was right. She wasn't an artist and would never be able to make a living painting. Doing what she loved had cost her everything. If there had ever been any chance of a decent relationship with her parents, she would have been a nurse or something.

She stepped from the tram and crossed the street to the long, open park separating the two museums and continued toward the Van Gogh. Even though the summer day dripped with humidity—what more could she expect in a city laced with canals?—the heat never approximated what Fort Worth endured for most of July and August. Thin perspiration coated her brow by the time she presented her monthly pass and pushed into the air-conditioned main floor. What she wanted was the next floor, which in her opinion held the best of the best.

After waiting patiently for the small elevator only to find it stuffed with people, she dashed up the stairs. A man broke away from the group and did the same. He looked somewhat familiar, though she couldn't remember where she'd seen him. Probably at one of the museums.

She worked her way to the front of the admirers of *Wheatfield with Crows*. A simple painting full of wind and dashed landscape, exciting enough to keep her interested. She checked to be sure her camera still had the flash suppressed and began clicking at various details.

෨෬

Richard received Maarten's text, *Found her at the Van Gogh. She is making lots of photos.*

Richard returned an immediate reply, *Stay with her. I'll be there in fifteen.*

They hadn't lost her. She could have gone underground for a month while working on more canvases, and he had to leave before then. Richard fast-walked from the block with three galleries, crossed an open mall, and slipped into a taxi that had just left a passenger.

As he rode to the museum, his phone dinged again. Maarten sent him a couple of pictures taken from her side along with the message, *Stay back. One at a time. I will not lose her again.*

As he arrived and fumbled with Euros to pay the taxi, he got another message.

She passed the sunflower paintings. Photographing Wheatfield under Thunderclouds *from every angle and distance.*

He turned from the departing taxi and texted, *I'm outside. Let me know when she leaves.*

Maarten replied, *It could be hours.*

Richard sat on a bench near the museum's front in full sun, which would have him well-baked in less than a half hour. He'd have to find a better place to wait. He spoke into text, *Spent the morning cruising art galleries enough that they're getting suspicious of me.*

Maarten flashed back an update. *Dropped the bug in her shoulder bag. Photos from several angles, including her ears.*

That was good. Lots of criminals were identified by their ears. Surely Interpol had a record on her.

She's on the move. Following downstairs.

Richard rose, blotting perspiration from his face, and stood in the shade of a large tree bordering the park.

Maarten sent one more text: *Here she comes now. Yellow T-shirt over jeans.*

Richard lifted his cell to his lips. *Eyes on her.*

Richard stayed put under the tree while she ate a homemade sandwich and drank water from a bottle out of her bag. He didn't expect such thrift from a crook. Maybe she hadn't scored a big sale yet. He got in line at the ice cream booth and bought a cone of chocolate.

She threw her paper napkin away, drained the water bottle, and put the empty back in her bag. To his surprise, she came to the ice cream booth. He couldn't hear her words, but the guy seemed to understand her. Soon she took a place under an umbrella table where she dipped into mint ice cream drizzled with chocolate syrup. So she had a sweet tooth.

He didn't leave the area, but stayed out of her direct line of vision. When she got up and tossed her napkin in the trash, he spoke another text to Maarten. *Walking down the park toward the tram or the Rijks.*

Got her.

Richard finished his ice cream and fought the urge to follow the woman. No need to set off her alarms. The bug would lead them to her. Five minutes later, he ambled along the sidewalk that ran the length of the park.

Apartment just off tram line five, Maarten wrote.

Richard waited well out of sight, then boarded the next tram.

Some fifteen minutes later, Maarten called. "I've got her residence. She used a key to get into a house on Oosterparkstraat."

Kendra dashed up the stairs and opened the door to her Dutch digs. Its stuffy air, heavy with the smell of vintage oil paints, puffed in her face. She dropped her shoulder bag on the single bed and hurried to push up the window. Strange. A man stood on the sidewalk across the street looking up. A very ordinary-looking man in a tan T-shirt and jeans. She couldn't tell much about his height or face from the third floor. He could be anybody or nobody.

She pushed aside the thin, gauzy curtains to admit as much light as possible and turned to her painting. Enough of the complicated milkmaid.

But it really was rather good. She snapped a photo with her cell phone to send to her roommate in Texas. Then she leaned the painting under the window to dry further and set up a new canvas.

Before spreading paints on the palette, she transferred the photo of *Wheatfield with Crows* to her computer and brought up the first whole view. Moving between the shots, she studied the swirling sky and waving grain. Her heart pounded with the energy of creation. With only a few hours to spare before her six o'clock appointment with Mr. Appelhof, she could divide the canvas into the painting's major areas and lay on the background colors.

Van Gogh. Exciting blues and yellows, warm red-brown ground, green grass to the side of the road ruts. Squeezing the oil paint tubes, mixing colors, choosing just the right brushes that research indicated he had used, she stilled the quiver of her hand and made the first strokes dividing the canvas into sky, wheat field, and road.

All too soon, she had to dress and catch a taxi to the gallery address. Irritated at both the interruption and expense— though it would be refunded later—she considered her tourist wardrobe and chose the only possible combination. The black slacks and her best silk blouse had to do. In fact, it might bolster her spirits to be treated as an art professional. She decided to take the Kimbell Museum's request as a compliment.

She set to work on her appearance, adding the eye makeup she only wore when she didn't want people to think she was under twenty-one. Twisting up her hair helped, too. Thank heaven she'd brought the low pumps in case she went to a decent restaurant.

After hurrying a couple of blocks down the sidewalk, she hailed a taxi and gave him the address.

Richard took Maarten's call, which began with a Dutch swear word. "She just left here at a gallop, and she didn't take her denim bag. I can not trace her. And she is not wearing the tourist things."

"Okay, now what? This may be the one time we really need to follow her."

"Wait. She's getting into a taxi. I've got the company name and car number. I'll call it in."

Within a few minutes, they had the taxi's destination. "The Applehof Gallery? Hey, I know that guy," said Richard. "We had a good conversion about the fraud market last week. I didn't tell him I'm with Interpol this summer. I'm on my way."

"What if she's dealing through him?"

"What if she's *trying* to deal through him, but he's honest? I'll let you know."

Chapter 3

Entering the gallery fifteen minutes early, Kendra found it a tastefully appointed shop. Paintings displayed by track lighting occupied well-spaced positions, not crowded in jumbled presentations like some stores she'd seen.

"May I help you?" The fine-suited man with a dash of gray at the temples rested an admiring look on her.

"I have an appointment..."

"Ms. Cooper? From the Kimbell?" He extended his hand, which she shook. "I'm Stefan Appelhof. I've been expecting you." He smiled with genuine warmth.

"Kendra Cooper. It's a pleasure to meet you, sir." She liked the man instantly.

Within her line of sight, just over Mr. Appelhof's shoulder, hung a modern painting which attracted her attention.

He followed her gaze. "It's quite fetching, isn't it? One of our finest local artists. The Kimbell would do well to invest in this young man. In very few years, he will be a big name."

They drifted together to the painting, and Mr. Appelhof gave a history of the artist and his blossoming recent success. As he kept talking, Kendra became impatient to view the Breitner floral she'd been sent to check on.

The tingle of a bell hanging above the front door drew their interest when a tall man entered.

"Ah, Dr. Reed. Welcome back to my shop. Can I help you with something?"

"Perhaps I could have come at a better time. I see you're with a customer."

This little errand for Mrs. Odem could take longer than expected. Kendra tried not to appear irritated at the disruption.

"It is quite all right. Ms. Cooper, may I introduce you to Dr. Richard Reed, art professor at... It is Yale, perhaps?"

"Emory, in Atlanta, actually."

"Pardon me. Emory University." His gracious smile turned to Kendra. "We had a very interesting chat when Dr. Reed visited the gallery last week."

Her gaze dropped to Dr. Reed's long chin. This was the guy who followed her out of the Rijksmuseum yesterday.

"Dr. Reed, this is Ms. Kendra Cooper, of the Kimbell Art Museum in Fort Worth, Texas. Ms. Cooper is here to see a lovely painting which has just come into our possession. Perhaps you would like to see it, too?"

"By all means."

"Let me escort you to my office...as soon as I turn the sign around. We won't be interrupted while we talk. I usually close at six during the week." In a few quick steps he uninvited any potential customers and then showed Kendra and Dr. Reed to his private space dominated by a large, antique desk. "Please be seated while I take the painting from our vault."

Kendra lost herself for a moment in a lascivious mythology scene on the left wall. Roman gods captured semi-nude nymphs in some fertile valley. Not a genre she appreciated, but Mr. Appelhof's view from his desk no doubt kept him stimulated in his love of art. She took one of the royal blue velvet-upholstered chairs as Reed lowered himself in the other. His long limbs possessed strength and grace.

"You're here to represent the Kimbell?" Reed's expression came across as polite but skeptical.

"The director, Mrs. Odem, asked me to check out a

painting this gallery is offering for sale. Just a first look to consider whether we might be interested."

"I see. Not your usual duties for the museum, I take it." An almost-smirk lent a curve to his upper lip. He would be a good-looking man if not so uppity. The only friendly thing about him was his softly tumbling curly hair, and he wore it trimmed on the sides and back, more like a businessman than an art professor.

"I'm pleased to be at the disposal of the Kimbell. It's fortunate that they can call on me at this time. Perhaps save someone a trip to Europe."

Mr. Appelhof entered bearing a small frame, which he turned toward Kendra slowly, with a sense of drama. Breitner's still life, a vase of anemones in red, purple, and pink blooms in a ginger jar, drew her smile.

She stood and took the frame in her own hands. The simple impressionistic rendering was altogether delightful. But was it Breitner? "You'll provide a copy of the provenance, I presume?"

"Naturally, my dear." He stepped to his desk and retrieved a folder. "Unlike some of Breitner's pieces, this one was never confiscated by the Nazis. It has been in certifiable possession of its owners and their antecedents since its purchase in the early 1900s. The stamps and seals on the back of the canvas all agree."

"Remarkable." She studied the swath of color at the base of the vase. It seemed to her that the painter had improved upon the original muddy shade. She had been tempted to do the same thing a couple of years ago when she'd copied Breitner. She compared that tone to the colors of the flowers, which were *not* brighter than expected, so it wasn't simply a matter of cleaning the painting. "Remarkable, indeed," she muttered. Not quite right, but almost. The signature declared the painting an original.

She didn't know what to say to this very nice man with happy expectation lighting his eyes, nor exactly what to tell Mrs. Odem. She decided to toss the ball to Professor Richard Reed. Let him stake an opinion on the painting. She extended it to him and found him looking at her, not at the painting. The frequent smirk had been replaced by a thoughtful squint.

The room held its breath as he grasped the frame.

Reed pondered the canvas for a full fifteen seconds. "Lovely. Breitner could say so much about the condition of the world by the droop of a blossom."

A long exhale from Mr. Appelhof gave the air permission to circulate again. "So well put, Dr. Reed." He nodded to Kendra. "Then we'll just secure this in the vault until you've communicated with your Mrs. Odem, shall we?" He extended a hand for the treasure, accepted it with respect, and held it against his chest, now showing only the back of the canvas as if their time to view it had run out.

This posture gave Kendra the distinct impression that he knew it was a fake. "We would have to x-ray it. There would be tests before a purchase is made…"

"Certainly. We would have them performed for your museum and provide certified originals of the results."

"Thank you, but I'm sure the Kimbell would insist on examination by its own experts." She could have said more about the sale being dependent on verification, but didn't want to challenge the gallery owner further.

"Please excuse me for a moment while I safeguard our little masterpiece here. I'll be right back." Mr. Appelhof gave a gentlemanly bow of the head and left with his treasure.

"What did you think?" Dr. Reed spoke in a low voice after the door had closed.

Kendra caught his eye, then she gave him a tiny shake of

the head.

"Why?"

How dare she question the opinion of a European art professional? But she did. "The base color is brighter than the original anemone painting."

"Maybe a cleaning of the old varnish improved the color."

"Maybe. We'll see what the x-rays and dating indicate." She was probably wrong and would have to be careful how she reported to Mrs. Odem. The Kimbell validated each acquisition with certainty, so her opinion represented a mere bump in the road to a purchase.

Their conversation halted when she heard Mr. Appelhof's approaching footsteps. He opened the door with a flourish and a grand smile. "Ms. Cooper, Dr. Reed and I are invited to a private reception on Saturday evening in the home of a collector, Mr. De Roos. I understand he has a new acquisition to show off. I'm quite sure I could add your name to the guest list with a quick phone call." Mr. Appelhof waited for her answer with eyebrows lifted. "Mr. De Roos would be delighted to have a representative of the Fort Worth Kimbell Museum attend."

The warmth of a flush came to her cheeks. What an opportunity to meet exciting art fanciers. To be admitted into the home of a Dutch collector. "But…I have nothing to wear."

The men burst out laughing.

"Women say the same thing in every country, don't they, Dr. Reed?"

"Exactly."

Mr. Appelhof turned gentle eyes to her. "What you have on is fine. Quite sophisticated, actually. Don't give it another thought."

"I would be delighted to attend, but I am serious about

my clothing. I came as a tourist and brought no evening attire." Not that she had money to buy a cocktail dress worthy of the occasion.

"And I am serious in assuring you that guests will not care what you wear. Many will be of my age or older, and they will be jealous of your youthful complexion and…ah…form. You will be well received."

"I'd love to go, then." Wait until they heard about this in Texas.

Richard recognized this as a sterling opportunity to become better acquainted with the woman who either was his quarry or had connections that would lead him to the forgery rings he sought. Her cognizance of a probable Breitner fake tripled his interest in her. She had spotted a variance he sensed but couldn't quite name. Once she identified what was wrong with the painting, he completely agreed.

Mr. Appelhof showed them around his gallery for about a half hour, expounding on several of his favorite acquisitions. His monologue often highlighted stories of how they came into his hands and the wealth and prominence of his clients.

More interesting to Richard were the canvases he pointed out as copies. Kendra, too, scrutinized these and once asked if more light could be put on a certain canvas, since Mr. Appelhof had turned off most of the track lights at the shop's closing time.

Richard observed over Kendra's shoulder, close enough to inhale her pleasant, clean fragrance. He fixated on a tendril of hair that had fallen from the casual twist on the back of her head. Her move to the right, perhaps because he leaned in too close, brought his attention back to the painting.

He wondered what she had seen. A Dutch windmill, an eighteenth century copy of Gabriël, the water's reflection of the structure with rising white clouds in the blue sky in the background projected the peace any Dutch citizen would relish. While he couldn't read the signature of the copyist, it hadn't been falsely signed as a Gabriël original. "Quite good, don't you think?"

"Very good," she replied. "Excellent control of the blues." She moved into the next room, which contained several modern pieces not at all to his liking.

Richard took the break in conversation as an opportunity to say farewell. He had her name and home city now. They weren't going to deal for counterfeit art in front of him. He shook hands and made all the right social noises and departed.

He wondered if Ms. Cooper might be entirely legitimate, in Amsterdam representing a fine Texas art museum. On the other hand, such a setup would make it possible for her to buy and sell fakes internationally. Discovering such a dealer had even larger significance.

Richard was pumped at the prospect of bringing her down.

So she would also be at Saturday night's reception. He had to review Interpol's photo and biography files of possible suspects and people integral to the Amsterdam art world before then.

The guest list likely included the most significant European collectors, at least one of the Germans who claimed to be discovering art confiscated by the Nazis, and a random assortment of art dealers. He hoped Alexander Holt would attend, because the wealthy investor had attracted the interest of Interpol on a couple of recent sales from his personal collection.

This event would tax his ability to remember dates and

obscure details and his helpful degree of photographic memory. Maarten had no James Bond invention or invisible camera to wire him with. He had to record all the names and faces with his own brain cells.

More than that, seeing how Kendra reacted among the cast of characters might tell him a lot. Her social interaction at the event would probably reveal if she already knew certain of the players. She might troll for buyers of her own. Surely she was more than the innocent Texan tourist she pretended to be. He counted on that.

Chapter 4

When Dr. Reed had left the gallery, Appelhof stepped toward Kendra. "Please join me for a light repast. A little 'brown restaurant' around the corner offers light meals, and we'll be able to continue our discussion."

Her stomach grumbled at the mention of food, and she placed her hand over her middle. "A brown restaurant?"

"Sort of like an English pub, with authentic wood walls. And, well, they're smoke-stained over the years. They always have good tapas to go with one's wine or beer. My favorite is nearby."

Her light lunch had completely run out. "I could go for some tapas."

Kendra walked with Mr. Appelhof—who insisted she call him Stefan—to the "brown restaurant" around the corner from his gallery. He led to a small, round table. When she sat, he took a place beside her, perhaps because it was a noisy, folksy place. Judging by the menu, food came in a poor second to wine, beer, and the hard stuff.

"Let me order a plate of various snacks for us," he offered. "Some kippers, sausages, and such." He spoke to the waitress, and soon they had a fine assortment of canapés, a Diet Coke for her, and a local beer for him.

"So tell me, how do you fill your after-work hours in Texas?"

"I try to get a little outdoor exercise, walk the

neighborhood… Mainly, I like to paint."

"What sort of things? Modern?"

She ducked her head. "I do copies of the seventeenth and eighteenth century masters." Tilting her face sideways, she shyly looked up to check his reaction.

His brow lifted. He looked pleasantly surprised. "Tell me more. Whom do you copy?"

"I just finished Vermeer's milkmaid, and started a van Gogh this afternoon. The purpose of this three-week vacation in Amsterdam is to study the originals."

"What do you do with your copies? Sell them to collectors?"

"That's the idea, eventually, if I can paint them well enough. My graduate professor said I could make fairly good money, and… I need it to pay my education debts." That was too much information. She felt herself falling off the Kimble's marble pedestal.

To her surprise, though, Stefan's interest did not waver. "Have you been painting during your vacation?"

"Yes. Here, I'll show you. I made a photo today to send to a friend." She brought up *The Milkmaid* and passed her phone to him. Then she reached over and flipped the display to the van Gogh completed on Monday.

"This is yours? You did this?" He stretched the picture. Concentrating on the tiny representation, he seemed quite impressed. "I'd love to see it. May I come to your apartment, perhaps tomorrow after I close the gallery? No, I could come before opening in the morning."

Why would he want to see her paintings? Did he have a reason to move from pub chat to action? She considered her rented room, the disheveled appearance of the easel, canvases in various states, and the usual bedroom mess. She didn't want him going there.

"Better yet, let me bring a couple of them to your gallery. I have these two that are dry enough, if I'm careful."

"Are you sure? I'd be happy to send you a taxi so you don't have to bring them on the tram."

She agreed to the arrangement, charged with such excitement that her stomach protested further food.

ৎৄৄ

The following morning she rose with the sun, much too early to take her paintings to Stefan. She'd made tremendous progress, totally lost in her work, when a scratch at the door startled her. Inhaling deeply, she straightened, stepped back, and surveyed the canvas.

The scratch came again, this time with a snuffing noise and a meow. Lost in the world of the wheat field, she didn't want to be disturbed. But a woman's voice traveled through the door as if she were speaking to a pet or child, and then she knocked.

Kendra rested the brush on her palette, which she placed on the bed over a newspaper. Opening the door, she found her landlady's mother-in-law picking up a cat by the middle.

The woman held the squirming cat and looked around Kendra into the room. "Sorry about the cat, dearie," she said in a strong British accent. "He thinks this is his room. He used to be my granddaughter's pet, you see, and this was her room."

"Oh. And you live upstairs now, don't you?"

"My room is just up there, at the end." She pointed toward the stairs. "This was my home before Hattie turned it into a apartment house. Not that I mind, really. One must pay the bills."

The cat, a plump adult with graying black and white fur, leapt from her grip and dashed under the bed. Kendra went to her easel, afraid he might knock it over and ruin her painting.

The elder Mrs. Graham dropped to her knees on the rag rug by the bed and cooed to the cat. "Come out, now, Boots." She rose and scanned the room. "You're an artist? Oh, *The Milkmaid*. You did that?"

Kendra shrugged. "I'm not an artist, but I like to try to copy paintings sometimes. I've never tried anything as hard as *The Milkmaid* before. As you see, I didn't do very well."

"I beg to disagree, dearie. That's excellent. You got the soft light on her face perfectly. And the folds on her blue skirt. Why, that could hang in a museum."

"That's very kind of you, but I never feel my copies are good enough. It's just a way to pass the time." That wasn't true. The burning ambition to copy the masters kept her awake at night. She'd saved for three years to make this trip when her salary barely supported her. But just one good canvas could pay back the trip expenses and more.

This sweet old lady and her cat interrupted that goal.

The elder Mrs. Graham bent again to the task of coaxing her cat from under the bed. "Come, Boots, come to Mama. Treat? You want a treat?"

Kendra slid the easel into the corner and knelt on the other side of her narrow bed. She reached toward the cat and gave it a shove. The cat scooted toward her mistress, who got a firm hold.

Propping against the bed, the old woman pushed to her feet. She tried to shift the cat and smooth the bedspread.

"Don't worry about that. I'll do it." Kendra wanted the lady to leave. Now, with her cat.

"I'll just get out of your way. Sorry to be a bother."

"Don't be concerned. Glad to see you again." And glad to close the door behind her. Kendra stretched her back. The morning light streamed in. She should dress and go to Stefan's.

She went to the window and rested her eyes, staring into the distance.

A black Mercedes had parked on the street. Most residents of Amsterdam didn't own cars, preferring bikes and walking. The younger Mrs. Graham even did her grocery shopping on her bike with a large wire basket in the front.

Kendra could barely see the outline of a man sitting in the car. She wondered who he was waiting for. The man raised something to his face, probably a cell phone.

She closed the window and pulled the curtains, wishing they offered more privacy. She was uncomfortable with only the thin, white fabric hanging loosely from a rod. A girl alone had to be careful.

ৎঙ

When she stepped from the taxi with copies of Vermeer's *The Milkmaid* in one hand and van Gogh's *Wheatfield with a Reaper* in the other, Stefan opened the gallery door and welcomed her. After paying the taxi, he turned to help her inside, his eyes as wide as his beaming smile. Taking the larger one, *The Milkmaid*, he led her to a back room with a wide work table and strong lighting. He placed it on an easel and backed up to admire it.

"Amazing." His whispered word held reverence. He studied it for some time.

She placed the other canvas on the work table, aware of the tremble in her hands. Her stomach churned. Showing her work to others, having them judge her performance, always made her nervous. This ranked with reading an English paper from the front of her fourth grade class. Worse yet, like showing her painting to her father.

Without warning, Stefan turned and embraced her,

squeezing hard. Caught off guard, she didn't know what to do with her own arms, so she left them uncommitted at her sides. When he pushed back, grasping her shoulders, he glowed as if he were a proud parent. "Marvelous. Your work is…perfect."

She broke his hold to point at the canvas. "No, not perfect. Getting the soft sunlight coming in the window from the side… I did as well as I could, but—"

"Nonsense, dear lady. If anything, you painted it better than Vermeer."

She bent her head as warmth rushed to her cheeks.

"Tell me, what is your goal? Come sit here and talk to me about your intentions, because this is so great an accomplishment."

She accepted the offered chair, a straight-back wooden seat, and he took the other one. "My graduate professor said he could help me sell them to collectors. As copies, of course, not frauds. I still have a lot of college tuition debt, and my salary at the Kimbell is quite low." She swallowed hard, her eyes glancing away to the cluttered workroom. Then she looked directly at him. "I need the money. Plain and simple."

He nodded slowly. "What arrangements do you have with this professor? How did he plan to sell them, and what will his commission be?"

"Um, I actually haven't talked to him for a couple of years. This is all fairly theoretical."

"Then let's talk specifics. You're good. I can sell both of these to collectors this week. In fact, I can call several people this afternoon, and I'll wager my collectors will pay more than the Americans of your professor's acquaintance."

His fixed gaze had fire in it. The air in the musty room held still.

"Commissions usually run about forty percent," he continued. "I would accept twenty-five."

Tears filled her eyes, and her lips quivered. Of all he had said, what mattered the most was "you're good." Then her practical side lurched forward.

"How much do you think you can get?"

Kendra took the tram back to her neighborhood and rushed down the sidewalk to Mrs. Graham's house. She skipped up the steps with wings on her feet, delighted to get back to her canvas. Having left *The Milkmaid* and *Wheatfield with a Reaper* at Stefan's gallery, she was eager to finish the second van Gogh.

She had to remind herself to slow down and concentrate. Painting should be about the pleasure, not the pay. Inching past enlargements of hundreds of tiny strokes became tedious enough that she determined to do something entirely different next.

The painting came to a stopping point as the sunlight faded. She would let the oils dry overnight and take another look in the morning. Perhaps tomorrow she'd return to the Van Gogh Museum to study the works of ol' Vincent's prolific friends. Though she rarely did the same painting twice, she had a hankering to repeat Rousseau's *Tiger in a Tropical Storm*. Her first attempt, languishing in her dad's hall closet, could be improved upon. Selling a new one, maybe to Stefan, would taste of vindication.

She arrived at the museum Saturday morning at the opening hour. Her plan was to drink in as much inspiration as possible, take dozens more photos before the weekend crowd blocked her access to the best paintings, and leave time in the afternoon to shop for something to wear to the reception tonight. Hattie Graham had given her the address of a good second-hand shop to check out.

By noon tourists swarmed the place, and hunger drove her back to the simple food stands between her two favorite museums. After waiting in line to buy her standard lunch, she claimed one of the last remaining tables.

Munching on her sandwich, she gazed at the milling tourists and imagined them in the colors of Cezanne's palette. A gentleman carrying a wurst and drink cup approached from her left. "Mind if I join you?"

She usurped a table to herself and spotted only one other unoccupied table. The man, wearing crisp slacks and a button-down shirt, had a gray Vandyke beard. His mild accent was probably Dutch. He looked okay. "I don't mind at all. Have a seat."

He scraped the folding metal chair against the white gravel and took the place across from her. They agreed that the weather was absolutely marvelous, and he began to eat his sandwich. After swallowing the first bite and taking a drink, he looked up and caught her eye. "Are you American?"

She figured that much was obvious, so she confirmed his assumption.

"Enjoying our museums just as a tourist, or do you paint?"

That caught her by surprise. Was it printed on her forehead? "I have a professional interest in art, and I paint a bit when I have time. How about you?"

He shook his head gently, with a slight smile. "My talent is limited to appreciation of art." He extracted a card from his man-purse. "My name is Alexander Holt." He placed the card beside her wurst's paper wrapper. "I enjoy collecting art. Perhaps we could chat sometime about what you do."

Now the conversation became a bit too personal. She didn't reciprocate with her contact information. "I really must be going. I have so little time to see so much. Have a nice day."

Richard took Maarten's call on the first ring. "Our patience pays off, my friend. Yesterday she takes canvases to the gallery of Appelhof. Today she makes contact with Alexander Holt in the museum garden. I think our suspect gets a bit careless."

Chapter 5

The summer Saturday evening in Amsterdam brought thousands of people into the streets. Kendra peered from the taxi, which rolled slowly along the narrow single lane between a canal and a solid row of tall brick homes.

"These are some of the most expensive homes in all of The Netherlands," said Stefan Appelhof. "See the elaborate gables?"

She craned her neck to catch a glimpse of the architectural embellishments above the third or fourth floor. Family crests adorned many of the homes. The taxi waited for a turn to release its passengers in front of a door admitting well-dressed couples.

She shouldn't have come. "Mr. Appelhof, I'm not sure about this. Look at that woman's dress." She wanted to be here, tonight, with these people, but not in the little black dress she'd bought second-hand.

"Remember, my dear, I'm Stefan. I thought we settled that. We're business partners now." As the couple in front of them was greeted, he stepped out and extended his hand to her. "Please, don't be concerned. You'll be the loveliest lady at the party."

Before leaving the cab, she touched the back of her hair, twisted into a French roll, to make sure it remained in place. She took his hand and exited, straightened her posture, lifted her chin a smidgen, and smiled at her fatherly date. He offered his arm and returned her smile with a twinkle in his eyes.

Together they approached the front door, where a butler accepted the invitation card from Mr. De Roos.

Kendra had heard these homes were compact to the point of being cramped, with stairs to the upper floors like ladders. This one, however, opened into a large, uncluttered room for its elegant guests to gather. A quick measurement by eye indicated the neighboring residence had been combined with this one, creating the luxury of space.

"Each of these houses directly on a canal is worth a couple of million, at least." Stefan spoke quietly at her ear. "De Roos had an architect gut two of them and redesign the interior."

A small man called Stefan's name and advanced with hand outstretched. Kendra only understood the first words of his Dutch greeting. "And you must be Ms. Cooper, of the renowned Kimbell Museum," he said in English. "What a pleasure to have you visit."

She assured him the pleasure was hers, while noting the green silk neck kerchief which complemented his eyes. A rather French fashion statement, but she had seen all manner of dress among the art collectors in Texas. This gentleman, less than her own height, wore a suit worth at least as much as her monthly salary, but his gracious welcome put her at ease.

A waiter followed the host with a tray of drinks. She took a crystal flute of champagne with the intention of holding it for the next two hours. Especially because she, moving out of her element, language, and comfort zone, determined to remain alert.

"Have you come to Amsterdam on a buying trip, Ms. Cooper?" Mr. De Roos seemed to be memorizing her face. For one moment, his attention fixed on her alone.

"Not at all. This is just a personal vacation to enjoy the art of your country."

Mr. De Roos's expression clouded as if he didn't believe her or didn't want to believe her. After all, her date for the evening was a prominent gallery owner.

"The Kimbell contacted me earlier this week and asked me to meet with Mr. Appelhof—Stefan," she continued. "Thank you for allowing me to join your lovely event tonight."

Another couple entered, and Mr. De Roos's eyes flickered in their direction. "Stefan, please show Ms. Cooper around. We'll move into the other room in a few minutes."

With this polite dismissal, he moved to greet the most recent guests. Kendra had had her five minutes of private time with the billionaire.

Stefan guided her around the room to show the magnificent collection of art on its walls. "I've attended his showings of a new piece before. When everyone is here, he'll invite us past those closed double doors to reveal what it is." He nodded in that direction. "The room beyond those doors is normally a formal living room, but they'll have some of the furniture removed so we can flow through it tonight."

"You don't know what painting we're going to see?"

"Rumors abound, but for security reasons he doesn't tell until it's properly hung and security-wired. Ah, the lovely Katrina De Roos, talking to the elderly couple with their backs to us. You'll meet her before the night is over."

An elegant, thin woman in a full-length fuchsia dress seemed engrossed in conversation across the room. Her bare shoulders and arms proved her to be well exercised, and she measured, no doubt, a bit taller than her husband.

"Meanwhile," Stefan said as he directed Kendra with a touch at her elbow, "may I show you their van Gogh?"

The midnight blue painting highlighted by a piercing quarter moon took her breath away. Imagine having such a treasure in the front sitting room of a home. Barely controlling her eagerness, she moved around another couple to drink in the dashes of color. "From his best works, the year before his death," she whispered. "Amazing." The Museum of Modern Art in New York City had owned the original *Starry Night* for decades. This had to be one of the series van Gogh painted from his asylum window. The swirling yellow and blues bore exactly the same brush techniques.

"Did you bring your camera this evening, Ms. Cooper?" A familiar voice, so close that his breath brushed her neck, pulled her back from her reverie.

She turned to face her handsome adversary. While he didn't wear a tux like some of the guests, he'd changed to a fresh suit, shaved, and—yes—splashed on an intriguing fragrance. "Good evening, Dr. Reed. And no, I seem to have left my camera in my room, along with my diamonds and everything else I should have brought to this occasion." Her tone matched his sarcasm.

"But you have one perfect gold chain. It's all you need." With a slight smile and tip of his head, he deflated the balloon of tension encircling them.

She touched the strand which she always wore, often hidden beneath her blouse. It was her only valuable jewelry. "It belonged to my mother."

"Your mother had excellent taste."

Except in men. "Thank you."

She lifted a hand toward the van Gogh. "Have you seen this?"

Kendra discussed the painting with Stefan and Richard, admiring the beautiful madness of the design until the double doors opened wide for the party to enter the living room. Dazzled by a chandelier of dozens of electric candles, she was swept along by the guests past an antique tapestry on the wall to the left. A few steps farther and on the right, a magnificent

Paul Gauguin, straight from his Tahitian period, claimed pride of place under a track light.

She controlled her urge to push through the crowd and park in front of the painting. She'd never seen a Gauguin outside of a museum, nor ever expected to. One of his paintings, now over a century old, sold for $300 million last year. She could only speculate on the price of this piece.

Space opened in front of them, and Richard guided her forward with a hand at the small of her back. A thrill spread from that warm spot, causing a weakness in her knees. She steadied herself before trusting her legs to move closer to the painting. He had no right to cause such a reaction.

At her other side, Stefan put a hand on her elbow. Without looking at either man, she wondered if jealousy ran between them. Did the widowed Mr. Appelhof consider her his *real* date? She stepped into an opening between other viewers through which the men couldn't follow. At last, she had a clear view of the three partially clothed Tahitian women lounging with clear blue water behind and a palm tree overhead.

So completely Gauguin. Simplistic. Lots of primary colors.

She could do that.

The thought startled her. Had she become a copyist to the degree that she only considered the grand masters as fodder for her imitations?

She slipped sideways, allowing others a clear view. Tracing a finger along a carved whirl at the corner of a deeply polished antique bookcase, she scanned the titles. All about art, naturally. The title on frauds burned its accusations toward her. But she was innocent. She'd never signed a painting as the original artist. In fact, she never signed paintings. If someone else added the artist's signature to her canvas, she'd be complicit. And maybe out of debt. Just a few really good ones would suffice.

A flash of fuchsia came into her peripheral vision at the same time Stefan drew near.

"Stefan, how kind of you to come." The hostess leaned in for a light double kiss, a touching of cheeks in the French fashion.

"Allow me to introduce Ms. Kendra Cooper of the Kimbell Museum in Fort Worth, Texas. Kendra, may I present our hostess, Katrina De Roos."

She also received the double kiss, the brush of a butterfly wing on her cheeks. Kendra fought the urge to say she was *just* an employee, an art librarian among many. Instead, she tried to respond in as gracious a manner as the fine lady before her.

"Have you met Dr. Reed?" Stefan motioned to Richard as he joined them. He seemed smoothly accustomed to Katrina's greeting, in his own element chatting about the new acquisition and other works of art in the previous room.

More hors d'oeuvres, wines, and champagne arrived on silver trays served by waiters who artfully moved among the guests. Kendra held her warming champagne glass and accepted a bite of smoked fish on a circle of whole grain bread. Her glance drifted a few feet past the immediate conversation circle, and she spotted a tall, slender gentleman with a gray beard. Where had she seen him before? Maybe not in a tux or with the elegant woman at his side.

He looked up and their eyes locked. The man in the park this afternoon? He raised one eyebrow and gave the tiniest nod with a cryptic smile, then re-engaged in conversation with his own circle. How unexpected to see him here.

Stefan introduced her to other guests, remaining by her side like a perfect gentleman. She wondered if he knew the Breitner still life was a fake. Fortunately, she didn't have to tell him. Mrs. Odem could handle that messy palette. Kendra didn't get paid enough to tell a European gallery owner he dealt in frauds.

The new Gauguin impressed Richard. This family had some serious money—probably more than his own—and they knew how to use it. Collecting and preserving the arts, fostering their appreciation in modern society, and thereby insuring the continuance of the culture made De Roos a leader in The Netherlands, perhaps all of Europe.

Richard could resign from Emory, manage his portfolio himself, and collect or deal in art for the rest of his life. He chose to work at a day job, though, and aspired to be department chairman someday. Productivity pleased him, and contact with the students provided a way to express his responsibility to God. Fortunately, his parents agreed someone as blessed as he should be making a contribution to others. This summertime gig with Interpol fit into that idea. But soirées with the art crowd always stirred up an evaluation of his purposes.

Richard scanned the room to identify as many of the art players as possible. Before attending tonight, he'd reviewed Interpol's files with photos and data, which he had pored over many times in recent weeks. At least three of the men and one woman among those briefs stood with him in this room, and he needed introductions—as someone from the Atlanta art nobility, not as an Interpol specialist.

Rather than use Mr. Appelhof, he would ask the host or hostess to introduce him to one of them. His opportunity appeared when Mrs. De Roos began a conversation with Mr. and Mrs. Bakker. He moved in and, as politely as possible, caught the eye of the gentleman.

Katrina De Roos angled in a way that let him into their conversational group, and she introduced him smoothly, without grasping for his name.

"Good evening." Richard offered his hand to Mr. Bakker, who seemed puzzled but shook it anyway. "It's a pleasure to meet you. I understand you have a fine collection yourself, with a special interest in landscapes, isn't it?"

The hostess graced Richard with a smile. "Dr. Reed is a professor at Emory University. We are pleased he was able to join us this evening." Though a full professorship remained a goal to be attained, he didn't correct the hostess in front of her guests.

Mr. Bakker brightened at this information. "Ahh. We have a single daughter studying art in New York." The chitchat began with that introduction, and then he was able to build on Bakker's acquaintance with Mr. Holt to get that introduction.

Alexander Holt's trimmed gray Vandyke beard came with a firm handshake but cold eyes. His tall, thin wife in an elegant black dress stood beside him, and neither participated in the discussion of the Bakkers' daughter in America. Mrs. Holt wore an expression of terminal boredom, and her eyes connected with no one, especially not her husband.

Wanting to get off the match-making train of thought which occurred too frequently, Richard directed the conversation toward Holt, learning of his interest in the eighteenth century masters. He could talk on that subject well into the next year.

Bakker gave him a business card and then Holt followed suit, implying permission to contact them after tonight. Richard offered them one of his university cards. He couldn't have hoped for better contacts, and all without mention of his Expert Group status with Interpol.

Trays of brandy and liqueurs were passed along with

truffles, and the party began to wind down. He continued to circulate among the guests to meet every person possible. Nothing could be better for his investigation and research than a gathering like this one.

At times he checked the position of Kendra and Mr. Appelhof. She seemed to be the new darling of the party. He guessed her sweet face and simple clothing challenged no one, which made her acceptable and non-threatening. Her attachment to the Kimbell gave a certain celebrity status, and the Dutch categorically loved Americans.

Right now, she listened with rapt attention to a gentleman holding forth on his desire for contemporary artists to incorporate techniques of the impressionists in their work.

Richard tuned his ear back to the conversation with Mrs. Bakker, who wanted to know if he could introduce her to the lovely American girl.

"I would be delighted." Stepping back, he opened the circle and caught Kendra's eye.

Mrs. Bakker's expression clouded when she learned her name. Obviously, she had expected a Bass, Carter, or Richardson. "Cooper? I don't believe I know that name."

"No, you wouldn't," Kendra replied with a soft voice. "My family isn't prominent in the Texas art world." The slightest tint of a blush lit her cheeks. "But I'm well aware of your family's contribution to the arts, Mrs. Bakker, and it's such a pleasure to meet you. Monet is my very favorite of the grand masters."

Well done. She's not only thinking on her feet, but she's done research as well.

When that conversation ended and only a handful of guests remained, Richard ambled over to where Kendra and Appelhof took a last look at the Gauguin. "Could I give you a ride? I have a car parked in the square behind this block, complements of its Interpol registry."

"Thank you, young man, but I'll escort Ms. Cooper home."

"Oh, no. It's much too far," she protested. "I've rented a room some distance out. I came to your gallery this afternoon by tram."

Appelhof touched her upper arm and smiled down at her. "Then I wouldn't think of letting you return alone. Amsterdam is wonderfully safe, but a lady should be properly attended."

Seeing Appelhof's possessive move ruffled Richard. He was much too old for her. "I doubt you'll find a taxi here on the canal. You'll have to walk at least a block to the square. My car is parked there. Shall we walk together?" He suddenly found it important to be the one taking Kendra home.

"A lovely idea." Kendra's acceptance postponed the decision until later, giving control to neither man. She led the way to pay compliments to their host and hostess, and each person gave their thanks for the evening.

As they strolled back through the first room, she drifted toward the van Gogh she'd been admiring when he arrived. "I just want one more minute with this beautiful painting." But one minute became three, and Richard and Appelhof wandered over as well.

"It isn't the same."

Her whispered words puzzled Richard. "What isn't the same?" He drew closer to her and to the painting.

"This isn't the same painting we saw before. The dashed lines—see? There's a little curl at the end. Especially in the moon. And look here, where the night blue and black swirl with the yellow. The strokes bend with the motion. Van Gogh would never have done that."

He drew closer and squinted at the tiny details she'd pointed out. A flush hit his head, almost like a bright flash in his eyes. By gum, she was right. How had he missed something so apparent to her?

Richard gave room to Appelhof, who pushed in from the side. The gallery owner tilted his bifocals and studied the painting up close. "You are sure the strokes were not the same earlier this evening?"

"Positive."

While Appelhof continued to scrutinize the fraud, Richard decided to take action. "Then we'd better tell them."

Chapter 6

Kendra waited with Stefan at the fraudulent van Gogh in the front room while Richard returned to the living room where their host and hostess chatted with the last guests. He strolled cool and loose, like tall men do when they haven't a worry in the world. Then he joined in the conversation until the De Rooses walked the guests toward the front door. When the group passed Kendra and Stefan, the host cast curious glances their way.

The butler let the other guests out, and Richard motioned toward the faux van Gogh. "Mr. De Roos, I think we have a problem."

Kendra and Stefan stepped away from the painting, opening the view for the others.

Richard nodded in their direction. "On our way out, Ms. Cooper noticed something."

Her heart flipped. She asked herself again how sure she was. Being put in the position of judging the authenticity of an extremely valuable painting made her feel like the walls were closing in. Her breath caught in her throat.

De Roos's guarded perusal turned from the art to her. "And what is that?"

She swallowed and inhaled, then lifted her chin to a more confident level. "Excuse me, sir, but did you have this painting exchanged during the evening?"

His eyes widened to full alert. "Exchanged for what?"

"For…a lookalike. A copy." The van Gogh signature made it a fraud, but she didn't use that word.

"Not at all. This is the original…" His words dribbled off.

"You see, Mr. De Roos," she said while pointing to the painting's moon, "these short dashes should be almost straight even though, together, they create the curve of the quarter moon." He approached, and she gave him time to scrutinize the landscape from a few inches away. "And the yellow dashes of the swirling night sky, here among the blues and black. They shouldn't have curls at the ends either."

De Roos stumbled back, his jaw dropped and his face lost its color. "Gunter! Call the police!"

Luuk De Roos urged Richard, Kendra, and Stefan to remain long enough to be interviewed by the police. Two arrived immediately, followed by a detective within a half hour. After flashing his badge, he joined in the questioning of the household staff and additional employees hired for the evening. Not being trained in crime investigation, Richard hung back and only participated when the police asked questions.

The chef had already reported by then that some of the temporary workers had left after the serving of the truffles ended. No other foods were served, only champagne and liqueurs as the presentation of the new acquisition wound down. His attitude left no one wondering whom he blamed for the theft.

Richard, Kendra, and Stefan Appelhof were retained until two a.m., with cautions that they might be called back later. Richard promised to get Interpol involved, and that alone allowed them to be released for a few hours' sleep. They again said goodnight to the host and hostess and left together.

Seeing no taxi patrolling the area, the three walked toward Richard's Interpol loaner in the next block with Kendra between both willing escorts.

"What led you to go back and examine the van Gogh tonight?" Richard said to Kendra.

"I didn't go back to examine it. I simply wanted to see it one more time before leaving."

"And the discrepancies were that obvious? Humpf. I was a little bleary-eyed by then." In his few years of teaching, he wished he'd had one student as sharp as Kendra.

Richard needed this woman. As the Godfather said in the movie, "Keep your friends close, but keep your enemies closer." He didn't know which role Kendra played, but she had the sharpest eye for detail he'd ever seen. If there were an innate, intuitive gift for artistic perception, she possessed it.

Either she pointed out the theft in all honesty, or she had fingered a fraud to keep down the competition.

"Please allow me to take you home, Stefan. And I can easily deliver Ms. Cooper to her doorstep. Interpol has loaned me a car, and I may as well use it."

"Thank you for the offer, but I insist on escorting the lady home."

The world turned at a slower pace on Sunday morning. Kendra woke wishing for her church in Fort Worth, not only for worship but also to be with her friends. She'd been in Amsterdam a full week, and hardly spoke to anyone except her landlady and the mother-in-law. She had lots of time to rhapsodize over the grand masters of art, photograph their works and attempt to paint them, but she lived in a vacuum. If

Lori had been able to come, they'd be talking about colors and techniques. Maybe painting side by side if they'd gotten a larger room together. But Lori's boyfriend wanted her to save her vacation to spend with him. She hoped they'd marry, and she'd need those days for a honeymoon.

Some people had boyfriends and hopes for marriage. Kendra had neither at the moment and pretended it didn't matter. The men she met in the art world hadn't been great date prospects so far. How sweet it would be to share love and art with a man.

Kendra showered and dressed, but had nowhere to go. Maybe out for some truly excellent coffee and fresh bread for breakfast.

She left her room, noticing the Mercedes no longer parked on the street. Feeling a sense of relief about that, which she couldn't put a reason to, she ambled along the sidewalk a few blocks to a café with wobbly round tables outside.

Indulging in strong coffee first with a cinnamon roll and then a cappuccino, she tried to come up with a plan for the next almost two weeks. Brochures she'd brought along in her shoulder bag showed museums of every imaginable kind, every point in history, as well as all kinds of crafts and sciences. Diamonds, photography, churches, houseboats, the Sloten windmill, tulips—they all had their own museums. Yesterday's thought of renting a bicycle came up again. About the time the caffeine hit, she decided she could use some exercise and outdoor time.

Upon returning to the apartment, she paused on the stairs when the landlady opened her door and greeted her.

The younger Mrs. Graham wore an anxious line on her brow. "Would you like to go to church with me? It's just a couple of blocks away. You might find it interesting."

"Is it in English?"

"Sorry, but I could translate for you. Mother Graham and I would love to have you with us."

"What kind of church is it?"

"Lutheran. What are you?"

"I go to what we call a Bible church. Non-denominational Protestant. Really, I wouldn't understand a thing in your church. I wouldn't even be able to sing the hymns. Thank you so much for the invitation, but I think I'll take a bike ride this morning." They parted cordially, and Kendra went to change into shorts.

Walking back to the café area, she found a bicycle rental shop and chose one with a small basket for her bag and maps. Bikes whizzed by in singles and groups, everyone seeming to know where they were going and needing to get there in a hurry. Her sense of purpose faltered. She stopped and straddled the bike and pulled out her city map. Nearby she found the Oosterpark, which she hadn't seen yet. An entrance beckoned to her.

Peddling at a leisurely pace around the central green lawns, she stopped to admire one of the monuments. She hadn't ridden a bike in years, so her thighs needed the rest.

Hairs raised on the back of her neck when the man behind her passed and then stopped as if admiring the curved central lake. She had no justification for thinking he might resemble the man outside her apartment yesterday afternoon, yet the feeling remained. He looked familiar in a nondescript way. She tried to remember when he'd begun cycling behind her, and decided he'd entered the park right after her.

No one in their right mind would be stalking her. She had nothing of value.

❧❧

Richard drained his coffee and responded to a call from Maarten, who was trailing Kendra. "I think she made me. I say we get out of here and try to get a search warrant tomorrow."

"What's the chance she's delivering a canvas by bike?"

"Not unless it's a small one rolled up in that denim bag she always carries."

"You're still getting a signal?"

"Yes, but if she ever cleans out the bag, she'll find the bug. It just looks like a tiny, round battery. She may not know what it is."

"We're wasting a beautiful Sunday." Richard motioned to the waiter that he needed change for a large bill. "Why don't you go home to your wife and kids? I'll hang around the park for a while, then go back toward her apartment house. I'm hoping we have enough evidence for Interpol to request a search warrant. See you tomorrow."

Even criminals and police needed a day off. They would learn more very soon. Meanwhile, he tried to stuff his frustration into his pocket with his change.

Kendra brought her full intensity to bear on a new canvas Monday morning. Copying the great masters would be so much easier once she returned to Fort Worth. If she borrowed the Kimbell's equipment overnight, she could project her art photos onto a canvas and outline the major elements of the design in a few minutes. Marking all the placements with a tape measure had been tedious.

Copies had to be correct, or she'd waste all that work. She staked a lot of hope on what, in reflection, had been casual comments by Dr. Rollins that he could help her sell fine art copies. The tension created in her life by debt plagued her every day, especially every payday. Her paycheck wasn't enough to pay off her college and grad school loans, and it wouldn't be enough for a long time. She had to do this, and she had to get it right.

She roughed out the design of *Wheatfield under Thunderclouds*. If she put the horizon in exactly the right location, the placement of the sky—beautiful dashed blues— then the patches of fields would fall into place. The earlier painting with crows proved her efforts were on the right track.

By the time the sun had shifted from shining its brilliance directly through her window, she realized she had to either have lunch out, an expense she'd rather avoid, or buy something to eat in her room. She smiled as she covered nearly authentic seventeenth century oil paints with modern plastic wrap. The white paint, having more lead content than the others, required special precautions. After wiping smears off her hands, she stuffed some money and the room key into her pocket and descended.

Hattie Graham stopped sweeping the front walk and stared at her with trouble in her eyes.

"Good morning, Mrs. Graham. I'm headed to the grocery. Can I pick up anything for you?"

She looked down at the cobblestone walkway. "I have what I need."

Missing the usual friendly exchange, Kendra paused. "Is something the matter?"

"No." But her expression belied the slow shaking of her head. "Not with me."

What a strange reply. "Is your mother-in-law okay?"

She glanced toward a third floor window. "She was fine this morning. She'll be downstairs in a few minutes to have cold cuts and cheese with me."

"Okay, well, I've got to pick up something for both lunch

and supper. See you in a few minutes."

Thunder rumbled overhead, and the bright morning was quickly becoming dark. No wonder she'd lost her natural light through the window.

Both women looked up at the clouds rolling in.

"Kendra?"

She turned, wondering what trouble played on her landlady's face. "You don't…um…have drugs up there, do you? In the room?"

"No." Kendra answered emphatically, with heat rising to her cheeks. "I don't do drugs. Why do you ask?"

Mrs. Graham shook her head again and swept the walkway with vigor. "Just making sure."

They had enjoyed each other's company over supper twice. Some suspicion had erased that easy sense of companionship and replaced it with this awkward exchange. Kendra wondered why doubt had come between them. "Sure I can't get you anything while I'm out?"

"Thanks for asking. I don't need anything right now."

As Kendra rounded the corner, two black Mercedes cars cruised by in the direction of her apartment house. She watched as three men and a woman got out and spoke to Mrs. Graham. Looked like someone was in trouble. Maybe one of the other renters had drugs. She had only passed them coming and going, and they didn't appear to be deadbeats. In a country with legal pot sold openly in stores, heavier drugs might be circulating.

Hurrying to the neighborhood market, she felt an urgency to return and find out what was up. What's more, a light sprinkle started to fall, and she hadn't brought her umbrella.

After making her purchases, she requested an extra plastic bag to put over her head. As quickly as she could return without slipping on the wet brick sidewalk, she entered the apartment house, pulled off the head cover, and started up the stairs to her room. At the halfway turn, she saw Hattie Graham standing at her open door talking to a woman in police uniform.

Gasping with shock, Kendra dashed the rest of the way up. "What's happening? What's going on?"

Chapter 7

The policewoman pushed back against Kendra's shoulder with an open palm. "Ms. Cooper, please remain outside."

She blinked when the officer used her name, then she glanced at Mrs. Graham. She must have given them information. That explained their awkward exchange as she'd left. Kendra stung at the betrayal.

"But what…? This is my room. What are you doing in my room?" She could see one man and woman in police uniforms, a man in a worn suit and tie, and Dr. Richard Reed in khaki slacks with a casual dark green knit shirt.

The guy in the suit propped her new Van Gogh copy on the easel and approached the door. "I'm Detective Maarten Alders. That's Dr. Richard Reed, Art Experts Group for Interpol." He motioned to the man she knew as an art professor. "You're under arrest for art forgery," he said in Dutch-accented English.

Interpol? "Dr. Reed and I have met, but the introduction didn't mention Interpol." Her mind raced through their two meetings searching for any word that could be misconstrued to incriminate her. "I was told he was an Emory professor."

Dr. Reed turned from inspecting her canvases. "Assistant professor, actually, on summer leave to assist Interpol with this investigation."

Alders took handcuffs from his wide leather belt. "Turn around, please, and put your hands behind your back."

"But I didn't... Those paintings aren't..." She didn't turn around and instead propped her hands at her waist. "How dare you burst in here and search my room? Do you have a search warrant?" She didn't know if Dutch police required one, so doubt replaced a portion of her indignation.

Detective Alders reached for a folder on her bed and pulled out an official-appearing paper. Of course it was all in Dutch, so she couldn't read a word except her name. She handed it to Hattie Graham, still hanging around just outside her door.

"I've already seen it. It's real, or I wouldn't have let them in. It says they're searching for art forgeries." The scorn on her face had settled into an eye-shifting apology.

"But I haven't. These paintings—"

"You're telling me you didn't paint these forgeries, Ms. Cooper?"

"No. Yes, I painted them, but they aren't forgeries." Exasperation scrambled her words.

Dr. Reed motioned toward her canvas still on the easel and told the uniformed officer to take it out to the car.

He lifted the Van Gogh with both hands and started toward the door.

"Be careful. Watch out." Panic rose in her voice, the pitch increasing toward a shriek. "The oil isn't dry yet. You're going to ruin it." She blocked his exit at the door.

Maarten grasped one of her wrists and slapped on a cuff. "Step aside, miss. I caution you not to resist arrest."

"It's raining." Her voice cracked, and sudden tears spilled down her face. "Please don't take it. I worked so hard ..."

The policeman, shorter and younger than the others, paused and looked to the detective, then to Reed.

He was bent down inspecting her copy of *Tiger in a Tropical Storm*, which leaned against the far wall. He picked it up and joined the group at the door. "Do you have any other forgeries, Ms. Cooper?" Just Saturday night they'd used each other's first names. She'd thought he was a new friend, another American in a strange city.

"They are copies, true, but you can't say they're forgeries. Look." She pointed with her trembling free hand to the bottom of the Van Gogh the younger policeman held. "Do you see Van Gogh's signature on this painting? Okay, it isn't finished. But there's nothing illegal about copying a painting if you don't try to pass it off as an original."

At least not in the US. She felt her face drain with the realization that she hadn't specifically checked the Dutch laws. But Dr. Rollins said she could, and he wanted her to. He said he could sell…

The four invaders paused, confused expressions among them.

Kendra held her breath and tried to stop the flow of tears. She didn't pull back her handcuffed wrist, nor did she offer the other one. "It's an art student technique. My professor encouraged me to try it."

"Did he encourage you to sell it?"

She glanced away, not able to admit she aspired to be good enough to sell a copy of a great master. "Not to deceive anyone. Not signed as an original."

Reed motioned for the others to join him on the far side of the narrow bed. The young policeman left the painting against the wall near the door, and the detective attached the other handcuff to the foot of the metal bed. The three police mumbled together in Dutch, with the American looking on in apparent confusion. Then they switched to English, but she still couldn't hear well enough to understand what they said. She looked at Mrs. Graham, who turned her face away.

The huddle dissolved, and Reed stepped closer to Kendra.

"We'll leave the paintings here in the room. You will come with us for an interview at the police station."

It wasn't a question.

Alders released Kendra's handcuff from the bed then removed the other handcuff from her wrist. She'd had to bend to hold that position for several minutes, and her back complained. She straightened and scanned the place that had been her studio, her sanctuary. Much too crowded with the four intruders taking up the precious little space around her single bed.

Dr. Reed picked up her palette from the newspaper spread on the foot of her bed. He stared at the colors, then lifted the plastic wrap from one edge and looked closer. The man and woman in police uniforms seemed to be waiting for orders. Even Alders looked to Reed. She wondered what part he played in this charade.

He looked up from the paints and replaced them on the newspaper. He didn't just drop them, or allow the plastic cover to stir them together. His motion came across as almost reverent, showing his understanding that an artist's palette was personal. "Let's go."

"Am I under arrest?" She wanted to cry so bad her throat ached, but dared not give in to that weakness.

He and the detective, whose name she no longer remembered, shared a glance. The detective shook his head. "No, you're coming in of your own volition to help us answer some questions," Reed said. "It'll make you look better in this process."

She nodded and reached into the wardrobe. When she turned quickly with a foot-long black object, the three police officers went for their guns.

Kendra felt the blood drop from her head. With a slow movement to her side, she raised the item which had nearly cost her life. "It's an umbrella, guys. It's raining out there."

With a collective sigh, the officers returned to a more relaxed posture, but the air in the room carried a charge high enough to strike lightning.

Reed waved her toward the door.

"Is there anything I should bring?" She picked up her denim shoulder bag. "You want to look through this?"

The detective accepted the purse, took a quick look, and gave it back. "Bring your passport."

She took it from a drawer in the wardrobe, feeling everyone's eyes on her back. Then she left the room with male and female officers in front and the other guys behind. Locking the door, she wondered why she bothered. As she passed her landlady, she controlled the urge to smirk. The elder Mrs. Graham, her tilted eyebrows a mask of dismay, stood on the stairs to the upper floor cuddling her cat.

"It's going to be okay, Mrs. Graham. Don't worry." She felt closer right now to the elderly woman than her landlord, Hattie Graham, her former best friend in Holland.

The five of them trundled out into the cars under a light rain. Though she crossed to one of the Mercedes in a few steps, she made a point of using the black umbrella. Then she closed it to slip into the back seat where Richard, ignoring the rain, held the door for her.

She knew no one else in Amsterdam except the two Mrs. Grahams, yet it mattered to her that the handcuffs had been removed. The disgrace of being led out as a prisoner would have been too much to bear.

She wanted to pray but didn't know where to start. She'd been assured that copying the techniques of the great artists— okay, copying their art—wasn't a crime. Having no sin to confess, then, she launched into a jumbled mental cry for help, the black mass of a plea for mercy.

The cloud's silver lining was thankfulness that her father hadn't seen this. She needed to keep him from ever knowing, or he would throw it in her face for the rest of her life.

୨୦୧

Richard sat beside Kendra in the back with Maarten driving as their car led the other one twenty minutes through the city. Her jaw clamped tight and her fingers shook until she clasped both hands in her lap.

He wanted to calm her, and it upset him that she triggered his sympathy. His reputation as a distant—perhaps too cool—art professor rested on the need to maintain proper separation from his students, an emotional group of young artists. He refrained from speaking about anything but the weather in order to tape her whole story at the police department.

When they got there, she had to yield her bag, including her cell phone and her passport, before being ushered to a small room occupied by a metal table and three chairs. She cast a glance at the one-way glass and frowned. A little intimidation would work well for them.

Alders and he took one side of the table and directed her to the middle of the other. While they expressed no rudeness or belligerence, neither man smiled.

Alders placed a tape recorder at the center. "This interview will be taped. Please state your full name for the record."

"Kendra Lorraine Cooper. And I would like to know yours as well."

"I am Maarten Alders, as I told you before at your apartment, and also with us is Dr. Richard Reed."

"What do I call you? Officer Alders?"

He nodded. "Detective Alders will do."

"But Dr. Reed, you are not in the Amsterdam police? What is your association?"

Maarten raised his hand. "We'll be asking the questions."

"I don't mind. I think she has a right to know whom she's talking to." Richard captured her eyes, a lovely combination of hazel. With her wet hair and the insecure rounding of her shoulders, her lack of confidence stimulated a protective urge. At least he could be nice. "As I've told you before, I'm an art and art history assistant professor at Emory University in Atlanta, specializing in seventeenth and eighteenth century works. I'm on a short term assignment with Interpol's Experts Group." He nodded to Maarten to continue the questioning.

"Please state your permanent address and profession."

"I live at 4320 Birchman Avenue, Fort Worth, Texas, 76107. I'm a librarian at the Kimbell Art Museum in Fort Worth."

"So you have—what?—a bachelor's degree in library science?"

"My bachelor's is in art history, with a minor in art. Then I have an MSLIS—Master of Science in Library and Information Science."

They knew all this, but it had to go on the tape. Besides, the information-gathering became part of the process of warming up the suspect. Get her to tell the simple stuff. Get her talking and sharing information.

Richard propped his elbows on the table and adopted a friendly demeanor. "Tell us about painting copies of major art works. Why do you do it?"

"It's—like a hobby. A way of appreciating the masters, learning what it took for them to paint how they did."

"But you sell them, don't you? I mean, it's a lot of work." Richard tried not to look threatening. "A painting like that takes a long time."

She ducked her head. "I've sold a few to friends, just for a hundred bucks. And sometimes at art shows."

Her apparent transparency became disarming. "Why? With your talent, you could be making a good living painting fakes."

"I prefer the term 'copy.' And yes, a good copyist can make a living that way. But I'm still learning. I'm not that good."

"I beg to differ with you, Ms. Cooper." Richard leaned back and dropped his hands to the table's edge. "What I saw today was excellent."

She blushed—actually blushed, dropped her head but angled it aside. The slightest upward curve touched her lips. Did she not know?

"You're very good," he continued. "Good enough to be selling copies as originals. The skin tones on your copy of *The Milkmaid* rival the original." Maybe a stretch of the imagination, but she hadn't finished it yet.

"*The Milkmaid*?" Her eyes moved about as if she were trying to connect thoughts. "When did you see *The Milkmaid*?"

Again the men exchanged glances before Reed spoke again. "It was for sale at Appelhof Gallery. You took it there on Friday. The day after we met."

"You've been following me?"

"Not me personally, Ms. Cooper. Interpol and Amsterdam Police have been tracking your movements for several days. You're a first-rate copyist. Plenty of dealers both in Europe and the US would fence art for you."

"But that would be dishonest." Her wide-eyed look was either total innocence or a well-practiced act. "Besides, how could *The Milkmaid* be sold as an original when the original is hanging right there in the Rijksmuseum?" She threw a gesture wide as if pointing to the museum. "And the Van Goghs, too.

Who's going to buy a fraudulent painting when the real one is currently on display?"

"Lots of collectors, actually. Wealthy art fanciers who want much better than prints in their homes." Richard thought of the Gainsborough-style landscape in his parents' home. It would be child's play for her to paint something like that. "Or an art thief who's planning to steal the original and needs a good copy as part of the ruse."

Her head popped back and her eyes went wide. "You think that's what this is? That I'm part of some thief's plan? Like what happened to Mr. De Roos?" She scraped her chair back. "No way." She stood and paced. "I didn't sign my copies, remember?"

"You said they weren't finished," countered Maarten.

"No, and I probably won't finish them until I get them home. I'm here for three weeks' vacation to enjoy the art and absorb as much of the culture as possible. Then it's back to my job—"

"—and your debts from college and grad school," threw in Richard. Again, he sensed he'd caught her off guard. "You're vulnerable if not culpable, Ms. Cooper. If you haven't sold a copy as an original yet, you're ripe for the picking."

She lifted her chin with a sniff. "That would be against my moral code."

Maarten waved to her chair. "Please be seated, Ms. Cooper."

Instead, she braced her arms on the back of her chair. "You have no evidence of wrongdoing. You have no reason to keep me here." Her voice had an extra tremble, as if making a dare she couldn't back up. "Pardon me, but my vacation clock is ticking. I'll see you back at the Rijks, I assume. Good day, gentlemen."

So she had recognized him. And neither one of them

could follow her unobserved anymore.

She paused as if wondering whether they'd stop her, then marched to the door, opened it, and slammed it behind her.

Richard dashed out and followed her to the front desk.

"I'd like to have my purse and passport back, please."

Richard nodded to the officer at the front desk. He took the items from a locked basket in the next room and produced a receipt for her to sign.

"May I offer you a ride home?" Richard gave her his universally-agreed winning smile.

"I'd rather take the tram."

Chapter 8

Kendra's head churned with the afternoon's experience. She'd never had lunch, because the police were at her apartment when she returned with food. Her stomach hurt with hunger and the acid of stress. Arriving at the main door, she inhaled deeply and sighed out a ton of tension. Inside, Hattie Graham's door opened at the same time she entered.

Her landlady stood there, not speaking, with her eyebrow raised in question.

Kendra remarked, "I'm back."

"They didn't keep you?"

"Of course not. I'm not guilty of anything." Kendra lifted her chin and flashed a glare at Hattie.

"I'm … sorry. About letting them in. But they had a search warrant. I couldn't keep them out. They would have broken down the door if I hadn't used my key."

"I know. You do what you have to do." It was just that … Hattie believed them. All that friendship and trust had been washed away with the wave of a piece of paper. Kendra took the first few steps before the landlady spoke again.

"Um … I was wondering … You're going to stay here?" Looking up the stairs, her voice tinged with a whine, she wiped her hands on her apron.

Kendra's breath halted as she turned around. "I have no intention of moving. The police have cleared me. I have almost another two weeks in Amsterdam."

They stared at each other from across a breach. Kendra briefly considered moving her two suitcases, easel, oils, paintings, and trying to find another apartment. Wasting more of her vacation time. "I paid you in advance for the three weeks." She didn't suggest a refund, because she didn't want any talk of a move. She hoped Hattie didn't want to part with the money. Maybe she had already spent it.

"Of course." The landlady turned and retreated to her quarters.

With the last bit of adrenaline burned out of her system, Kendra trudged up to her room. Her first thought was to eat a sandwich and flop on the bed to totally relax, maybe even sleep. Seeing the room in disarray following the invasion of the booty snatchers, she immediately moved things back into their places. She put the canvases where they had been, set up the easel in the right place with the second Van Gogh on it, and leaned the tiger against the far wall. She moved the one straight-back chair to its little table, and closed the wardrobe.

Finally she made a sandwich with extra ham and cheese, poured some water, and thought a quick prayer before chomping down.

Slumped before the table, she savored every bite. The fragrance of oil paints combining with ham and cheese smelled like home. The stench of having been violated remained only in her mind.

A scratch came at the door. Boots. The cat with three white feet and one black, unbooted foot. Hattie Graham didn't want her friendship anymore, but Boots did.

She opened the door and cooed to the cat, which sprang onto her bed. Kendra dashed to move her palette to the safety of the table. "You think this is still your bed, do you? Well, it isn't, but I don't mind if you come for a visit. In fact, I'm kind of glad to see you. Someone else's cat is better than no friend at all."

She put the last corner of sandwich in her mouth and ran a hand over the sleek fur. Boots responded by flipping over to expose her belly. Kendra stroked her a few times, then cuddled her in her arms.

Someone knocked on the door. "Kendra, is Boots in there?" The elder Mrs. Graham's British accent identified her.

"Yes, ma'am." She opened the door, still holding the pet. "I guess she was just checking everything out."

"Dearie, I'm so sorry those people came here this afternoon. Please don't blame Hattie. They had that search warrant, and she couldn't—"

"I understand. But believe me, I'm not selling frauds to anyone. I'm just an art librarian on a vacation. And I don't know anything about forgers in this country or my own. I couldn't help them at the police station."

"Would you like a little tea and poppy seed bread? I went downstairs to Hattie's and baked this afternoon."

Kendra wondered again why Hattie kept her mother-in-law stashed on the top floor. Perhaps to maximize on room rental. "Thanks, but I just ate."

The last thing she needed in her system was a food that would test positive for drugs.

Richard swallowed his pride and called his Interpol handler while Maarten listened from the confined office where they worked. "This woman we've been following is a remarkably good copyist, but we can't pin a crime on her. She may even be one of the artists we're searching for, but she hadn't signed any of her paintings. And like she said, she can't pass them off as originals when the originals are hanging in museums right here in the city."

"Then maybe she's preparing copies for a steal and switch." Van Der Veen's raspy voice sounded none too pleased.

"Same thing occurred to me. Thought I'd give the museum managers a heads up, just in case." Richard took a gulp of what he promised himself was absolutely his last coffee of the day. Until after dinner tonight. "The thing is, this woman acts naïve—and maybe it's just an act. But I get the feeling she could be manipulated easily. If I stay in contact without being too much of an irritation, she may lead us to the people running the scam. Because I'm convinced she isn't the head of it."

"Okay, so what's your next move?"

"Maarten and I are going to continue interviewing the gallery owners."

"Remember, Dr. Reed, this is Europe's artistic heritage we're trying to protect. Not just the value of stock in museums and galleries."

"Yes, sir. We're on it." He'd spent time in every course he'd taught on how Hitler's destruction of art was an attempt to change Europe's culture. The *Führer* wanted to erase its history and redirect the minds of its youth. Van Der Veen didn't need to lecture him.

They signed off, and Richard chugged the rest of his coffee. Maarten raised an eyebrow in question as they both stood.

"He thinks I've forgotten why I've been brought over. He never was in favor of my coming for just the summer. If I can't at least push the investigation forward before I leave in August, my name's mud."

"What's next? Back to the art schools? Are you still interested in that kid who turned out Picasso-style canvases?"

"Not at all. He's not worthy to clean brushes for someone

like Kendra Cooper. Let's prowl the art dealers. The honest ones have the most to lose."

Richard and Maarten wasted a couple of hours in the art district concentrating on a short list of known forgeries which had passed through Amsterdam galleries in the previous decade. The only thing they learned was that Kendra's paintings had already left Appelhof's gallery with new owners. Alexander Holt had bought *The Milkmaid*, still unsigned. The legal transaction left them no avenues for protest or arrest.

As they left the gallery, Maarten motioned toward a coffee house. "Let's take a load off our feet."

"At a coffee house?" Richard looked incredulous.

"Yes. A coffee *house*. It's the coffee *shops* that sell marijuana and drugs."

Richard followed him to a shaded outdoor table, feeling the need to re-think their investigation. "You know, I think Kendra Cooper is innocent. I just wish she'd sign all her paintings."

"I am a policeman for a few years now, and this woman … She does not fit the psychological profile of a criminal. Maybe she walks the line, I don't know. She needs money, and that makes her a risk." He stared into the distance. "I think you should talk to her again. Not in the police building. Get a little closer. Perhaps you learn something, like if Holt made a pitch to her."

"I doubt she has any interest in talking to me. Afraid I stepped in it pretty bad."

"Stepped in what?"

"Never mind. An American expression." Richard tracked on the bicycles whirring past. They made him want to take a day off in the park.

"You could apologize."

His attention zapped back to Maarten. "Why? Okay, we accused her of being in a fraud ring. But it was all in the line of duty. We had our reasons."

"Apologies work with women. Especially like her. What is she, a Christian? I saw her bow over her wurst in the park." Maarten swore and shook his head. "She's got it bad."

"Yeah." Agreeing to that statement pricked Richard's conscience.

"But you see, that's the kind of woman who respects an apology. You go talk to her. You'll see."

ဓာ

Kendra recognized Dr. Reed's number and came close to not answering the phone. She barely said hello before he launched into a bumbling apology.

"We were so wrong. I feel really bad about that. I thought maybe I could make up for it by taking you out to dinner."

Words wouldn't come. Was this a new pick-up? Arrest a woman and then make up by offering to take her for a date? "Sorry. I need to make up for the time I lost today." She was willing to bet very few single women turned this guy down when he asked them out to dinner.

"The museums are nearly closed for the day. Give yourself a break and take off the rest of the evening. We need your help. Since you're not part of the fraud ring, maybe you can help us re-think our investigation."

She hated the expression, "I don't want to get involved," but that's exactly how she felt right now. "Don't you understand? I'm not a fraud artist. I don't know what you're asking about."

"Are you in your apartment right now?"

She hesitated, wondering if he knew. Not given to lying, she considered dodging the answer then answered, "Yes."

"Look out your window."

After putting down her brush, she went around the easel and peeked through the thin curtain. Dr. Reed stood in the street below, holding his cell phone to his ear and lifting a bouquet of colorful mixed flowers.

"Please come down. Let's have some coffee or whatever. I admit I was wrong about you. I need your help."

He had her at the word "need." She was such a sucker for that word. "Okay," she said as if agreeing to go to her worst friend's birthday party. "Just for a few minutes."

She took her sweet time leaving the room and coming downstairs. She left her hair in a ponytail gathered into a rubber band at her neck and didn't put on lipstick.

He came to the sidewalk and handed her the flowers. "Hi."

"Hi."

Kendra noticed as her landlady turned away from her sitting room window, which was open to the fresh summer air. Hattie Graham had witnessed the scene.

Kendra stepped over blooms in the flowerbed, called Hattie back, and handed her the bouquet. "Would you please put these in some water for me?"

"Well, I ... ah ... sure."

Kendra returned to the sidewalk. "You wanted to talk?" She had no intention of making this any easier for him.

"There's a little pizza place a couple of blocks from here…"

"Do you see me holding a sign, 'Will talk for food?' I'm not hungry." A half-truth. Her travel budget required stringent means.

"Then let's meander in the park." He motioned toward the park where Maarten had followed her last Sunday, and started walking. After a few steps, she followed.

ᔕᦂᦔᔒ

Richard tried to act relaxed, like this conversation was no big deal. "What are you painting now? Or what is your next project?"

"Finish Rousseau's tiger, and maybe do a bright Cézanne. Something cheerful. Or a landscape."

Her voice carried the slightest tremble of fear. She didn't realize he was completely harmless. He didn't carry a gun, and even when he'd questioned her at the police station, he didn't think he'd been threatening. Except for breaking into her apartment and searching among her personal belongings, he reminded himself. "How long do you plan to be in Amsterdam?"

"August sixth. Eleven days. The time is going by too quickly."

"Is there any chance of your staying longer?"

She flashed a quizzical look. Then a shrug. "I have a job. I have to be back."

"I know what you mean. I plan to work with Interpol until mid-August, then return to Emory. Sliding in at the last moment before classes start."

Half a block later, he ventured another question. "Is this your first time in Europe?"

"First time. I'd like to come back and see more. Especially Austria."

"Beautiful country. You should paint it. You're very talented, you know. You've matched the techniques of the masters. That's how you recognize frauds, isn't it?"

She nodded sullenly. "What is it you want to know?"

Now inside the serene garden, he admired the open lawn without answering. "How long have you known Alexander Holt?"

The question surprised her. "I don't know him at all. We were introduced at the De Roos showing, but I'd met him in the outdoor food court near the museum." She recounted the accidental meeting at which he gave her his card. "And then at the De Roos's he acted as if he didn't know me."

"You know he bought *The Milkmaid* from Stefan Appelhof, don't you?"

She gave a gasp of surprise, her smile lifting her face for the first time since he'd lured her out. "No, I didn't know. Since Stefan hasn't called, I assumed he still had her."

They rounded a curve in the walkway, and the pond's center fountain spurted water in a graceful geyser.

"We have reason to believe Holt may have sold a few fakes into the European art market."

"Why don't you just get a search warrant and see what he's hiding in his underwear drawer." Her immediate retort came with the sharpness of a palette knife.

"Ouch. Okay, I deserved that. But tell me what you would look for if you thought a counterfeit painting lurked in a private collection."

"What can I tell you that you don't already know? For a reproduction, each stroke and color has to be perfectly like the original. That requires tons of patience. Most painters just won't do it." She sat at a bench and stared toward the fountain. "Study the most complicated parts, and see how close it comes to the original. That's why I take so many photos in museums and then enlarge them on my computer. A lot of painters don't even use the right brushes."

She watched a toddler stumbling with her ball on the

lawn. "And then there's the color mix. We have tubes in pre-mixed shades that never existed before. For an authentic-looking copy, you have to use only the colors available a century, two centuries ago."

The more she shared, the more he admired the perfectionism of her talent. He still didn't understand why she limited herself to tediously copying the work of others.

Chapter 9

Now that Richard had complete information on Kendra Cooper, he had verified her identity, residence, and employment at the Kimbell Museum. Everything checked, even her monthly pass at the museums in Amsterdam. She was who she said she was. But so much more. He'd seen her indignant during their raid. He'd seen her timid and insecure. Saturday night, he'd seen her work the art crowd like a well-placed museum professional.

Lost in the recollection of her grace and disarming charm, he startled when his phone rang. Van Der Veen's office number at Interpol. "What's happening there, Dr. Reed?"

May as well get the bad news out. "Discovering more crime but fewer criminals."

"I heard about the theft at the home of De Roos. You were there, *ja*?"

"Right. Probably a catering employee who did it. The local police are working on it, but I registered our interest in the case." He'd shown his Interpol ID primarily to extricate them from the post-midnight investigation. He'd made no promises about searching for the thief, since that had nothing to do with his work at Interpol.

"I have here something I want you to see in Hungary," Van Der Veen continued. "A merchant in Budapest has several paintings he claims belonged to his family before the war. He says they were taken by the army of Hitler, and now they are being returned through an underground Jewish group of which I have never heard. And I thought I knew them all."

"And you doubt their authenticity?"

"It would be too easy to slip in a few frauds. For that matter, the paintings seized by Hitler may have been frauds. A lot of wealthy people had copies made for their country homes or to take the place of art they had to sell. This isn't just a contemporary crime, you know."

The shift to Budapest sounded like a whole new can of worms. "When do you want me there?"

"Yesterday."

Richard's first thought surprised him—that he'd be leaving Kendra, sacrificing any chance to get to know her better. "I might be able to hop a flight tomorrow, if—"

"I expect you at my Budapest office as early as possible." Van Der Veen's coarse voice and Dutch accent made that decision final.

Did Richard dare ask? Would inviting Kendra Cooper sound as if he weren't sufficiently qualified alone? In a reckless moment, he realized he didn't care. This was just a summer liaison with Interpol, an interesting experience which would look good on his résumé. "There's a woman who works with the Kimbell Art Museum of Fort Worth who's vacationing here right now. She has a keen eye for copies. Spotted the fraud Saturday night. Mind if I bring her?"

Van Der Veen said nothing.

"I mean, if she's interested," Richard added.

"I can't give her a salary. Hotel and expenses, or just add her to your account."

"We're talking separate rooms, of course."

"Of course. I might find some bonus funds if she becomes valuable to the investigation, but I'd rather you didn't mention that."

He wouldn't, but might consider sweetening the pot if she hesitated. His family trust fund ran wide and deep enough that he could do anything he pleased. Especially on a paid summer in Europe.

He was glad he hadn't mentioned earlier that Kendra Cooper was his prime—and only—suspect.

Quivering with excitement, Kendra left her discussion with Stefan Appelhof. If he sold the two paintings she'd taken him for the kind of prices he expected, that would recoup the cost of her trip and bring down her college and grad school debt a few thousand dollars. Less debt meant less interest on the debt, which meant she could pay off the rest sooner.

She hurried to the boarding house, hoping to finish one more painting to leave with Stefan at the end of next week, when she'd be flying back to her day job. Already her mind swirled with questions about what the European art market wanted compared to what sold well in America, and whether she should try to ship canvases back to Stefan from Texas later. She took a mental pause to thank God for the means of paying toward her debt, which she took as further confirmation of His direction to stay in the field of art despite her parents' objections.

After jogging upstairs, she rattled the oversized key in her door and threw it wide. The almost-finished painting no longer propped on the easel waiting for her attention. Her mouth dropped open, and she gasped. Maybe she'd put it against the wall? Making a full turn around the room, which was small and had no hiding places, she realized someone had taken it and a couple of other unfinished canvases. And her computer with its hundreds of art photos, the vast wealth of her trip.

Beneath the usual smell of her oil paints and solvent floated the odor of the intruder. He'd left a ripe underarm impression on the air of her closed room. Or it could be a woman, but she didn't think so.

Wave after wave of shock washed over her. She dropped on the chair at the narrow table she used for a desk and caught the mirror's reflection of her mouth hanging open, her face white.

Then a full fury hit, and she dug in her purse for Richard Reed's card. Her fingers trembled as she punched the numbers on her cell phone so hard she broke a nail.

Reed answered with a calm, pleasant greeting.

"What have you done with my paintings and my computer?" she blasted through the airwaves. "Are you not convinced yet that I'm not a criminal?"

"Excuse me? What are you talking about?"

"If you got another search warrant and raided my room, you're going to look really silly this time. And there's nothing—I mean absolutely *nothing*—on my computer to interest you except a few hundred amateur photos of museum art."

"Kendra, are you saying a team has searched your room again?" His voice held none of its usual confidence.

"I assume so. Just like last time, I wasn't here when the breaking and entering happened." She intended for her accusation to sting.

"What was taken?"

"My laptop and the van Gogh copy I hadn't finished yet. And another one in progress. Stefan has the other two on consignment." Thank heaven she took them to him as soon as he called, or she would've lost so much more.

"Have you spoken to your landlady about this?"

"I just got here. Just entered the room and found this …

this … *desecration* of my privacy and theft of personal belongings."

"Kendra, back out of the room without touching anything." His smooth tone of authority had returned. "Don't touch the door handle again. Wait right there. I'm coming."

"You didn't do this?"

"I definitely didn't, and I'll call Maarten and the police chief to find out if anyone from the station knows about it. Please back out and stay put. It'll take me about fifteen minutes."

Kendra did as he ordered. Wandering out in a daze, she descended to Hattie Graham's door. She knocked and waited and knocked again. Hattie didn't open up, so she returned to her own floor and sat on the top step. Boots the cat joined her from the third floor, meowing and pawing at her leg. When Kendra smoothed her fur, Boots climbed into her lap, circled, and made herself comfortable.

Tears spilled down Kendra's cheeks. In so few minutes she'd gone from rhapsodizing about her future to wondering why the world wanted to thwart and complicate her life.

"Boots?" the elder Mrs. Graham called from the top story. "Where are you, sweetums?"

Kendra looked up the next flight of stairs, causing more tears to fall. She should tell the lady she was borrowing comfort from her cat, but she knew her voice would crack if she spoke.

"Boots? Oh, there you are. My goodness, she likes you." Mrs. Graham held to the banister as she took each careful step. She looked directly at Kendra when she neared the bottom. "What's the matter, dearie?"

Kendra shrugged, unwilling to speak of the immensity of her loss and the sense of being invaded.

"Is it your boyfriend? Did you have a spat?"

Kendra shook her head, wondering what the dear old lady was talking about. "I don't have a boyfriend."

"I mean the young man who came for your things this afternoon. He told me he was your boyfriend."

"What?" Her head jerked toward the elderly woman. At that moment, someone rang at the outside door. Probably Reed. "Wait. I'll be right back. Don't go away." She flew downstairs, checked through the small window, and let him in. "The lady who lives upstairs, the owner's mother-in-law—she said my boyfriend came for my things this afternoon. I don't have a boyfriend." She spun around and ran back up to Mrs. Graham with Reed right behind.

The urgency of their questions seemed to upset Mrs. Graham. "I was in the kitchen making my afternoon tea biscuits when he rang the bell. He asked about you. He said you were in a bind and had sent him to pick up a couple of things."

"So you let him in the front door?" Richard spoke in a deferential tone, probably to avoid sounding like he accused her of bad judgement.

She flushed and looked to the side. "I did, but I waited at Kendra's door and watched to make sure he didn't muck up her room."

"Wait a minute. You mean you let him into my room?" Kendra's blood pressure spiked. A flush of anger, not embarrassment, heated her face.

"He only took the things you asked him for, some paintings and one of those little computers."

"But I didn't send anyone for anything. You opened my door to a thief and let him take the only things I had of any value." Kendra dropped onto a step, shaking her head. The dizziness she'd felt before had become a pounding headache.

Tears came to Mrs. Graham's eyes, and her mouth

trembled. "I didn't know. I thought I was doing you a favor."

Hattie Graham entered with an armload of groceries in time to hear her mother-in-law's last sentence. She placed the bags on the bottom step and came up slowly, frowning like the evil witch of the north. "What's this? What's gone wrong?"

Kendra kept her head down, too overwrought to repeat the story. Richard Reed recounted it to Hattie, who gripped the rail and shook her head with her mouth hanging open.

The elder Mrs. Graham wrung her hands while tears streamed down her cheeks. She reached for a handkerchief from her worn sweater pocket and blew her nose. "I'm sorry. I'm so sorry. I thought I was helping."

Richard pulled out his phone. "May we sit somewhere I can ask a few questions about this fellow?"

Hattie suggested they all go into the downstairs parlor. As they did so, Richard made a call, apparently to Maarten, and reported that police would soon be there to take a statement and begin an investigation.

Kendra had little hope her computer would be recovered before she left Holland, and she certainly didn't have time to start another painting to leave with Stefan. The ancient oils would never dry enough.

Criminals knew about her. They knew where she lived. One had entered her room and taken what he wanted.

After Maarten and another policeman had come to interview the elder Mrs. Graham—who remembered little except that the guy was "nice"—Richard asked Kendra if she would please come have a cup of coffee with him.

She stared at him as if he had gone bonkers.

"Just for a few minutes. I'd like to propose a suggestion."

He placed a hand on her back and motioned toward the door. She put one foot in front of the other while twisting to look at the ladies, but she said nothing as they left the house.

Wanting to put her at ease, he measured his pace so she wouldn't have to stretch to keep up. "I received a call from my Interpol chief this morning. He wants me to participate in the examination of an art collection which has recently surfaced."

He glanced down at her, but her face remained clouded, unchanged from the robbery interview.

At the café on the corner, they entered a bricked area off the sidewalk which was delineated by a low metal fence. They took a seat at a tiny round table. He ordered a coffee and raised an eyebrow to her.

"Cappuccino, please." She dropped her hunched shoulders and leaned back on the flimsy chair. "A collection that just surfaced?"

So she had been listening.

"Fifteen paintings, several artists from Rembrandt to Picasso. They're supposedly coming out of some place they'd been hidden in Budapest, where Jewish sympathizers protected them during World War Two. Their provenance at that point puts them in various cellars and secret rooms of palaces from the era of Queen Sisi."

She tapped a forefinger on her chin, and her eyes, listless before, now darted about without focus. "First you do x-rays and chemical dating, naturally. Make sure those dates agree with the provenance for each one."

"Interpol is already working on that, painting by painting. They should have results by tomorrow."

"Are all the artists significant? I mean, we would know how Rembrandt painted in the 1640s and what his subjects were. It may not be so easy to check styles and dates for lesser known artists. Can you get the data you'd need for every one?"

Richard shifted in his wobbly chair. "I don't have a list yet of the artists and paintings. I'll find out more when I get to Budapest."

She aimed a look at him. "You're going to Budapest?"

"Yes, and I'm offering to include you, for as long as you're available."

Her head snapped back as she gasped. "Me? I'm leaving on August sixth."

"I realize that, but this is the chance of a lifetime to view works the public hasn't seen for seventy-five years. With your sharp eye and artistic insight, you'd be a huge asset to Interpol. They're covering your expenses, and there's a five thousand dollar bonus."

Her mouth opened in a perfect oval. Maybe he had gone too high.

"Look, your computer has been stolen," he continued with his most convincing explanatory tone, "the works you'd hoped to finish this week are gone, and there probably isn't time to get another painting done and dried enough to transport. Come with me to Budapest for a week. I'll get you on your flight home on schedule."

Her expression passed from stunned to clouded. Then she blushed. "I don't … I can't … I won't travel with a man. I'm not that kind of girl."

He pretended to be offended. "I'm not proposing anything improper. You'll have your own accommodations in a fine hotel. We'll work on the project together, as well as other Interpol investigators. This is your chance to do something significant for the world of art. Consider it a gift back to the grand masters."

He watched this appeal wash over her, thinking the last bit pure inspiration. What more could he say to convince her?

Assume the sale.

"You can pack all your things out of Mrs. Graham's house so you don't have to return here. Then you'll be ready to fly home when you leave Budapest."

"Why me?"

How could he put this so as not to offend? "You imitated the great masters. The paints, the brushes, the exact strokes. Who better to recognize the original?"

She tapped her chin with a forefinger again, which he now recognized as her thinking mode. "I need to talk to Stefan about the two paintings I placed with him."

"No worries. Holt has already bought *The Milkmaid*. I'm sure Mr. Appelhof be able to sell the van Gogh, too, and wire the money to your bank account. And I'll return here eventually, so I can help with that."

"What if the van Gogh doesn't sell?"

"If he's that interested, he knows it will. He's well acquainted with his market and his potential customers."

Kendra responded to her cell phone's ring. After greeting Stefan, she listened while Richard sipped coffee and acted as if he weren't there.

"Already?" Her face lifted and her eyes widened. "Today? Sure, I can. About two? ... See you then." Wonder and delight brightened her complexion as she turned to Richard. "He has sold both paintings. Oh, this is marvelous."

She clasped her hands prayer-like in front of her lips, but her smile stretched wider. "When can we leave for Budapest?"

Chapter 10

Kendra accepted Stefan's gallery check for nine thousand dollars. Six and a half for *The Milkmaid* and two and a half for van Gogh's *Wheatfield with a Reaper*.

"I didn't charge a commission on these, my dear. I'm hoping you'll let me handle all of your work in the future. Consider me your agent. We can make beautiful music together." Standing rather close for a man conducting a business transaction, he smiled down upon her with something of a flushed face. Close enough that she smelled the coffee on his quickened breath. No longer fatherly, as she'd thought of him the night they'd first met, his remark sounded like a pickup line.

She couldn't think of a man his age as a romantic interest. She stepped back and raised her hand with the check between them, dipping her head as if for a closer examination. "I thought the buyers were going to be here. I wanted to meet them, and wore the same slacks and silk blouse as before. It's the only clothing I have with me that doesn't look like any other tourist."

"Don't be concerned about your clothing. You're absolutely lovely. But the buyers have been in and out during the day. Both are businessmen who make quick decisions and get back to work. They thanked me for calling them first and wish to be notified of your coming releases."

Kendra suspected that Stefan simply bought the two

paintings and would later sell them for a profit, if possible. She decided his earning on the sales didn't matter, though she'd rather deal with an impeccably honest person, especially if he were going to sell for her again. But with extra income like this, she could retire her education debt within the next year.

"I hope you will not leave soon, Kendra. You could rent a nice apartment and stay for a while. Turning out works this rapidly, you would make a comfortable income."

"Oh, no. My job at the Kimbell means a lot to me. I *must* be on the plane on August sixth."

"Your loyalty is charming, dear, but you've found a way to make a living in the art world. That is not a trivial matter. I could help you find a place—"

"I'd rather discuss the possibility of shipping art to you from Texas. And I don't actually turn out works so quickly. I'd put a lot of study into those two and made several rough attempts before coming on this trip. This final period of van Gogh's works had captured my attention for years, as had *The Milkmaid*. She is so delicate, so difficult to paint that I may never attempt another Vermeer portrait."

"Then perhaps something simpler. A landscape, a still life. I have clients who only buy still lifes."

"Like the Breitner Mrs. Odem asked me to check out?"

He paused, holding his breath before easing it out slowly. "With your talent, you could paint one of those a week."

She turned and put the check in her little black purse. The air in the gallery suddenly became stifling. He knew the Breitner was a forgery.

And he knew she knew.

෧∘ෂ

Kendra excused herself from the gallery as soon as

possible with the intention of cashing the check before leaving for Budapest. That way, she wouldn't be left holding a worthless piece of paper if something went wrong. But how to do that in Amsterdam?

She disregarded the idea of calling someone in the Kimbell's accounting department. She didn't want them to know about her business on the side. Her father had a good plumbing business in Texas, but she struck his name off the list of choices in the space of a gnat's breath. Instead, she sent a text to Richard Reed, and he called her back in a few seconds.

Outdoor sounds formed the background of his greeting.

She said hello and got right to the point. "I have a US dollar check on a bank in New York which I want to cash and somehow deposit the money in my own account, or maybe wire it there. How can I do that?"

"Hmm. That's a good one. Where are you right now?"

"Outside Stefan Appelhof's gallery. Why?"

"I'm in the area too, gleaning more information from gallery owners before we leave. Let's meet in about fifteen minutes at that café around the corner from his shop."

"Okay, but it's getting late. I need to do something with the check today."

"Who's it drawn on?"

"Appelhof's gallery account with Citibank in New York City."

"I'll make a couple of calls to people who would know. See you at three."

Kendra window-shopped, her hand tight on the thin strap of her black purse. Amsterdam's pride in its safety mocked her trembling insides. The check was too important to her future life to lose.

Soon she spotted Richard a block away, striding the cobblestoned street toward her with his phone to his ear. A smile rose on her lips and in her mind.

As he approached, he punched it off and waved at her. "Shall we go in?"

"I'm too nervous for more coffee, and I don't need anything to eat. Why don't we just take that bench for a moment?" This had to be quick.

The street, blocked off from traffic in what the Dutch called a shopping mall, offered a nearby bench which she led them to.

"May I see the check?" Richard's voice was kind, not demanding. Perhaps she'd gotten off his most wanted criminal list.

She took it from her purse and handed it to him.

After a moment, he gave it back. "It's in dollars. You can't sell it to a bank in Amsterdam without paying an exchange fee now and another one when it's transferred to the US. I've asked my advisors, and the best way to handle it is to express mail it to your bank. It'll get there in a couple of days."

"But what if it's cancelled or lost, or not good anyway? I wanted to get it cashed immediately and then deposit cash—oh, I don't know." She bent her head and closed her eyes for a moment, trying to shake the frustration of almost having so much money—but not quite.

"You'd pay exchange fees twice, and there would be a delay, too. Appelhof's gallery has a good reputation. His record as a businessman is solid. Express mailing it to Texas is the best option by far. Would you like me to go with you to the post office? We can get it off this afternoon."

His suggestion surprised her, but considering her lack of knowledge of even where a post office was, much less how to get registered mail to the US, she accepted.

He loped along the cobblestones while she endeavored to keep up. "Tell me something, Dr. Reed—"

"—Richard, please. We're going to be working together for a week."

"Are we going to be looking for fraudulent art, or the artists, or the dealers?"

"All of the above, I suppose. Any one may lead to the others."

"What about Appelhof? I think he knows the Breitner is a fake."

He paused, so she stopped also. His blue eyes searched hers. "Do you have any proof of that?"

"No, just the way he acts. Remember how briefly he showed it to us the afternoon I met with him at the gallery? I felt then that he at least suspected it was a fraud. And then today he suggested that I could turn out one per week. He asked me to stay in Amsterdam and keep painting copies."

"That's what you do, isn't it? And it seems to be working out well for you." He motioned toward her purse.

"But I don't want to become part of some fraud ring. I'm not entirely sure he won't have someone else paint Vermeer's and van Gogh's signatures, though a museum or collector with any savvy at all knows to test the age and x-ray the layers of a painting."

"That's the conundrum you're in, Kendra. Your best motives could be bent to criminal results."

Stefan may not be a gentleman or the innocent gallery owner she had thought. He probably fenced forgeries and could fence her copies as well. Her signatures, small in the right corner, could be over-painted with that of a grand master. And the two she'd rushed to him yesterday had no signatures at all. Why had she hesitated and left them blank?

Her one rationalization came in handy, that if she copied art on display in museums, she couldn't be accused of fraud. The originals were public.

Richard rested his large, warm hand on her upper arm. "You're an excellent artist. Why don't you paint your own creations?"

His gentle touch jangled her insides so much that she couldn't even pull up her stock answer to the question.

ೞ✤ೞ

Richard thanked Maarten for picking them up before daylight the next morning and driving them to the airport. With his suitcase and two of Kendra's, they needed his help.

The airport, in frantic activity, swirled with passengers and bags. Maarten swung a case onto a cart. "I'll be in touch with you as the investigation proceeds. Hope to see you back here in a couple of weeks."

They shook hands and slapped backs, then Kendra stepped nearer. "I don't suppose I'll see you again. I'll be flying home in nine days. Thanks a lot for the ride … and for believing me. It's reassuring to be working with the good guys."

He laughed and shook her hand. "Glad to have you on our team."

After their check-in, Richard led Kendra to the executive lounge. "We'll board soon, but we may as well be comfortable. Besides, we should use the time to speak confidentially about the case." He touched the small of her back, directing her to the reception desk while admiring her new navy blue suit and pale blue blouse. She must have bought that after they parted at the post office yesterday. The subdued outfit looked professional, a very good choice for their trip.

She paused as he checked them into the spacious lounge, and then chose a seat in a small nook with a side table and lamp. Richard left his briefcase with her and went for their coffees. He returned with a plate of breakfast finger foods as well.

"Cappuccino, right?" He placed the foamy cup on the table near her and took the other seat.

She chuckled. "Cappuccino is usually an afternoon indulgence, but thank you."

"Have a nibble. This is sausage in a roll, that's cinnamon, and I think the other has apple. I got two of each." He slid a clean plate from beneath the loaded one and passed it and a paper napkin to her.

"This is so fine. I'm not accustomed to traveling in luxury." She took one of each item and bit into the cinnamon roll first. "Mmm. Light, and not too sweet. Thanks."

"My pleasure." He tasted the sausage roll, thinking it really was a pleasure to provide for a woman who didn't expect it. The women in his life typically acted as if they deserved the impossible and wanted it now. Like Taylor. In retrospect, thank heaven the wedding never happened.

They chatted about the weather, their rush to pack and get to the airport, and her impressions of Amsterdam. Nothing consequential, yet so agreeable. During his second cup of coffee their flight was called, and he hadn't mentioned their business in Budapest at all. They entered before the masses and took their seats in business class.

After take-off, he opened his briefcase and gathered what little firm information he had on the newly discovered art in Budapest.

Her hair, clasped at the neck, draped over her shoulder. "I went to a library last night and used their computers to look up information on Hungary. Its history, especially through the war, and what happened to the Jews." She turned to him, her expression strained. "They were pushed into two ghettos where thousands died of starvation and disease. They'd been living and working in that city for generations, and suddenly they were treated worse than animals."

He nodded. "It happened all over Europe. Hard to understand." He scanned his papers. Many Jews were wealthy, productive citizens before the persecution. Sponsors of the arts. "Hungary had been such a rich nation during the reign of Queen Sisi. The castles and palaces still stand side by side along wide boulevards. Many have been converted to public buildings, museums, and government offices. If we have time, I'll take you to a few of them. And to the renovated synagogue. It's quite an experience."

"You've been there before?"

"I spent a few summers in Europe during college and grad school." He chuckled. "Studying art, right?" He glanced past her out the window. "I had some good times."

When she didn't respond, he again felt the gap between them. His privileged family provided so many advantages, including travel. For the next few days, he would be responsible for getting her about the city safely. Though she had great knowledge and sophistication in the art world, he had brought her into a criminal investigation without any training. Nor did he have any.

He handed her the page listing the artists and titles of the fifteen paintings they were going to evaluate. "If we meet local art connoisseurs, we'll be introduced as art historians, not Interpol officers. If we see the owner of the paintings at all, we want to keep him at ease as much as possible."

She studied the page. "A Rembrandt self-portrait, of which there are about sixty known in the world; two Picassos, a Monet seacoast—he's rarely copied because of the complexity of his tiny brushstrokes … This is going to be interesting."

"I'm glad we have the Internet to help with the research. So much information instantly available. Oh, by the way, have you heard anything about your stolen computer?"

She winced. "Not a thing. And I wasn't backing up everything since I got to Europe. Traveling on the cheap, you know. I only have the photos still in my camera. It was in my purse."

"You'll have access to a computer at Interpol. But a lot of our judgment will be intuitive." He closed the lid of his briefcase and accepted another cup of coffee from the attendant, but Kendra declined. "Your brush strokes and careful shadings of *The Milkmaid* are remarkable. How long did it take you to paint her?"

She chuckled. "Ten years and two weeks. I've had a fixation on that painting for a long time and made a lot of starts. I brought my best canvas rolled up in a tube in my suitcase and finished it after seeing the original."

"An oil? Wasn't it damaged?"

"Not too bad. It had dried for months."

He followed her glance out the window, where a bright blue sky soared above an endless cushion of puffy clouds.

"The same way with the van Gogh," she continued. "I'd begun that one by projecting a really good photo onto the canvas, using museum equipment after hours. All those frantic brush strokes… You know he painted more than one canvas a day in his last months?"

"It must have been easier for him to create the painting than for you to copy it."

Her face pulled in a sardonic smile. "You better believe it."

"You didn't answer me yesterday. Why don't you paint original works?"

She turned away from the window but avoided his eyes. "Because I'm not good enough."

"Who told you that?"

"My father. He refused to help pay for my college. He said painting was child's play, not real education. My sophomore year, I gave him a copy of Rousseau's *Tiger in a Tropical Storm*, which I thought he'd like. It's still in the hall closet."

A weight landed on Richard's chest. His parents had been quick to praise every drawing he'd done as a child, every canvas he'd ever painted as an adult. That this woman had become a fine artist without any affirmation or financial support astonished him.

"I called him last night, just to tell him I had an opportunity to go to Budapest and work with some art experts on old paintings."

"What did he say?"

"Nothing much. Wanted to make sure I was still coming home on schedule. He was afraid I'd lose my job and would never be hired by anyone else. I think he still considers my position at the Kimbell a fluke."

Her cheerful expression had turned ashen. He wanted to fold her in his arms and assure her that she was simply magnificent. Her hands lay in her lap, trembling slightly.

With an impulsive move, he placed his hand over both of hers. "You're nervous about the trip. Do you have fear of flying?"

She turned sideways, pressing her back against the plane's bulkhead. Either by intention or accident, her hands moved from under his, so he pulled his back. Not like him to be so bold.

"Not really. I've only flown a few times before, and I liked it."

She propped with her hand over her mouth, staring past him. Then she dropped it, inhaled deeply, and refocused at him. "I have something to confess." As she said this, moisture came to her lovely hazel eyes, now a fine shade of blue-green. "The only reason I knew the Breitner was a fake was because I'd copied that painting. I knew the color beneath the vase was supposed to be dull. The copyist did what I wanted to do—he brightened the color. I'm not an expert on Breitner nor any other fine artist."

He studied her face, her complexion as smooth as Vermeer's milkmaid. But unlike the milkmaid, her eyes told of her insecurity. "*Au contraire*, my dear. You are an expert because you have copied Breitner, Vermeer, Rembrandt, van Gogh, Rousseau, and I don't know how many others. You have reproduced their paints … duplicated their brush strokes … I know their works from pictures, museums, and art history books. You know them in your heart." He motioned toward her chest, but came nowhere close to touching.

She blushed and broke contact with his eyes.

"More than that, you have an intrinsic feel for art … for the elements in a painting that make it great. That's something that cannot be taught." He smiled and lifted her chin so she had to turn those beautiful hazel eyes back to his. "I know, because I try so hard to teach people who don't have it."

Someday Kendra would discover how special she was. He wanted to be there when it happened.

Chapter 11

Kendra gripped the arms of her seat as the airplane braked, forcing her body forward. She hadn't flown enough to get over the thrill and the fear, though Richard had sat calmly beside her the full two hours. She followed him through the swarming passengers to baggage claim in the Budapest airport, where he hoisted their suitcases onto a cart. Such a relief to have a man handle her bags.

He pushed the bags to the front car of the taxi line and gave instructions to drive to the Marriott Hotel on the Danube River. "We'll drop the bags there and head over to the Police Palace, where Interpol has its offices," he told her quietly as the car accelerated.

"Police Palace?"

"You'll see why it's called that when we get there."

Although they arrived before the hotel check-in time of three p.m., accommodations were available when Richard showed his passport and Interpol ID. She enjoyed the excellent service and sense of respect in this world-class hotel, to the degree she'd never experienced in her usual cheap hotel stays.

Kendra's room, located several doors from his on the eighth floor, provided everything she might wish for. Decorated in muted tones of blue and gray, it begged her to pull back the quilted comforter and sink into its high bed. She resisted the temptation, freshened up, and responded to his tap on the door ten minutes after arriving.

He'd freshened up, too. He looked good and stood within an aura of men's cologne. "How's your room?"

She opened the door wider and swept her arm in an arc. "Marvelous. I wish I could spend the day here."

"Not a chance. Van Der Veen is waiting for us at Interpol, and he's not a patient person to work for."

Kendra's stomach turned to lead during the taxi ride. She doubted she'd be any help in identifying the fifteen paintings. She'd accepted under Richard's pressure, giving in easily for selfish reasons—free travel, a bonus, and a glimpse at works unseen by the public for seventy-five years. Now came the time to prove her worth, and she had no faith she could do that.

The blue glass exterior of the national police headquarters rose high in a huge circular structure on one end and a rectangular extension to the left, also encased in glass. Kendra craned her neck to see the remarkable building called the Police Palace. A tall communications totem pole stood atop the center of the round part like a proud decoration on a flat-topped hat. She'd never seen such a construction before. Richard's touch on her elbow reminded her to quit gawking and go inside.

After passing through security, Richard greeted a medium-height man with thinning gray hair whose barrel chest strained the buttons on his dark suit. Even she, unaccustomed to firearms, noticed a bulge that indicated he was packing.

"May I introduce you to Mr. Klaas Van Der Veen?"

Richard's Interpol handler managed a smile without losing the worry wrinkles on his forehead. "A pleasure to have you join us this week, Ms. Cooper." His motion toward a bank of elevators included them both. "Let's go directly to the fifth floor. We have much to show you."

There they entered a room that would have been spacious if not for the worktables and easels set up everywhere.

Protective muslin drapes covered most of the frames. To the left, one of Monet's beachside paintings captured her. She drew near, hardly daring to breathe. Van Der Veen turned on more lighting, and the work beckoned her to climb into one of the fishing boats in the foreground and cast off into the shimmering water. About thirty inches high and forty wide, the painting pulled her to become absorbed in its scene.

"It's held up well," Richard murmured near her right ear. "Probably done in the 1880s. A little cleaning of the varnish and it's good to go." He withdrew tortoise-shell reading glasses and looked closer.

"May we turn it over and check for stamps on the back?" She made the request reverently, like asking to go up to the altar of a cathedral.

"That's what we're here for." Mr. Van Der Veen joined them. "The Monet is most likely an original. The x-ray and dating of the paint checks out. We're trying to eliminate recent copies."

Kendra touched one finger to the canvas's outside edge where dabs of paint would have been covered by a frame. "One thing I don't understand, sir. The authentic oils take two to three years to thoroughly dry. Nothing younger would ever pass even a cursory inspection. How do criminals expect—"

"They try to dry them artificially, which creates artifact. But they counterfeit the stamps and stickers on the back as well, and that's enough to fool collectors eager to get a good deal. The seller gives some convincing story about how the painting has been concealed for decades and lets them discover the fake provenance as if he doesn't know what he's got. Eager buyers fall for the bait when discrepancies look them in the face."

Richard prepared a cloth-covered space over a work table and gently rested the frame face down. Together they studied all identifying markers through a magnifying glass supplied by Van Der Veen.

With permission, she took photographs and made notes, moving with reverence around the painting. "Where did these fifteen paintings come from?"

"A Hungarian man claims that a Jewish-Hungarian underground group dedicated to restoring art contacted him about pieces that had belonged to their families before the war." Van Der Veen's voice took on the resonance of a lecturer. "He said they were found in the false wall of an old house here in Budapest when it was being renovated, and were then turned over to the Jewish group, which contacted him."

"Then how did Interpol get involved?"

"We were alerted by an art dealer the Hungarian tried to sell them to. A different department of Interpol is checking his story. The dealer doubted the veracity of some of the paintings and had been burned before. So he called the Hungarian police, and they contacted our art fraud department."

Van Der Veen drew them deeper into the room. "Come. Look at the two Picassos." He uncovered two framed paintings a little over two feet tall.

Kendra did an internal roll of the eyes. Nineteen thirties Picassos, the sort of cartoonish, brightly colored drawings with black outlines. She respected the artist's adventurous experimentation, but it wasn't a genre she cared for. Therefore she knew less about it. She'd studied what had been required of Picasso's work, no more. Following the process, however, she would examine the provenance and signs of aging compared to the scientific tests. She bent to the task, hoping the rest of the paintings were more like the Monet.

"I'll be over at the Rembrandt self-portrait. It has some curious overpainting I want to look at again in light of these test results." Van Der Veen left them with the Picassos.

Richard quirked a one-sided smile. "Don't you wish you could get paid what Picasso earned for these glorified doodles?"

"Better yet, I'd like to have what just one of them sells for now. His *Nude, Green Leaves and Bust* recently went for over a hundred million dollars, and he painted it in one day."

Kendra used the magnifying glass to study one painting while Richard turned the other over to check its marketing trail. "I posed a question to you that I often use to check the artistic sophistication of my students. You didn't fall for that."

"Glorified doodles?" She considered an answer that would gently express her opinion while still sounding like an art professional. "I think a lot of his paintings show a heavy dose of humor, but it's more than that. Showing two sides of a woman's face … It's like an author writing a character's words at the same time he tells what the character's really thinking in contrast. People aren't always who they appear to be." She flipped her painting to record and photograph its markings.

"Anyone in mind when you say that?" His mutter contained amusement.

"Everyone. No one in particular." But now that he mentioned it, he ranked high on the list. Who was this man, and why had she begun to care?

"Dr. Reed, Ms. Cooper, what do you think of this self-portrait?" Van Der Veen in effect called them to the Rembrandt. They pored over the painting until sandwiches were brought in for lunch.

As the three removed heavy brown paper from crunchy buns layered with ham and cheese slices, Van Der Veen pulled a rolling office chair from one of the worktables and took a more casual pose. "Talk to me about the Rembrandt."

Richard deferred to Kendra with a nod in her direction. "She's our resident expert on Rembrandt."

She ducked her head at the compliment, hoping the Interpol director didn't know she'd earned her "expertise" by copying Rembrandt. But she did know his manner of applying paint and the brushes and strokes he used, so she tackled the answer. "The self-portrait has some poor overpainting. I think he wore a different hat in the original. You know, Rembrandt had a large studio with several protégés, and he often allowed them to make additions or corrections to his originals if a painting didn't sell. These self-portraits were popular. He made over sixty of them."

Van Der Veen took a long pull on his Coke can. "The tests weren't perfectly conclusive. The blotchy areas in the x-rays leave us wondering."

"That's further indication that they were painted in his era. Lead used in the pigments, especially white, block the x-rays." Surely he knew that. Was this a test of her knowledge? She tried to balance sounding like a pro and yet not lecturing the expert. "But then, it's possible for a modern painter to formulate those paints. Not particularly safe to work with, but I've done it."

"Have you now?"

"It's in my master's dissertation. I'd be glad to give you a copy—if my laptop hadn't been stolen. I could get to the file if I could access my off-site backup."

"Please do. I'd like a copy. In fact, it might be useful to this project. I'll see that you have computer time—"

"She can use mine," said Richard. "We'll get you the file." He eyeballed Kendra, and she gave a confirming nod.

"Let's call it a day." Richard checked his Patek Phillipe wristwatch, a gift from his father when he got his doctorate.

"It's six o'clock." His back and eyes felt the strain, but they'd made great progress on the fifteen paintings. Not one appeared to be a contemporary copy, though the Rembrandt that had a lot of bad over-painting and a simple Monet landscape were suspected of being copied in or close to their original era. The Monet was particularly good.

He removed his reading glasses and massaged the bridge of his nose.

"I'm ready. We're not going to finish all these today." Kendra sighed, then she gave him a tired smile. "Pacing is important."

"Want to see some of the city tonight? They really turn on the lights, especially along the Danube." He offered in as calm a manner as possible, hoping to move their relationship out of the workplace and into ... well, something potentially more personal.

"I'd love to. But first I have to download my dissertation file."

"My computer is back at my hotel room. Didn't think I'd need it today. We can do that before dinner. And you'll want to go with me, because ... " He reached for an inner pocket. "I have the magic card." He held up a metallic blue charge card with a wink.

The taxi fought through evening traffic, winding around wide boulevards cut by tram lines. He invited Kendra to his room, which was identical to hers. "I'll set up my computer and power up. I hope the Wi-Fi here is good."

She remained near the entry as he worked. "I suggest you use the Internet cord. It's marginally more secure for a public Wi-Fi user."

Grumbling, he attached the cord provided in the desk drawer. "I suppose so. Okay, the hotel guest password works." He rose when the computer awoke and he'd typed in the password. "Have a seat."

She brushed a hand lightly over the silver laptop, letting her fingers trail along the narrow edge. Then she settled in and logged onto her off-site backup while he went to brush his teeth and not look over her shoulder. He exchanged his suit jacket for one of tan suede.

In less than a minute, she had downloaded the file to his computer. "There it is. Respect the copyright, but you have permission to use the information."

"Thank you."

"Why do you think Van Der Veen wants my file? Would he know my dissertation includes details on formula and preparation of seventeenth- and eighteenth-century pigments?"

"It does? I wouldn't have guessed that." The woman kept surprising him.

"If fraudulent paintings turn up with my formula, will I be suspected of creating them?"

Kendra's level of fatigue floated somewhere in the range of waking consciousness only due to the prospects of seeing Budapest and having dinner with a handsome man with an expense account credit card. This evening would be exciting on several levels.

Richard guided her down the elevator and out of the building. "The hotel has a good restaurant—we could even eat outside—but there's a charming small place a couple of blocks from here I'd like to introduce you to. Okay if we walk?"

"Definitely. We've been inside all day, bent over tables and easels. I need the exercise."

She'd invested in two light suits and a comfortable pair of professional-looking shoes, largely on her one credit card, before leaving Amsterdam. Pleased to have better than her tourist clothes, she felt confident of her appearance beside the well-attired professor as they walked together through the lobby. Several heads turned, evidence they made an attractive couple, which gave her a charge.

He directed her from the hotel drive-up area to the left, away from the river. Sidewalks yielded to cobblestone streets, still visible in summer's late sunlight. Swiveling her head to see the elaborate building façades, she stumbled on the irregular surface. He reached a steadying grip on her elbow, then offered his arm.

Unsure whether to take it but thinking it would be rude to decline, she slipped her hand around his upper arm. The soft suede, supple and warm, excited her fingertips. They walked that way for at least two blocks, with her becoming more comfortable at his nearness. She inhaled his warm fragrance, an interesting combination of what he'd splashed on and what was particularly him.

"Here's the restaurant, right where I left it years ago."

Dark walnut panels and columns lined the walls, and the tables bore burgundy cloths and napkins. Each one had a small candle. The waiter seated them, lit their candle, and replaced the miniature shade over it. Without being asked, he gave them menus in English. Was it that obvious?

"Hungarian goulash really is the national dish," commented Richard. "And do you know the national condiment?"

She browsed the list, holding the menu to receive enough light, reviewing a list of condiments in her mind, and came up blank. "No idea."

"Paprika. It's in most of their foods, so they're reddish."

"Then I'll go for the cultural experience. Hungarian goulash, please."

He nodded and ordered the same for both of them when the waiter returned.

They chatted throughout the dinner about the paintings they'd examined that day. With her hunger satisfied and, in the dark, comfortable surroundings, she stifled a yawn. After a rushed yesterday loaded with ups and downs and then a short night, they'd departed Amsterdam early this morning. All this settled on her shoulders. She chided herself for not being a sparkling conversationalist though she desired to keep him interested.

Richard seemed distracted by two men who had entered and taken places at a bar that ran on the inner wall of the restaurant. She didn't recognize them, but they did appear to be watching by way of the mirror's reflection. When she noticed, they turned away and gave full attention to their beers.

The portion was too large for her, though Richard managed his well. He requested coffee for them with a dessert resembling apple strudel. She only ate a few bites, so ready to return to that high bed and soft comforter in her hotel room.

"Shall we stroll back to the river?" Richard asked. "You really have to see the Royal Palace all lit up."

"Of course, but I'm fading fast. Let's not stay out late." Would she ever get another chance to be with Richard like this? Her fatigue curtailed the night of a lifetime.

Still out of sight of their hotel and enjoying the cool of the evening, Kendra noticed that Richard turned several times and looked behind them.

"Kendra, I'm a bit uneasy about the two guys at the bar in the restaurant. They're behind us, walking fast enough to catch up with us."

She stifled a reaction to check them out and tightened her grip on his arm. Her heart pounded with an unreasonable fear. A walk on the empty streets of a strange city didn't seem so relaxing all of a sudden. "Do you think they're…"

"I don't know."

≫≪

At the corner, Richard waved at a policeman a half block away and turned in that direction. Approaching the man, he called out. "Would it be possible for you to walk with us a few minutes to the Marriott?"

The young fellow smiled. "Are you concerned for your safety, sir?"

Richard tilted his head toward the two men, who paused at the corner and then turned to the right. From this distance, he noted only their medium height and dark clothes and couldn't be positive they were the same guys who watched them in the restaurant.

No, wait. The stockier of the two had an irregular step. He sort of kicked his right foot out before he put it down.

The policeman motioned toward their hotel. "The streets of Pest are quite secure, but I would be happy to accompany you and your lady."

As they covered the final moments to the hotel, Richard patted her hand. "We'll see the palace some other night."

"I would like that. I want to see everything I can."

The lit-up Royal Palace, where Congress now met, was a night sight, but there remained much to experience in the day. "We won't work on Sunday, so I'll take you to the Buda side of the river."

"The Buda side?"

"Budapest—which you've probably noticed they pronounce *Budapescht*—is two cities on opposite banks of the Danube." They rounded a corner near the hotel. "See the hills? That's Buda. We're on the Pest side, and it's fairly flat." His talking was as much to calm her tension, which he felt in her grip on his arm, as to educate her.

They thanked the policeman at the front door, and Richard tried to give him a twenty Euro bill. He wouldn't accept the money, but smiled as if he appreciated the gesture.

Richard entered the Marriott, then motioned for Kendra to come through the bar area and out on the patio, which was just a wide sidewalk and tram track away from the river.

"Ahh, how beautiful." She turned toward the Royal Palace, which appeared, in the total wash of strong lights, to be constructed of pure gold. "I've never seen anything like that."

"It houses the Budapest History Museum and the largest library in the country, and their congress meets there. We may be able to see part of it on Sunday." While she drank in the brilliant palace, he watched her face. Showing her Budapest put magic in his evening as well. Made him want to take her to Paris. To Vienna.

A light sprinkle began, and they re-entered the patio door. After passing through the elegant bar, they continued to the elevator. Waiting a moment for it to arrive, Richard glanced at the fancy gift shop about ten yards away. Inside, behind its glass showcase, two men looked back.

Chapter 12

Kendra appreciated that Richard ushered her to her door and paused until she had it open. He seemed very protective of her, something she'd always desired of a man yet rarely experienced from a date. At home, her mother always had to lock up the house at night. If she ever married, she'd explain to her husband how much it would mean to have him protect her.

"Would you like to meet for breakfast downstairs at about 7:30?"

"Sure. See you then."

"The hotel has a decent gym. Want to work out before breakfast?"

She laughed at the thought of expending time and energy on healthy exercise when she could barely hold her eyes open. "Thanks for the invitation, but probably not tomorrow morning." She stood there, not wanting to say goodnight but needing sleep.

"Don't forget to turn the dead bolt and swing the privacy lock on the door."

She promised and stepped inside. After securing the door, she prepared for bed. With a groan, she remembered hearing the ding of a text message which she'd ignored during dinner. The temptation ran strong to postpone finding out who'd sent it, but she'd wonder all night. She touched the commands on her phone.

Someone named Alexander Holt, who said he'd met her

at the De Roos showing, had bought *The Milkmaid* and wanted to talk to her about other art she might be willing to paint for him. She vaguely remembered the man, well-dressed as they all were that night. Ah, yes, the silver-bearded guy who bore a resemblance to the actor Donald Sutherland in younger years. Cold eyes, strong handshake.

Responding could wait until tomorrow. She rested her head on the feather pillow with a sigh, and dreamed all night about making fraudulent paintings for the *Hunger Games* president.

Since she woke early and didn't want to disturb Mr. Holt with a phone call before breakfast, she texted him: *What other paintings did you have in mind? I'm flying home on August 6th but could ship them back from there.*

While she applied her minimalist makeup and combed her hair back into a clasp, her mind tumbled with the challenges of safely transporting new oil paintings from Texas to Amsterdam.

Mr. Holt called before she left for breakfast. After a pleasant greeting, he cleared his throat. "I would like to have duplicates of several paintings. Would you consider reproducing Rembrandt's portraits? Or *Return of the Prodigal*? That has a lot of dark background. Perhaps it wouldn't be too difficult."

Explosions popped in her brain. "Not too difficult? His background isn't just dark. It's multi-layered with myriad detailing. That's a very complex painting. The facial expressions are intense."

"*The Prodigal* might be a long-term goal. I saw the van Gogh you placed with Appelhof. We could start with a couple of his simpler paintings, perhaps the sunflowers, while you develop more intricate ones."

This guy obviously had no idea what it took to put paint on a canvas. Besides, she could only imagine facing those garish yellow and orange sunflowers—and did he imply several of the series?

"And, naturally, I'd like you to sign the Vermeer I bought," he continued, "duplicating his signature consistent with the period. That should come first."

"I won't sign Vermeer's signature to a copy. That constitutes fraud. The signature must be my own."

"Really, my dear? Kendra Lorraine Cooper? What value would that have?"

Her knew her middle name? Her insecurity loomed in this battle of words. She bolstered her courage by sending a quick prayer toward the ceiling. "The value of a well-done copy, which apparently is about six thousand, five hundred dollars."

"You're talking peanuts, young lady. That painting, properly dried and embellished with a little fabricated history, could be worth millions."

"But the original is right there in the Rijksmuseum. Why would anyone pay—"

"Who's to say that's the original? Some authorities estimate that nearly half of all fine art in museums and private collections today are copies. Let's return to the point. You have debts to pay, and you work every day for a museum that doesn't appreciate your talent. Work for me, live well in Europe, and all that will be in the past." He took a drink of something, probably his morning coffee, while she remained speechless. "And I do insist that you remain in Europe. Transporting newly-painted art always leaves its mark. I will ensconce you in an apartment with excellent lighting—not like the apartment house you've been staying in—and provide your supplies. Return to Amsterdam and allow me to show you what I can do for you."

The part about college debt must have come from Appelhof. *Gee, thanks, friend.*

Holt knew too much about her. An eerie feeling prickled the back of her neck, like spiders walking down her spine.

Her mind reeled with the possibilities. Life in Europe painting the grand masters. A future without debt and freedom to indulge in travel, restaurants, and a decent wardrobe. Having her work appreciated, not stashed in her father's closet. Temptation raged a war against her principles, which had gotten her exactly nowhere in the art world. Her hand trembled as she held the phone to her ear. Such power spewed from the small device, the power to change everything.

"Thank you for the offer, but I can't accept." She cut the connection before giving Mr. Holt time to even say goodbye. The hotel room came back into focus around her, and disappointment settled on her shoulders.

She could be wealthy, an artist of value.

She could be one of the criminals she assisted Interpol in finding.

Richard tapped on Kendra's door. When she answered, she appeared to be ready but distracted. She rushed around closing her suitcase and making her bed while he stood at the entry.

"Don't bother. They'll take care of that."

"Oh, yes, I guess so."

The way she avoided his eyes bothered him most. "Is everything all right? Did you sleep well?"

"Sure. Just let me get my … " She dropped her phone in

her old denim satchel, checked to be sure she had her key card, and they left.

Not a smile. No warmth in her hello. Maybe she would tell him over breakfast.

The full restaurant area downstairs had been converted into one enormous buffet with cold cuts, cheeses, a hot food line, and fruits and juices in different areas. People with plates swirled everywhere. She seemed stymied by the variety, but eventually collected a plate of choices. As he returned to the table, he found her there with head bowed, presumably in prayer. How touching. He sat quietly and motioned to the waiter for coffee.

When she lifted her head, he organized conversation to ferret out her change in mood. "Are you concerned about the two men who followed us last night?" He'd scanned the breakfast area for them and, as far as he could tell, they weren't present.

She blinked and looked around. "I'd forgotten about them. Do you think they were dangerous?"

"Probably not." They'd scared him silly, especially because he wanted to protect her. "Just the same, I reported the incident to Van Der Veen before I went to bed. He's having a car sent to pick us up at 8:30."

"Thank you."

Richard indulged in marvelous European cheeses and breads while Kendra sampled bits of each item on her plate and drank two cups of dark coffee. He tried to start a conversation with her, but nothing worked. Maybe she wasn't a morning person, but it looked more like worry. He wished she trusted him enough to share what concerned her.

On the way to the Police Palace with an Interpol driver, he outlined his objectives for the day. "We didn't even uncover all the paintings yesterday, and truly examined only five of the fifteen. Let's look at the other ten and see what we have. Any we can confirm as most likely originals we'll put aside. What we suspect needs a closer look we'll get to as soon as possible. I'm hoping there aren't many in that category."

"Sounds like a plan. My understanding of this job is that we're looking for contemporary criminals, so if we think a painting was copied a century ago, we report our suspicions and move to the next one." She looked to him, her voice stronger now.

"That's correct. Our employer is Interpol, not art galleries and auctioneers, though Christie's and Sotheby's would certainly be interested in the results."

"I wonder where the fifteen paintings were found, and who claims ownership now. Somebody somewhere has a lot of money riding on our findings. And I question whether the two men following us last night were hired by the owner."

So she was concerned. He hoped to dispel her anxiety. "We don't know for sure that they were following us."

"No, but they turned the opposite direction after they saw us talking to the cop. Then they showed up at the hotel."

He didn't know she'd seen them in the gift shop. Not much got by this woman. Again she showed her fierce independence. Most of the women he'd known would turn to quivering gelatin if they thought they were in danger.

Too bad Maarten couldn't come with them from Amsterdam. He'd feel safer with his police buddy.

After arriving at the Police Palace and going through the security check, they rose to the fifth floor and entered their work room. Van Der Veen stood in the center of the room drinking from a disposable cup. He must have just arrived.

"Dr. Reed, Ms. Cooper, good morning."

"Good morning, sir." Richard pointed toward the paintings they examined yesterday. "I suggest that we move these five paintings out of the way, grouped on the large table there to the right. As we examine each of the remaining canvases, we'll move it to the confirmed ones when we're finished. The doubtful ones, starting with the Monet landscape, can go to the left."

"Sounds good. Let's start today with this Breitner." Van Der Veen pulled the muslin off a bright still life, just over a foot tall by about nine inches wide.

"From Breitner's 'Anemones' series?" Kendra sped to the painting, took the frame in both hands, and carried it to better lighting in their primary examination area.

Richard joined her, hovering at her shoulder. He brought a magnifying glass over the edges of the flowers and ginger jar vase. "Let's see the back."

After she rested it on its face, protected by padding, Richard compared the stamps and markings with its provenance notes and lab tests. "We can't jump to conclusions."

Kendra nodded. "This is me being calm and objective." She kept her head down and bit on her bottom lip.

"What's the chance of two Breitner paintings in his anemone series surfacing for sale at the same time?" Richard's muttered question expressed a hope that they were finally onto a lead.

"About as great as the probability that both of them are fake."

Van Der Veen approached and looked on from the far side of the table. "Have you found something?"

"Maybe," said Richard. He explained that an identical copy of this painting had been offered for sale by an art dealer in Amsterdam.

Van Der Veen drank the last of his coffee and tossed the cup into the trash can. "If we find one fraud in the group, suspicion is cast on the whole group."

Excitement rose in Kendra's search. Not only did she handle fine art hidden from the world for three generations, but the exercise had become a quest for the interlopers among the innocents. Never far from her mind lurked awareness that she could be the crook others sought in the future. An investigator might pull the muslin off a copy, saying that upon close inspection and testing, this one was most likely a fraud. The strokes were correct but not convincing, pretty but not perfect. Interpol would track her down and convict her.

She shook her head, trying to dislodge the accusations. She'd been right not to tell Richard about this morning's phone call.

Richard looked up. "What is it?"

She had to make up a reason to be shaking her head, fast. "You stare at these paintings long enough, and your vision goes blurry."

"Yeah. Ready for a lunch break?"

"Not hungry yet. Let's tackle that big one." She lifted the covering off a Thomas Gainsborough portrait of a woman in a wooded setting. "Sixty-two inches wide, ninety-four inches high. Life's too short to try to reproduce this one. You can almost feel the texture in her dress."

"Yes, and her tiny dog looks like he could bark himself right off the canvas." Richard came close with the magnifying glass, then stood back with a smile of admiration. "Okay, let's do the drill. X-rays, dating, provenance. I think we'll be able to move this to the confirmed group."

They spent less than an hour on the intricate portrait and made extensive notes on exactly why they confirmed this painting as an original Gainsborough. "This is a good idea," said Kendra. "We should be making a written list of points, pro and con, on each painting."

Van Der Veen looked up from inspecting the painting of a New Testament parable. "Excellent. I'll have clipboards and paper brought up after lunch. Are you ready for a break? Let's go down to the restaurant."

Over wursts, potatoes, and a sort of vinegar-laced slaw concoction, the Interpol agent reviewed what they'd evaluated so far. "You've made great progress. We've done at least a cursory inspection of eight of the fifteen." The statement came across not so much a compliment as a summary of where they stood in the process.

Nevertheless, Kendra and Richard nodded as they chewed. She took his comments as a warming confirmation.

Van Der Veen pushed back his plate when he'd consumed everything down to the last pickle. "Can we speed it up a bit? Work tomorrow also? I've heard rumblings about another collection we want you to see before you both return to the US. A larger one. Highly significant. It would be quite an honor for you to be called in. Quite an honor."

Chapter 13

In Klaas Van Der Veen's absence after lunch, Richard surveyed the job yet to be done in the workroom.

Kendra moved about the paintings remaining to be verified, paused over a landscape, and picked it up in both hands. "Hmm. Jean-Baptiste-Camille Corot. In pretty good condition, but rather dark. Could use a careful cleaning of all the old varnish." She turned to Richard. "You know what's strange?"

"What's that?" What was strange was the change in their relationship. She'd become a friend, a fellow professional. And now, working closely with her every day, sharing most of their meals, he looked at this woman in her all-business role and wanted more. A smile crept up on his face. But her question had nothing to do with his thoughts. He forced his mind back to the present artistic commission.

"These are all major artists. In this one room, we have two Monets, two Picassos, a Rembrandt, Gainsborough, Breitner ... and we don't know what else." She waved toward those still covered. "Each one of those would probably sell at auction for hundreds of thousands of dollars, and some of them for millions. Who owned this many of the masters when the war began?"

Her question was valid, and required serious consideration. Richard ambled over and looked at the Corot she held. "They're supposed to have all been in one gallery. Thousands of wealthy, well-educated Jews lived in Hungary. About 70,000 were shoved into the ghettos of Budapest to die of starvation and disease. These could be one gallery's collection when masterpieces became less valuable than a day's food."

He flipped over the Corot and tried to read details there. "The Germans confiscated all of their art and valuables, money, jewelry … everything. Non-Jewish Hungarians participated in the theft because Hitler couldn't spare enough troops to do the job. This group of fifteen canvases could be the culmination of thefts from those confiscations, by either Germans or Hungarians."

"I see. A person who had access to the stash may have cherry-picked some of the most valuable. Wouldn't the current owner be forced to return them to descendants of the pre-war owners?"

"It's often a long legal process to find the families, and they may have to sue for return of the property. While the ideal result is restitution of belongings to the rightful people, the detective work can go on for decades."

Kendra replaced the Corot on the worktable with care. "There's the history … and the mystery."

With this pronouncement, she angled her face to his, a wan smile adding to the Mona Lisa-like perfection of her hazel eyes, now more green against the landscape and her light green blouse. The years of self-discipline in contact with his female students threatened to weaken and dissipate. The physical attraction to a woman so lovely and so intelligent washed over him in a wave almost too strong to resist. He raised a hand to her shoulder.

Then he stepped back and broke the spell. "Yes, well, it will be interesting to follow these masterpieces in the news over the coming years. I'll make a list to keep personally, and try to stay in touch with the gallery owners I've met. They'll know what comes of them."

"But why would there be fakes among them? The Breitner copy resembles the one Appelhof wants to sell the Kimbell, enough that I think the same artist did them both."

"Quite possibly. Perhaps the owner realizes he'll lose most of the paintings to their legal owners, if they can be found, and hopes to make the fakes accepted in the good company of the verified originals. Who knows? It all comes down to greed one way or another."

He bent to study the landscape. "At any rate, let's not waste too much time on this one. Corot was one of the most copied artists of his century. He allowed his students to copy his work, and then he touched them up and signed them as originals. Literally thousands were produced that way, and pure frauds from other artists also passed as authentic Corots. If this painting doesn't appear to be new this decade, take it over to the non-suspicious group. It's not what Interpol's looking for."

He left her with that task, feeling the need for separation from the woman who drew his interest even more than some of the greatest artists the world had ever known. Attempting to appear focused, he proceeded to an Edgar Dégas nude woman drying her back after a bath. No, that wouldn't help get him in the correct frame of mind. He covered it and lifted the muslin off another Dégas, a brightly colored impressionistic painting of two ballerinas at the practice bar.

Flipping through reports of the scientific tests, he had doubts of its origins. The provenance appeared convincing and agreed with markings on the back. The shadows and modulations of orange and yellow in the background imitated well the techniques of Dégas, as well as the black outlines of the figures. Studying details under magnification, he muttered his doubts as Kendra walked the Corot to the collection of unchallenged canvases.

When she returned, she bent over the painting, which was about four feet tall and three feet wide and bound in an antique scrolled frame. "Have you got a live one there?"

"Not sure. The painting is excellent, but the tests don't agree."

She pointed toward a frosting of white on the girls' shoulders and down the arms. "Do the x-rays show that to be lead paint?"

When he'd located the film, he held it to the ceiling light. "Yep. Lead paint, but as you know very well, that can be formulated."

She craned her neck to get a better view, and the strands of her dark, silky hair fell across his arm. He could have moved his arm. He could have handed her the x-ray film. Instead, he inhaled deeply of her clean fragrance. A whiff of vanilla resonating with almond. She stepped back and looked again at the dancers while his heart soared to imaginary music.

"Sometimes you have to go with your instinct, Richard." She stepped over to their working materials and returned with a swab and solvent.

He gave her a cautionary look. "If this is an original, it's worth millions. Maybe hundreds of millions."

"I won't damage it. Right here on the edge, where the canvas bends around its frame … " She'd found an unvarnished area. Light as a butterfly's wing, she swabbed the tiniest bit of color with the solvent. The cotton tip came away tinged with orange. "If it hasn't dried since 1888, it's got to be a fake."

He exhaled a long sigh. "Too bad. Every art collector, gallery owner, and auctioneer wants to find that immensely valuable, overlooked masterpiece. I can't even guess what a Dégas ballet series painting would be worth. Well, let's check out the bather."

It, too, did not hold up under their inspection and the lab tests. Both the fakes were escorted to the losers' corner.

Klaas Van Der Veen bustled into the room about a half hour before five, the end of the workday. "What progress have you made?"

Richard reviewed details and summarized their conclusions as the three went around to each canvas. "So we only have four more to examine. We should be able to do that without difficulty tomorrow." He hoped they'd be finished in time to tour the city a few hours. Kendra had seen so little besides this room and the hotel. "What's the other collection you mentioned at lunch?"

Klaas breathed deeply, looking away at the floor and rolling his lips between his teeth. Then he faced them. "This has to be confidential. There must not be a leak. You cannot imagine the pandemonium if the art world and press found out."

Richard nodded, urging him to continue.

"Fifty paintings have been found stored in wooden crates in a cave."

"A cave? On the Buda side?" He assumed the Pest side of the city had no mountains that might form caves.

"In Austria."

Richard's head popped back in surprise, and Kendra gasped.

"Interpol will send you to Vienna on Monday, and from there to the site where they were found. Ms. Cooper, I'm trusting you with this information in the hope that you will accompany Dr. Reed. Your insight has been valuable this week. Will you go?"

Kendra stammered and brought both palms to her cheeks, then relaxed them to her sides. "I need to be on the plane Friday to return to Fort Worth. I suppose if Interpol could get my tickets changed to Sunday without additional charges, I could extend two days, but no more."

"You do realize what's at stake here, don't you? What an earth-shattering discovery this is? You're aware of the impact just one stolen painting has on the art and culture of Europe? *Woman in Gold*, for example. We're looking at crates and crates of fine art, still in the cave in Austria. Surely the Kimball Museum would allow you to take part in the greatest single art discovery of the century."

"A sabbatical," she whispered.

"Pardon me?" Klaas leaned closer.

"I don't know. I may lose my job over this, but ... I'll call my boss and see if she'll give me a few more weeks' absence. That is, if you want me that long. But I'd have to have a salary. I can't afford to stay as a volunteer."

Klaas grinned and spread his arms wide. "No one works in law enforcement for free. I'll have an employment package prepared for you. For the meantime, I assure you that all your expenses will be covered, plus a salary which will compensate for the high cost of living in Europe."

Kendra's eyes widened and her face blanched so much that Richard prepared to catch her if she fainted. Then a smile crept over her lips and widened to full beam.

She offered her hand. "Done."

Chicken with the ever-present paprika served on the hotel restaurant's patio satisfied and relaxed Kendra. Richard had ordered the steak, which he commented was tough but tasty. They sipped coffee and watched people stroll on the wide sidewalk beside the river. Flaming torches flickered into the dusk, and she reflected on how their partnership had grown during these two days. Replacing the initial animosity and suspicion, he now treated her like a professional.

"Daylight lasts much later than I expected," she said.

"Northern Europe's like that in the summer, but it gets dark early in the winter." Richard had been seated opposite her, his back to the Royal Palace. He scooted his chair around to the near side. "Amazing. It's an impressive building in the daytime, but breath-taking when all the lights are on at night."

"And the bridge. I'd love to walk across and find the cathedral marked on the hotel's tourist map."

"We should have time tomorrow afternoon. But see how that hill goes straight up? We'll take a city bus or taxi." He stared into the distance. "There's so much I'd like to show you."

Kendra's pulse raced. A few days ago, she didn't want to be in the same room with this man. He thought she painted frauds, and she thought he conducted a personal attack on her privacy, her art, and her income. "Instead of ruining my vacation, you're making it the greatest adventure of my life."

His eyes reflected the torch's flame. "I apologize, Kendra. We raided your room in some half-baked idea that we'd found a fraudulent artist. You're the best I've ever seen. It just made sense that you painted for a distributor and could lead us to the people we want to stop."

"I accept your apology, and I'll raise you one." She toyed with the moisture on her glass, and decided to take her own dare. Relaxed by the dinner and his apology, she realized she wanted to trust him. She told him about Mr. Holt's call and his insistence that she sign her copy of *The Milkmaid*.

"What did you tell him?"

"I refused, of course, and said I wouldn't paint copies for him." She looked away at the golden-lit palace across the river. "Strange. That's what I had hoped for—selling copies to collectors. But as copies, not frauds."

Richard propped an elbow on the table and leaned only inches away. "How do you feel about that now?"

"I love painting. I get excited just thinking about spending a day alone with a canvas and my palette. But the instant I sign Vermeer's or van Gogh's name, my product becomes a deception. A lie. And I become a criminal."

He signaled the waiter for the bill, which he presented within a few seconds. Richard signed with his name and room number, and the waiter thanked him happily before retreating.

"Interesting, isn't it? You can own a Beethoven symphony for a few dollars, a Robert Frost poem written on a page of notebook paper for a few cents. But an original Rembrandt costs millions."

"So true." She toyed with her water glass. "Mrs. Odem, my boss at the Kimbell, extended my leave for one week, but she said I should stay in contact with her if something exciting develops."

"One extra week. Then you need to return on August thirteenth?"

"Yes, and I've already changed my flight reservation, which cost Interpol a hundred dollars." Her life had taken a dramatic turn, and the ramifications of this new assignment caused a thrill to shiver down her middle.

"I can hardly believe they're paying me to do something so exciting in the art world." Then an unwelcome thought occurred. "When do you return to the US?" She didn't want to be in a strange European city alone.

"The same day as you. The thirteenth, and that's squeaking in at the last minute before classes start. But Emory's okay with that. My department head sees the value of my being here for this. I'm keeping him as informed as Interpol allows."

He drank the last of his coffee. "Would you like to walk beside the river for a few minutes?"

His apology made all the difference in how she felt about him. So few people admitted their wrongs and said they were sorry. She wanted to get closer to this man. "Sure. I need the exercise after two days in a room."

He stood and assisted with her chair, and then they took three steps down to the wide pedestrian walkway. Ambling toward the brightly lit bridge, they watched people of all types and manner of dress pass by. A street performer fiddled on a violin with his case open for tips. Playing with vehemence, he gathered a circle of listeners. When he ceased playing, they drifted away. Richard dropped a bill in the violin case. She admired his generosity.

"I could get tickets to a Hungarian dance performance tomorrow night," he said. "I think you'd enjoy it."

"I would." She should not be feeling this thrill down her middle. She remembered having a crush on her French professor in college, and she wound up in an awkward situation. That mustn't happen with Dr. Richard Reed. "How long have you been teaching at Emory?"

"Only three years, not counting a couple as graduate assistant. And you? How long have you been working at the Kimbell?"

"Two years, not counting interning during my master's. I volunteered as a docent sometimes in the summers, but I had to work as a waitress or any job I could find to stay in school."

"Was your father employed?"

"Oh, yes. He owns a plumbing company. He does very well."

"Then why didn't he cover your tuition and fees? You said he didn't consider studying art to be a worthy subject, but he should have honored your career choice."

She stopped and crossed her arms. "Dad didn't go to college. He's really smart and hard-working, but … Look, I had a younger brother who was everything he wanted. Brian, Junior—we called him Bry—was quarterback on the team, the center of Dad's life. He died in a car wreck his senior year in high school. He and his friends had been drinking. Dad never got over it. Still hasn't."

"I'm sorry."

"Mom and Dad wanted me to be a nurse or something 'useful.' Dad, in particular, doesn't see the point in art."

"I'm surprised you stuck it out. You must have a strong, independent sense of direction."

She dropped her arms and stepped close. "Yes, and right now it's telling me we should go back to the hotel. Did you see that man who just passed us? The one who sort of swings his left foot out before taking a step? Not exactly crippled, but there's a difference in his walk. One of the men following us last night did that."

Richard paused and made a casual turn. "The guy on his cell phone looking toward the statue in the little park? I think you're right. Let's walk a little faster. I don't think he'll try anything with so many people around. I'll call Interpol and request security. Who is he, and why is he following us?"

Kendra didn't answer, but remembered the creepy chills that crawled around her neck by the end of Mr. Holt's phone call yesterday. He intended for her to do exactly as he required. She'd refused to obey and hung up on him. It could be that she put both herself and Richard in an awkward—or even dangerous—position.

Chapter 14

Kendra and Richard set a rapid pace back to the hotel. In her haste and shakiness, Kendra stumbled on a tile in the walkway, but Richard grabbed her arm in time to steady her.

"Are you okay?"

"Yes, but I can't walk as fast as you." She liked his being taller than she, but that made his step longer.

"Sorry. Here, take my arm. These tiles are uneven in places." He placed her arm inside his and then slowed his long stride the rest of the way. Meanwhile, he phoned for a policeman to meet them in the lobby.

The comfort of his bracing arm warmed her like a fireplace in winter.

They ducked into the hotel via the restaurant patio entrance rather than circling to the front. While they waited near the check-in desk, Kendra's phone rang. She checked the caller ID.

"It's Mr. Holt. Should I answer it?"

Richard nodded. "Go ahead. He might answer some of our questions." He pulled her into a quieter sitting area. "Put it on speaker."

They'd barely exchanged hellos when Mr. Holt said, "I need your signature, Ms. Cooper. You don't want to try to leave Europe without doing me that favor."

"No way that's going to happen. I'm not even in Amsterdam any longer." She forced a strength into her voice in contrast with how her nervous stomach felt.

"I know exactly where you are. I can have the painting brought to your hotel room tonight. And remember, this is not a little pro bono work. You will be rewarded both now and for future pieces. I look forward to a long and mutually satisfying relationship." The muted, husky tone of this last sentence caused a shiver of revulsion to travel her spine.

"Mr. Holt, I do not wish to disappoint you, and I'm pleased you appreciate my copy of *The Milkmaid*. But as an art professional, I simply cannot comply with your request."

"It's ten p.m. The painting will be delivered in thirty minutes, and my man will wait downstairs after the delivery until you call him and tell him it's ready." He disconnected without saying goodbye.

The call left her trembling. She had no doubt that the two men who followed them through Budapest worked for Mr. Holt. He knew where she was, and he intended to have his way.

Two policemen entered the hotel, and Richard waved and approached them. He showed them his Interpol ID and asked them to join him and Kendra in the sitting area, where he made introductions. Richard made it clear than he and Kendra were working on an art fraud case and felt threatened by men who followed them in the area of the hotel.

Fearing they might be overheard, Kendra suggested they go up to her room. There she explained as quickly as possible, leaving out many details, why she needed protection.

"It's almost 10:30 now," Richard interrupted. "How are we going to handle this?"

A knock came at the door. "Maid service," said a woman's voice in accented English.

Richard and the two police dashed out of sight around the corner from the door.

Kendra chained the door and then opened it as far as that allowed. "I didn't request anything." A uniformed maid stood alone in the hall without a cart.

"I turn down your sheets? Towels?" Her wide eyes indicated a higher level of excitement than routine housekeeping normally stimulated.

"Thank you, but I don't need—"

"Let her in," commanded Richard.

She admitted the young woman, whose mouth dropped open when she spotted the police.

"Who sent you?" asked one of them.

"The hotel. I do this every night. With the chocolate. Here. See?" She dashed to the bed, placed a bon bon on each pillow, and swept a hand over the coverlet without turning it down. "You need fresh towels? I bring towels."

"No, thank you." Kendra cast an anxious glance to the men, wondering what to do next.

One of the policemen said something to her in Hungarian, and the woman scooted out.

"I think we missed an opportunity," said Richard. "She was sent to check you out, to see if you were alone. With the officers present, nothing will happen. I should have followed her to see whom she reported to."

After a call to their station, the police informed them that a guard was being dispatched to stay on the floor through the night. The two policemen and Richard remained in her room until he came. She sat on the edge of the bed while they waited, occasionally stretching her back. She ached from their long day bending over paintings.

After an awkward silence, Richard suggested they watch the evening news and found a channel with CNN in English. The men took the settee and desk chair. Kendra lamented this ending to her evening, which had been going so well until the dadblamed crooks showed up. This probably meant they wouldn't dare to attend the folkloric dance program tomorrow night, or see the cathedral on the heights of Buda on Sunday.

Her breakfasts and evenings with Richard meant more than visiting the tourist sights of a country she may never see again. She truly enjoyed his company. He made her feel special in his well-bred, gentlemanly way.

When the guard showed up and took his post in the hallway, the officers were dismissed with thanks. The room door closed, leaving Kendra and Richard alone inside.

He turned to her and placed his hands on her upper arms, looking straight into her eyes. "If anything happens, if you're afraid, call me. Okay?"

"I will." But if something went wrong, she wouldn't have time.

Richard slipped his key card into the gym door at six, pleasantly surprised to find Kendra jogging on the tread mill with the guard standing on duty. She gave him a wave but didn't pause her light-footed run. Her long ponytail swished back and forth, setting its own pace. He liked that they did this together. Her shorts showed off her firm thighs, as if she ran often.

She clocked four miles and left him lifting weights, saying she needed time to primp.

The guard remained with Richard and Kendra at breakfast, standing sentinel in the busy restaurant until the driver arrived to take them for their final morning at Interpol's room in the Police Palace. Richard did a constant scan for their adversaries of the previous evening, but didn't spot them. He suspected they worked for Holt, but his unplanned bumbling ruined any chance to know for sure.

After opening the locked workroom at Interpol the next morning, Richard uncovered the remaining four paintings. "We have quite a group of friends here. Seurat, Cezanne, Emile Bernard, and Henri Rousseau. I have to believe the person who tucked away these masterpieces was partial to impressionism."

Kendra moved slowly past the display on a long table. "If I were going to copy art purely to make money, I'd choose something simple." She paused in front of the Rousseau. "For example, this lion looking out of the jungle. It's childish. The lion sits up facing the viewer, not some sleek, well-muscled cat prowling for prey."

Richard brought the x-ray and dating tests for that piece, and it soon failed their examination. "Good work, partner." Their palms slapped a high-five, and then he banished the fraud to the other losers on the left. "Three more to go. What does your instinct tell you about this Seurat?"

She circled to the end of the table and peered at the park scene from the side. "His pointillism paintings would have been very difficult to duplicate, but this beach scene…not so much." The hazy depiction of sunbathers enjoying a lazy afternoon along a river resisted their efforts to prove it a fraud, however. "Did he not ever paint an actual face? Outlines are only hinted at."

The evidence all led them to believe the Seurat an original, as the Cezanne and Bernard also were judged to be.

Klaas Van Der Veen joined them for the last two evaluations. "So of the possible recent frauds, we have the Breitner floral still life, both Dégas paintings, and the Rousseau. Four out of fifteen."

She nodded. "And the Breitner probably was done by the same copyist whose work was passed for sale to Appelhof's gallery in Amsterdam. We've turned up at least one definite link to fraudulent art, and it connects to at least one of this group."

The discussion of that painting led to her informing Klaas about Alexander Holt and his purchase of her unsigned copy of *The Milkmaid*. "We assume the guys who've been following us work for Holt. There's simply no one else with a motive, and Holt is trying to intimidate me into painting for him."

"Finally we have a couple of characters to investigate," said Van Der Veen. "This is a significant break."

"I'm quite sure the same copyist painted both of the florals, because he made the same mistakes in both of them." Kendra tapped a forefinger against her chin. "What I don't understand is why he produced two identical paintings and released them within the same time frame here in Europe."

Klaas Van Der Veen chuffed an unhappy breath. "Criminals are more greedy than smart." He rested a sleek leather briefcase on a table and extracted a folder. "Please read this, Ms. Cooper. I've had our legal department prepare a contract for you, retroactively dated to the past Thursday, when you joined us to work on this collection. That's for the purpose of remuneration as well as to justify your hotel guard last night. Spend a few minutes reading it and sign it right away, if you would."

"Thank you, sir." She accepted the document and began reading.

Richard wanted to offer help in understanding the contract, but she didn't ask. To avoid distracting her, he motioned Klaas aside. "We'll be doing the tourist scene this weekend. I'd like to request an armed guard so we can move freely in crowds, especially at night."

"I've already arranged that. You'll be covered around the clock by someone from the Budapest Police Department. He'll be armed and prepared to arrest any suspicious persons."

"Great. I'd just like to show Ms. Cooper a few points in this fantastic city before we fly out."

Kendra waited for Mrs. Odem to come to the phone. Expensive minutes ticked by as a week-end volunteer rushed to find her, where she worked overtime to facilitate the setup of a new exhibition. She should have asked for a call-back, but didn't trust that would happen before she left for Vienna. Wiping her sweaty palms on a muslin cloth tossed on the table, she mentally worded what she'd say. I'm sorry I won't be able to return on time… No, better not start with an apology.

"Yes? This is Carla Odem. How may I help you?"

"A remarkable development has occurred. I recognized a van Gogh as a fake, and have been swept into an opportunity to work under a temporary contract with Interpol." She tried to project a confidence she didn't feel. "I've been asked to remain in Europe for a few weeks to authenticate a recent find—which I'm not free to talk about—and would like to take a brief sabbatical from the Kimbell."

"Kendra? Is this you?"

"Yes, ma'am. And by the way, the Breitner floral you asked me to check out is going to test as a fraud as well. In fact, I and another Art Expert for Interpol discovered an identical fraudulent painting this week."

"You're saying two of the same painting?"

"Yes, ma'am. Interpol is going to confiscate Mr. Appelhof's copy and put it through rigorous testing. But I'm not sure that's happened yet, so please don't mention it. You can just say the purchase is off the table for now."

Mrs. Odem stammered, which Kendra had never heard her do before. "I've already agreed to extend your vacation by a week. So you're asking for a sabbatical. For how long?"

"I'm not sure, but I am positive that my being on this team will eventually be enormous favorable publicity for the Kimbell. You can say that I'm on loan to Interpol for a few weeks."

"I'll need to hire someone else for a while … " Mrs. Odem's voice weakened as she spoke her developing thoughts. "Maybe two people. You've become indispensable around here."

"Thank you. I do want to come back. I love my job at the Kimbell."

After disconnecting, she crumpled against the worktable. She needed to go to the bathroom. "I'll be back in a few minutes. I'm going to change to my tennis shoes for our afternoon tour."

Richard broke away from his conversation with Mr. Van Der Veen. "Don't you want to call your family before we leave? And your roommate?"

She paused, aware that her whole setting in life had changed. "I'll e-mail Dad later. And I called my roommate last night."

"While you change shoes," Richard said, "I'll call Maarten and see if he knows of any breaks on the theft of De Roos's van Gogh. And maybe they've found your computer."

Her reflection in the restroom mirror showed her facial flush and perspiration. She dug makeup out of her back pack and did a quick touchup. After snapping a tight knot on her shoestrings, she took a few deeps breaths and thanked God for this marvelous opportunity. She stood on the cusp of a whole new world. She straightened her new pants suit and adopted a buoyant expression.

Only four days had passed since the reception, the theft of Mr. De Roos's van Gogh, and the "boyfriend's" theft of her computer and her remaining works in progress. Those events transpired in another country, before she traveled with Richard for this Interpol assignment. It seemed weeks in the past. No longer a tourist living on an amateur artist's budget, she now had a contract as an Art Expert with Interpol, an armed guard, and a handsome escort who shared many of her interests. This, too, would be a weekend to remember.

Chapter 15

Richard hailed a taxi at the front door of the Police Palace, feeling more secure about public transportation now that they had an armed plainclothes policeman accompanying them. He directed the guard to the front and seated Kendra in the back with himself. "Up to Buda, to the Matthias Church," he requested.

He turned to Kendra, whose wide smile spoke volumes. "We're off for the weekend, and I want to show you as much as possible in a day and a half."

"What a relief. But we did a good job, didn't we?"

He touched a finger to his lips and pointed to the driver. "Yes, we fulfilled more than the expectations of our employer." He wished for time alone to relish the success of their completed task. Perhaps tonight over dinner.

The taxi quickly crossed the massive chain bridge over the Danube, its stone pillars reminiscent of the Arc du Triomphe in Paris. Hairpin turns up the mountain led through a verdant residential area to the tourist center of Buda. Swinging left and right as the car climbed, he hoped the wurst they'd gobbled for lunch in the police cafeteria wouldn't be a problem. She hung onto the arm rest and still looked excited, so he guessed she was okay.

At the top they crossed Trinity Square, rejected a poorly-clad woman selling crocheted items, and entered the cool, baroque cathedral by the southern Maria Portal. Inside, they vied for a place among the swirling tourists to see the colorful frescoes on its walls and the various naves and stained glass windows.

"May we sit down for a moment?" Kendra asked. "I'd like to be still and take this all in."

He ushered her to a pew in the center, and their guard took a position at the end of the row. Unsure of her intentions, Richard waited for a clue. At first, she focused on the frescoes and made a few photos. Then she put her camera away and sat quietly.

"I've only been in a couple of cathedrals before, and those were in the US." She spoke quietly, though very few of the mass of visitors showed a reverent attitude. "This kind of church building isn't what I'm accustomed to worshipping in, but I respect the art and architecture. They show the devotion of its parishioners."

Richard shied away from a discussion of worship. "Quite a few kings and queens were married or crowned here, including Franz Josef I and the beloved Queen Sisi in 1867. This cathedral has been important in Hungary's history since the 1700s."

She relaxed against the pew, breathed deeply, and even closed her eyes for a moment. He wondered if she were praying. If she expected him to bow and pray in this tourist setting, she'd be disappointed. He was a high church kind of guy who kept his religious practices close on the inside.

With a serene smile, she shouldered her purse. "Ready to go?"

Pushing through the crowd to leave, they broke into the brilliant sunlight. The policeman whipped on his sunglasses and steadied Kendra's step on the rough stones with a hand on her elbow. "Over there, you see the city." He directed them to the bastion and its view of the Danube River and Pest side of

Budapest below. A cool breeze blew through the stone arches and around the spires. "I take your photo?"

They posed in one of the arches, but their guard urged them closer together. Richard scanned the crowd, becoming the guard while the guard became the photographer. He'd seen nothing to be concerned about, and moved nearer Kendra. She looked up at him, a bit of confusion showing in the tilt of her eyebrows. He simply smiled at the camera with an arm behind her, hand resting on her shoulder.

They spent a couple of hours touring the Royal Palace, though it no longer had any royal apartments to visit. Passing by the country's largest library, they cruised the National Gallery of fine art until her shoulders slumped and her eyes glazed over.

"Enough art for one day?" he asked. "It's getting late. Let's go back to the hotel and take a break before dinner."

Alone in the quiet of her room, Kendra stretched out on the coverlet and soaked in the peace. Intensely grateful to God for allowing her to be in this place at this time, she prayed for his direction in whatever came next. She could hardly imagine touring Vienna and examining an enormous cache of art with Richard. Van Der Veen indicated other researchers, including more permanent Art Experts of Interpol, would be involved in the evaluations, but only Richard mattered to her right now.

She'd gotten over his distrust of her last week. He had his reasons.

She sank into the feather pillow and pulled the coverlet over her legs to fend off the air conditioner's draft. When she'd almost dozed off, an unwelcome thought popped her eyes open. Richard would be leaving on August thirteenth, just two weeks away. He couldn't just request a sabbatical. He had classes to teach at Emory. And a life to live in Atlanta.

Her cell phone rang, and she checked the number. "Hello, Mr. Appelhof … Stefan."

"Alexander tells me you've left Amsterdam, and you resist all his efforts to have you sign the Vermeer." He used his smooth selling voice, almost a coo.

"It isn't a Vermeer. It's the copy of a Vermeer, and he doesn't want my signature."

"Why not sign it as Vermeer? The real one is hanging in the Rijks, so it isn't going to deceive anyone."

"Stefan, I don't have to tell you it's illegal. What if an art thief substituted my painting for the original? I might go to jail as an accomplice."

"My dear, what an imagination you have. Things like that happen on American television, not in the real world."

"If this is why you called, you're wasting your breath— and my international calling minutes." She should change the settings so only texts came in. Maybe Richard could show her how to do that.

"Alexander Holt is a close friend, an upstanding gentleman in the European art society. Your rejection appears rude and personal. He is a generous man, and tells me he has extended an offer which would be quite helpful to you. You told me you paint the masters because you need the money. If you would be reasonable and accept his offer, you wouldn't have to be so miserly about inconsequential costs like telephone minutes."

He thought she was miserly? Not wasting money made good sense. "I have to get ready for dinner. Please excuse me."

"Our friend is very charitable, but you don't want to cross him." Stefan increased his volume and spoke with a hard edge. "I advise you to work with him, both now and in future requests. Be free of your debts and enjoy life. Europe will be kind to you, and I can help." He sighed. "You're such a lovely young woman. I'd hoped to be able to introduce you to Amsterdam society…"

Was he hitting on her? She'd felt that he was interested the night of the De Roos reception and again when he bought her two paintings. She, however, viewed him more as a father figure, a potential mentor in the Dutch art scene. "I'll keep that in mind. Good evening."

Giving up on the nap, she re-applied her makeup from scratch and brushed the shine back into her hair, wearing it long and straight over her shoulders. Yesterday's suit and a clean blouse completed the picture. She wished for an enticing perfume or a third suit of clothes. A man like Richard would expect better.

He tapped on the door, and her heart flipped over. She inhaled and exhaled, calming and counting to ten before she opened it. "Good evening." She smiled in a way she hoped was pleasant without appearing smitten.

He'd shaved again and combed his sandy curls back into place. His after-shave lotion or man-perfume triggered the equivalent of a giggle in her middle. She looked aside, hoping not to give away her excitement.

The officer stood near his chair across the hall, ready to protect them from whatever. She acknowledged him with a nod, and the three of them boarded the elevator.

"The Hungarian dance program begins at 8:30, so let's have dinner first. There's a nice place I went to years ago. I hope they're still as good. I didn't ask the concierge. No need to advertise our plans."

Their guard paused at the hotel entrance. "You will be driven by an armed chauffeur in an Interpol car. He remains for the night, and I return tomorrow."

Richard shook hands with the officer, and both thanked him for his protection.

When they'd entered the car, Kendra turned sideways. "Is all this security necessary? Do you really think people in the art fraud industry would harm us?"

Richard looked down into her eyes for several loaded seconds. "Van Der Veen thinks you need protection, more than having me along. He says Holt can be a dangerous man."

"Stefan Appelhof called me this afternoon, trying to get me to work with Holt. I refused again."

Concern showed in Richard's expression, but not surprise. His large jaw clamped tight. "Yes, all this is necessary." He rested a hand over hers. "We must keep you safe." Then he moved his hand and glanced outside. Perhaps he heard the thumping of her heart and realized she'd made too much of his simple comforting gesture.

The chauffeur parked at a restaurant deep in the city, then accompanied them to the door. Upon entering, she found the restaurant to be small but elegant. The waiter seated them in a back corner with a view of the front door as if he understood the needs of a couple accompanied by a bodyguard.

The romantic restaurant, soft music, and candle on their table with a precious little shade over it delivered a tender, personal mood. She perused the menu, fortunately in English, which offered many choices. At those prices, the expense account mattered. She chose the lamb, a delicacy she had not enjoyed for a long time.

As they waited for their meals, Richard relaxed against his arm chair and smiled warmly. "Tell me about your aspirations in the art world. What do you hope will happen for you in the next ten years?"

The question caught her unprepared. Relieved he hadn't asked about her family, she organized some thoughts. "I enjoy my job at the Kimbell and the people I work with. Obviously, I hope to pay off all my debt, which I insist upon doing before considering marriage and a family. That's my long-range goal, though. And to keep painting. I love the painting and research into the grand masters."

The candlelight reflected from his clear blue eyes, and from there her glance drifted to his long, strong chin. He fiddled with his fork, then turned to her again. "Are you considering a prospect for marriage at this time?"

How much nicer than asking if she had a boyfriend. "No. In fact, I've avoided dating until I can get my life in better order. I paint a lot in the evenings and weekends, and don't go where single people gather to meet. Except church, and that hasn't turned up any potential love interests."

They both chuckled. "Church hasn't been good hunting grounds for me, either," he said. "But then, I don't go to the singles groups. At twenty-nine, I'm a bit old for that."

"How about you?" She wanted to know, and hoped reversing the question didn't come across as too forward.

"Recently broke up with a woman I'd thought was the one. Coming to Europe for the summer seemed a good way to avoid the fallout."

"Were you engaged?"

"Yes, but not living together. I was holding off on that until the ceremony. Which would have been Christmas, had it happened."

She'd like to ask what went wrong. Instead, she went for a safer topic. "Tell me about your family." Then she realized she'd opened the one subject she didn't want him to launch.

"Mother, father, younger brother taking over the family business. Fifth generation Atlanta, all into social life and support of the arts. My brother's married with two kids."

"What's the family business?" Probably something more

elite than plumbing.

"Mainly real estate and investment management. My great-grandfather set us up by owning a large farm in what became central Atlanta. Thousands of acres, which he continued to farm with hired help after the Civil War. We still have a nice plot for the house in Buckhead. You should come see it sometime, when we're both back in the States."

The thought sent tingles down her spine for several reasons, especially the implication that their friendship might continue after this summer. "Do you live there with your parents?"

His eyes crinkled with a smile. "I still have a room there for when I stay overnight, but I live in a condo near Emory. More independence and ties to campus life."

He sipped from his water glass. "I talked to my mother this afternoon. They'll be in Vienna a few days while we're there. I will absolutely have to pull away from the job for an evening to visit with them."

He looked up as the waiter approached. "Ah, here's our dinner."

Loud words at the entrance drew their attention away from the sizzling platter. Two men confronted the plainclothes policeman. One of them shoved him against the inner glass-paned door. At the sound of breaking glass, diners' heads jerked to the front.

Kendra recognized the wide cheekbones of the man who walked with a strange gait. She gasped. The fear of being found squeezed her heart. The unknown adversary had come for her.

Chapter 16

Richard grabbed Kendra's hand and pulled her toward the kitchen door, rocking their dinner table and swerving past the waiter. He looked back as he shoved her inside the steamy, fragrant room. At the entrance, their guard shoved back and pulled his weapon. The barman lifted a large handgun and shouted in Hungarian. The aggressors took off, pursued by the cop.

Richard whipped out his cell phone and called the number he'd been given for security.

The ponytailed barman's slight build disguised his ability to protect the clientele. With a wave of the revolver toward the ceiling, he gave a grim grin. "Don't worry. They not come back." He swaggered to the front with both hands on the weapon, held high. After squeezing through the glass French doors, he peered outside into the street, then retreated as the police guard returned breathing hard.

The officer spoke to the barman in Hungarian, apparently thanking him for the backup if body language sufficed. He slapped the guy on the shoulder, then he came to Richard at the kitchen door. They entered the kitchen together, and Richard put an arm around Kendra in a sideways hug. "Don't worry. They're gone. You're safe."

The plainclothes policeman smoothed a hand over his hair and adjusted his suit jacket. "They split and got away, but the street patrol looks for them. I requested a uniformed officer to join us. Please continue your meal."

A chubby man with neatly trimmed beard rushed into the kitchen. "I am so sorry for this unfortunate interruption. Please, come be seated. Your dinner is ready." He pushed the swinging door open, urging them to return to their table.

Richard nodded to Kendra, answering the question on her brow. With a hand at the small of her back, he led her to their table. The waiter swooped over with his loaded tray and served their meal, lifting covers which had kept the dishes warm.

"Thank you, God," whispered Kendra. Her animated expression showed no fear. His recent fiancée would have done a drama queen act worthy of an Academy Award, a total all-about-me scene. He appreciated Kendra's even disposition through all that had occurred this week and recognized her stability. As different as their stations in life were, she resembled his mother in that way. Queen Beatrice of the Reed family kept her feet firmly on the ground. An idea flitted past his mind of introducing them in Vienna. He thought they would like each other.

Kendra's eyes lifted to his. She brushed over his hand, just a second of warmth. "And thank you, Richard. I appreciate your protection."

The owner didn't retreat to his office, but visited each table offering friendly chatter and free wine. When he spoke to them, Richard responded congenially and didn't mention the incident. Though their appetites had dampened, the food came up to his expectations. Their previous mood, however, fled with the bad guys.

"Who do you think they were?" she asked. "If they are stalking me, then why? Is Holt behind this?"

He had no answers.

✥

Kendra agreed to continue with their plans to see the folkloric show, now with two armed policemen, one in uniform. While the crowd waited for admission in a long line out into the pedestrian street, her group of four gained entry immediately. They climbed to the mezzanine level, where she and Richard sat in the center front row and the guards took a stance at the rear sides.

For over an hour, five musicians in white blousy shirts played their hearts out with various stringed instruments and something resembling a stringed marimba. Men and women wearing colorful costumes tapped, hopped, and swung each other around with tremendous energy. They laughed, shouted, clapped, and appeared to be having a joyous party. The staged performance recreated, as much as possible, a festival in some town square, and she loved it. She applauded until her hands hurt.

As the performance closed, their guards whisked them out through a back stairwell ahead of the crowd. On the street, one preceded them on the right, and the other followed to the left. No cars drove there, so they strolled a couple of blocks to the nearest pickup point, her arm linked with his for support on the cobblestone. At least, that was her excuse.

Richard pointed out a shop whose customer line stretched past the front serving window. "Would you like some ice cream?"

"Thanks, but no. The lamb was marvelous. I don't need anything else until breakfast."

"Then let's return to the hotel. I'd like to get you out of the masses. We've been fortunate tonight, but I don't want to press our luck."

She nodded. "I agree. What do you think about our sightseeing plans tomorrow? I'd really like to go to the reconstructed synagogue and see the ghetto."

"Let's go when they first open in the morning. I have a totally unsupported theory that crooks don't rise early."

She laughed and gave his arm a squeeze. "Good. I'd really hate to miss my one chance to see Budapest. It's a fascinating city."

When they reached the car, the uniformed policeman said goodnight. The armed guard delivered them to the hotel and accompanied them to their floor. As Richard paused for her to insert her key card, the guard ambled down the hall, his back to them.

"Good night, Kendra. It was a pleasure taking you out tonight."

"Thank you. I enjoyed your company and look forward to tomorrow." Polite phrases strained to express her appreciation for their time together and all he had shown her today.

"See you at breakfast? Nine o'clock? The synagogue opens at ten. I'll knock, and the guard will go down with us."

"Great. See you then."

He leaned down and brushed her cheeks with kisses in the French style, the same way Mrs. De Roos had greeted all her guests. That gentle touch triggered a shiver down her middle and a desire for more. She stepped into her room, locked the door and set the chain in place with a swoon clouding her vision.

Chapter 17

Richard cleaned up from his morning work-out. Kendra must have slept in. He tapped at her room and waited while she peeked around the chain before opening up. Her caution reassured him that she took her safety seriously. "Good morning, Kendra. Ready for the tourist scene?"

She left the door open while grabbing her purse. Dressed in slacks and a cream silk blouse, she'd out-class the average tourist today. She must have slept well, because she looked bright-eyed and cheerful. He wanted to greet her with a kiss, but he suspected rushing their relationship wouldn't work with this woman. They'd known each other such a short time.

Professional distance would avoid awkwardness later. He certainly didn't want to create a long-distance relationship later.

"I'm excited. This is going to be a great day." When she smiled, her lips spread so wide. The mauve-tinged lipstick caught his attention.

After closing and checking the lock, she walked with him to the elevator. The guard followed, and they exchanged good mornings. "Are you so sure it's me they're following? Maybe it's you."

He shook his head. "We have no proof, but I think it's the man who wants your signature. He's trying to intimidate you into agreeing."

"He underestimates my stubbornness." She stabbed the

button for the main floor. "And if he's behind the theft of my computer, I'll make sure I bring that up if he calls again. Or maybe I'll call him. I need that computer, Richard. It's old and slow, but it has thousands of photos, old academic papers, studies on artists, even the research and recipes for historic oil paint formulae. I didn't use off-site backup as much as I should've."

Richard squinted. "I don't recommend that you call him. He may see it as a negotiation—your compliance for the return of the laptop."

"Yeah, I guess you're right. I hate it when the bad guys hold the aces."

They joined the other hotel guests swirling about the various buffet lines. After being seated and requesting coffee, they split in different directions for breakfast choices. His sweet tooth awakened by her enchanting lips, he gave in to the temptation of two bakery items.

He spotted her bowing over her plate and dallied before he returned to the table. While secure in his high-church religion, praying in public had never been the practice in his family. She made no great show, however, and reached for her coffee in a few seconds.

He placed his plate on the table and took a seat. "Found what you wanted for breakfast?"

"Oh, man. After living on pennies for so long, it was all I could do not to take bread, ham, and cheese and stuff it in my purse for lunch."

He laughed. "We're on a generous expense account. You can have anything you want for lunch. By the way, your old laptop is a PC, right?"

Confirming that, her eyebrows tilted. "Why do you ask?"

"A new one has been ordered. You'll need it for our research. And it's a keeper. You can take it home with you."

The action of reaching for her coffee cup froze, and her mouth opened. She leaned forward conspiratorially. "Really? Interpol is giving me a new computer?"

Interpol might not refund him the money, but he wanted to do this for her. Without lying about the source. "Don't question it. Just accept it, and be grateful."

She rocked back in her chair, still looking stunned. "I'm grateful, but I do still want my old one."

"You'll probably get it, eventually. Meanwhile, the new laptop should arrive tomorrow." He'd impulsively ordered it rushed from the US Wednesday afternoon after she agreed to the Budapest trip. If it didn't come by Sunday night, he'd ask Van Der Veen to get it to Vienna. "Let's visit the most important tourist sights today and stay in tonight."

She nodded her agreement. "Safer than roaming the city after dark." Her eyes darted to the guard in the corner. "By the way, did the Amsterdam cops catch the guy who stole it?"

"No, and they haven't found the canvases he took from your room." He watched her to judge how much that mattered.

A shrug told it all. "They weren't finished. I'll start them again in Texas, and they'll be better for everything I've learned."

"Did you hear what the man was expounding upon at the De Roos's house that night? About how modern artists should adapt the techniques of the grand masters in new compositions?"

"I've been thinking about that, but few modern artists are using oils. Acrylics are so much easier to use, they cost less, they dry faster ... Why go backwards?"

"True, but you could do it if you wanted to. You know more than most artists about the paints, the proportions, and the strokes they used." Professorial urges insisted that he pull her away from the limiting life of a copyist. "You could do original works unlike anything else being produced today."

She sipped coffee, her eyes turned down. "Maybe. But would anyone want to buy them?"

"Marketing is hard. It's like writing books. We all wish we didn't have to work to sell them. Sharing your vision, though, is worth the effort. If we only copy what was painted in previous centuries, we don't advance art. We don't express the world we live in."

Her expression had darkened. Maybe she didn't like the world she lived in.

Van Der Veen's call interrupted their pseudo-academic discussion with a request that he meet with several Interpol officers for a planning session on the Vienna cave expedition. "The paintings are still mostly in crates, and we want to discuss how best to extract them from the cave and use your limited time before your return to the US."

Richard shut his eyes tight and dropped his head. He so wanted to show this city to Kendra today. If he had to attend the planning session, she should at least go with the guard and see all she could. "Okay. You're right. We need to do that. I'll be there in a half hour."

Kendra's brow went up. "What's happening?"

He explained, and she had the kindness to look disappointed. "But you can go with the guard, and maybe I can meet you for lunch." He hoped the meeting wouldn't take too long. This day should have been for the two of them.

Top on Kendra's list to visit was the synagogue and ghetto. The guard, Péter, drove her and stayed by her side.

The normally silent shadow bloomed into a proud tour guide. "Pro-Nazi Hungarians bombed the synagogue in 1939. It was rebuilt in the 1990s."

The first sight of its two onion domes on tall octagonal towers surprised her, as did its dramatic horizontal brick pattern, alternating beige with red. Approaching the main entrance, she studied the brick pattern at her feet and discovered its menorah design.

Looking down and all around, some quirk of a tourist's gait caught her attention. She couldn't see the man's face as he hurried to purchase an entry ticket.

Péter directed her inside, giving the entry guard their pre-purchased tickets. The magnificent interior captured her attention, and she put away the ridiculous suspicion that their nighttime stalker might follow her here.

The opulent synagogue surprised her with several features more common in Catholic cathedrals, like the wooden pulpit extended midway over the main floor. "Look. See those pipes? They have an organ."

"It's a very fine one, too," said Péter. "Concerts are given by some of Europe's best organists. The acoustics are excellent."

"Have you ever heard it?"

"Once, years ago."

The brilliance of gold and geometric designs dazzled her. "I didn't expect it to be so rich."

"People with Hungarian Jewish roots, even Americans like Estée Lauder and Bernard Schwartz—your actor Tony Curtis—gave millions of dollars." His smile dimmed. "So few years after tens of thousands were starved to death here in the ghetto. About two thousand are buried in the courtyard behind the synagogue."

Kendra joined a group of tourists near the front to hear a man speak in English about the history of the building, its cemetery and museum. Péter remained standing in the left aisle. Though the sanctuary bustled with talks to many language groups and people entering, leaving, and churning among the rows and aisles, Kendra felt the sacredness of the place. As she reluctantly left through the side door with the others, she looked back at the center Ark and its gold embellishments.

She stumbled against a middle-aged woman. "I'm sorry." They both reached for Kendra's purse, which had fallen off her shoulder. Péter rushed toward Kendra when the fumble happened, but she waved away his concern. Then he accompanied her silently through the small Holocaust Memorial Park. They also took a half hour to see thousands of relics in a small upstairs museum.

"The tour through the ghetto is the kind of outside walking we ought to avoid today," he said. "Besides, it's all open streets now. Everything's cleaned up. Let me point out a few things and then return to the car."

As the guard recounted the grisly history of the ghetto, Richard called her. "The meeting's winding down. Would you like to pick me up and continue the tour together?"

"Yes. I'll see you in a few minutes." She gave Péter the change in plans, and they took off for the Police Palace.

Richard waited in the brilliant sun, a relieved smile stretched across his face. He looked so good in the fine, blue plaid shirt that picked up the color of his eyes. Péter had been an excellent guide, but her excitement piqued at having Richard along for the rest of the day.

He swung into the car beside her. "Hero's Square, please."

Along the boulevard, Richard pointed out palaces from the prosperous days of Queen Sisi.

"I had no idea Hungary had been so rich before World War Two," Kendra said. "The enormous art market and confiscation of important works from wealthy Jews begin to be more plausible. I wish I had time to see more. I honestly never thought of Hungary in any way other than as a Communist vassal."

Sitting together in the back seat of the black Mercedes, she twisted in every direction to get a better view as he and the driver showed her veritable castles that once belonged to nobility, most now converted into public libraries, public spas, and government offices.

"Travel does broaden the mind, doesn't it? History is so boring until you visit the places where it happened." Richard gave her hand a squeeze. "You can come back and see all this again."

When? The twelfth of Never? One trip to Europe per lifetime was more than she had ever anticipated.

At the enormous paved square, he leaned forward to speak to the driver. "Put us out here on the curb, and we'll walk over to the statues for a minute." To Kendra he explained, "There's no parking on the street."

"I'm supposed to stay with you at all times. We park by the buses." Péter pointed backwards to an area a short distance from the square which he'd just passed. However, he stopped the car as requested.

Richard opened the door. "We'll just be a moment. Don't worry. I'll be with her." He motioned for Kendra to exit with him, and she scooted over on the seat and took the hand he offered.

The guard's mouth hung open with no reply. As soon as Richard closed the door, he sped off down the block, having to circle to get back to the parking area.

Richard led her across the white- and gray-patterned

expanse to a semi-circular arrangement of statues centered by the Tomb of the Unknown Soldier. Backing this, a tall pedestal with an eagle at the top rose skyward. He read details from a tourist guidebook about each Magyar chieftain's and explorer's statue while she drifted nearer the sculptures.

When he looked up, she wasn't there. Little old ladies in tennis shoes, men hobbling with canes—no shapely young woman with long, silky dark hair. "Kendra?"

A muffled cry came from behind the stone figures. "Kendra?" he yelled.

Running footsteps on the right drew his attention. Péter, with his gun drawn, rushed around the end of the semi-circle of statues shouting in Hungarian. Richard broke from the crowd, circling the massive structure to find Kendra pushing and kicking at a man who grappled her waist and arm while a stocky woman held her other arm.

"She's got a needle," he shouted.

Kendra stomped on the man's instep and jerked her arm away from the needle, breaking it off in her skin. Péter shot at the man but missed, then ran forward and pushed him so that he stumbled and knocked his head on the paving stone with a resounding crack. The woman escaped while Péter slapped cufflinks on the unconscious criminal.

Two policemen on park duty jogged up. Péter instructed them to call an ambulance and keep the man under guard until it arrived.

Fright on Kendra's face turned to a dazed blank. She stared at her bleeding arm, then plucked out the broken needle in slow motion. Her knees gave way as Richard rushed up and scooped her in his arms. "Call another ambulance. That woman stabbed her with something."

Chapter 18

Richard carried Kendra in his arms across Hero's Square to the street while Péter raced for the car. He'd insisted he could get her to a hospital faster than waiting for an ambulance, and he had lights flashing and siren blaring when he drew up to the curb. Both men eased her onto the back seat, then Richard sat with her head in his lap.

He brushed her hair out of her face and prayed more fervently than he had for any reason in a long time. This was his fault. He'd wanted to show her the city—and the next one, and the next. Danger hadn't been part of his privileged life, and he ignored the signs because they were inconvenient. Now she paid for his carelessness.

Her soft cheek in his hand hadn't lost all of its color. Her eyelashes fluttered a bit when he stroked her face. Maybe she didn't receive the full dose of the injection, apparently an anesthetic. She would be okay. She had to be.

Péter screeched in front of the emergency entrance, hopped out, and opened the back door. "Sir, I have a suggestion. If you want to go in with her, you need to be family."

"Well, I'm not. I assumed my Interpol ID would get me anywhere."

"No, sir. Not a good idea in a hospital. Maybe they keep you away so you do not threaten the patient."

"What am I going to say? I'm her brother? I don't even

know her father's name or address."

Medical personnel burst through the admission doors apparently asking questions in Hungarian.

"Then say you are her fiancé. They will let you in with her."

Would it be wrong to lie in order to protect her? He gave a nod to Péter, called the medics to Kendra, then followed the stretcher as if he had that right.

After Richard had informed the medical team of her name, nationality, and what had happened, they invited him to have a seat outside her curtained treatment area. Ignored while nurses and technical people rushed in and out, he propped on his knees and resumed a repetitive prayer for her recovery, reciting pleading phrases like a Buddhist prayer wheel.

A short, middle-aged nurse came from behind the curtain. "Did she hit her head when she fell?"

"No, I caught her. She didn't fall on the pavement."

"Please fill out this form."

Her middle name? Her age? He thought it was twenty-six. Her address in Fort Worth? Time to call Klaas Van Der Veen.

Klaas cut off his attempt to explain. "Your guard already called from the waiting room. How is she?"

"I don't know. They're working with her now." Richard struggled to control his voice, his emotions. He closed his eyes and pressed his forehead between his forefinger and thumb. "They're trying to find out what was in the injection before they can treat her."

Klaas supplied information from her temporary employment form as Richard asked the questions. Not the ones about whether she was pregnant, lactating, or had HIV-AIDS as he assumed all those were a no.

"The guard reported the incident as an attempted

kidnapping. Do you agree?"

"Exactly. The man had a gun, but didn't try to use it. We don't know about the woman. She got away."

"How did they know Ms. Cooper would be at Hero's Square? Did they follow your car from the Police Palace?"

"Péter didn't think he'd been followed. He said a woman bumped into her in the synagogue and knocked her purse on the floor, so I riffled through it and found a bug, I think. Looks like a little round battery. I gave it to Péter to give to you."

"By all means, get it away from you and Ms. Cooper." He gave a long sigh.

"Do you think it will be safe for us to … proceed to the next city?" Richard's paranoia level had risen such that he didn't want to give any personal information on his own phone.

"If she is able, stay with the plan. Our men will go over the rental car you're driving from Budapest, and follow you well out of the city. The best thing for you both is to get out of the country. We've got the kidnapper, and anticipate we'll be able to get information out of him. Assuming he wakes up." He did a fake sort of cough. "Hungarian police do not have all the restrictions of you rights-oriented Americans."

They closed the conversation, and Richard resumed waiting. Since the patient form now included her father's name and contact details, he could call her next of kin. She'd told him enough about her father that he hesitated to do that, though. They didn't seem to be on the best of terms. Not if her copy of Rousseau's tiger was still in the closet. He put away his phone and resumed praying rather than frighten the man with incomplete information about her condition.

"I'll take that form now if you're finished." The nurse reached toward the page, which dangled from his fingers as he propped on his knees. He sat up and handed it to her.

Her face softened with compassion when she saw his

expression. She patted his shoulder. "Don't worry. Your fiancée is going to be fine. The doctor speaks with you soon."

His conscience pricked at the reminder of his lie. He'd known her just over a week, but their days working together made it seem like much more than that.

The doctor emerged shortly. His relaxed demeanor and the curve of his mouth calmed Richard's fears.

Richard stood to receive his handshake.

"She's going to be fine. She didn't get a full dose of the anesthetic, and the needle wound wasn't bad. Since all her vitals are good, I'm going to release her to sleep it off."

"You're not keeping her here until she wakes up?"

"There's no need. She's already responding to some degree. Take her back to your hotel, and stay with her until she's alert. Take care that she doesn't fall going to the bathroom, that sort of thing. She may be nauseated because of the anesthetic. I can give you a prescription for that, but it will make her sleepier. I suggest that you just let her sleep. Don't give her coffee or stimulants."

Richard winced at the thought of caring for her personal needs and functions, but he wouldn't leave her alone.

"I must ask another question." The doctor's tone dropped a level into a more serious category. "Do you affirm that the injection happened as you told it, by a stranger in a public place?"

"Yes, sir."

"You yourself did not do this, nor would you cause her harm?"

"No, sir. She and I are working with Interpol here in Budapest." He extracted his Interpol ID from an inner pocket and showed it to the doctor. "We had an armed police guard, but I ... I'd insisted he put us out at the curb and park the car. He's in the waiting room now if you want to speak with him."

"I spoke to him when you brought in the patient. Okay, let's get her into a wheelchair. The nurse will help deliver her to your car."

Richard made a quick call back to Klaas with updated information.

"Okay, I'll send two armed guards and a car to take you back to the hotel." Relief in his voice poured through the phone. "They'll stay with you through the night. We have someone at the hospital front desk now to arrange payment for her care. There won't be any charges to her."

After raising the head of the bed, the nurse spoke in a loud voice to Kendra and slapped her hand. "Time to wake up. Swing your legs off the bed."

Kendra's eyes fluttered. Richard stepped close and braced his arms around her. "Stand up, darling. You can finish your nap at the hotel."

Confusion wrinkled her brow, but she complied with their efforts to get her into the chair. He kissed her cheek and allowed the nurse to push her out. At the car, he strapped her into the reclining front seat. After arriving at the hotel, Péter located a wheelchair to get her to the eighth floor.

Uncluttered, neat and organized, her room didn't surprise him. Taylor had been like an untrained child, throwing around her clothes on chairs or the floor, the result of having maids since birth. Increasingly he realized his good fortune that she broke off their engagement. He hoped she and her new love found happiness together, at least until the guy's money ran out.

Richard turned down the comforter and sheet, removed her shoes, and helped her into bed still wearing her slacks and blouse. She sighed, rolled onto her right side hugging the pillow, and settled into a pattern of heavy breathing.

He watched the rise and fall of her chest from the settee,

thanking God for her safety. All this chase after valuable art seemed ridiculous in comparison to the life of one precious woman. He no longer suspected her of participating in the fraud industry. Her innocence radiated from her face. In a time when politicians and businesses flaunted the word "transparency," she was its poster child.

The strain of the day weighed on his eyelids. Somewhere during the pondering of whether they could proceed with the plan of driving to Vienna tomorrow morning, he drifted to sleep.

Kendra stirred first, throwing back the coverlet with a whimper.

Richard stood to check on her and massaged a cramp in his neck. "Hey, girl. You doing okay?"

She looked around the room, rubbed her eyes, and swung her feet to the carpet. "Need to go to the bathroom." Swaying on her first step, she grabbed his arm.

He walked her to the door, unsure of how much he could do in this role of caregiver. "Can you make it from here?"

"Think so."

Flushing and tooth brushing noises came through the door while he perched on the corner of the bed nearby. When she exited, she'd brushed her over-the-shoulder hair. "What happened? Did I pass out at the square?"

He reviewed the events of the eight hours since they'd met at eleven. "So you've been asleep, to some degree or other, for quite a while. How do you feel?"

Her hand went to her stomach. "Hungry. I haven't eaten since our breakfast here at the hotel."

"That's good news—hungry and not nauseated, that is. Want to go downstairs for dinner? I need to check on something."

"I'll have to put on makeup. Just be a minute."

She turned to go back into the bathroom, but he grasped her forearm and pulled her close. "You don't need makeup." She sank into his hug and wrapped her arms around him. "You don't even realize how beautiful you are."

She pushed back enough to look at him, smiling with a slow shake of her head.

"I'm so relieved you're okay." He held her again, relishing the warmth of her body fitting perfectly against his. Then he leaned down and kissed her gently.

Surprise lit her face, perhaps even amusement. In fact, he'd surprised himself. Not sure his momentary lapse could work out well for either of them, he backtracked. "Let's go find some food."

Péter had been replaced by a stocky, bald guy. Richard checked the man's ID and asked him to follow them to the restaurant. His hopes ran high that slipping out to Vienna without using any public transport would take them off the grid of whoever chased Kendra. A cave full of paintings awaited them. Now that Kendra was safe, he barely contained his excitement for this final segment of his summer with Interpol.

He paused at the concierge's desk to ask if he'd received a package. The young man checked a list and excused himself to the secure room for luggage. He returned holding a box with "RUSH" tapes and Overnight Delivery stamps.

Yes! Richard wanted to do a fist pump and crash his body into the concierge in a victory celebration. Instead, he slipped the fellow a good tip with all proper decorum.

He turned to Kendra, waiting with the guard. "Santa Claus just brought your Christmas present." He smiled so wide it felt like his face would break. He loved giving things to Kendra because she didn't expect them.

◦◦◦

Kendra's step still wobbled at times. She trembled inside, and Richard's kiss gave her an extra reason beyond the anesthetic. If he found her weakness to be a turn-on, he had a surprise coming. She thought of herself as strong and determined. Persistence made it possible for her to get through school without parental support, and she didn't have it within her to be a man's clinging vine.

On the other hand—he kissed her! Not in a demanding or possessive way, but with gentleness and caring. Her vague recollection of his presence at the hospital and then helping her to bed made her think he'd been with her all afternoon and into the evening. He must have stayed in her room to watch over her. For all her independence, that meant a lot. She craved a protective, loving relationship.

Entering the restaurant, she scanned the large area for dangerous strangers. The guard pointed out a table away from the window but with good view of the floor and a nearby exit. The waiter seated them there. The guard took his stance by a decorative dividing wall, and she tried to relax.

Richard put the box on the chair between them. "Don't let me forget that."

"What is it?" Reading the brand name, she hoped this wasn't a re-purposed box.

"Your new laptop. If you're awake enough, you can set it up tonight. I'll help you. If you want me to."

"For me to use in Austria? That's so great. I'm sure I'll need it to research what we find." Excitement at being connected to the world lifted her spirits and chased more of the fog from her brain. She should e-mail her roommate, and she ought to send a text message to her dad.

"Use it as your personal computer. Put everything you want on it. Download programs tonight. You get to keep it when you go home."

"Really? After a week's work for Interpol?"

"Consider it compensation for your old computer—which we still hope you'll get back eventually. They know we need the Internet for this job."

He raised the menu and studied the options. End of discussion, though she questioned Interpol's generosity. She'd bought her laptop when she began the master's degree, and it ran slow and sometimes froze up. She didn't expect to be able to replace it for at least a year.

The waiter returned for their selections, and she quickly chose a mild chicken dish. It soon arrived with a savory sauce and roasted potatoes. Richard's beef and sausage goulash ran red with paprika. The melded, steamy flavors heightened her interest in food, which had awakened more slowly than the rest of her. "Umm. This is going to be good."

While they ate, Richard supplied the details she'd missed this afternoon. "We surmise that the intention was to kidnap you. The woman who stabbed you with the needle left a stretcher and sheet. She escaped in a sort of van with a red cross on it, like a medical vehicle, but not the normal EMT truck."

"I remember a man with her, probably Hungarian. I'd walked around to see the back of the statues. He asked me to take a picture of them standing in front of the horseman and chariot near the center."

Richard's hand, reaching for his glass, paused in the air. "Did you get a photo of them?"

She shook her head, straining to pull back any details. "I wouldn't go that far away from you, so he grabbed me and then she came at me with the syringe."

"We got the man. He was unconscious and bleeding because his head hit the paving tile when Péter shoved him down. He's under guard in the hospital now." Richard sipped his wine, his face clouded. "He's in serious condition. He may not wake up."

"I can't imagine why anyone wants to kidnap me. Forcing me to sign a painting doesn't seem reason enough."

Chapter 19

Seeing the thrill in Kendra's bright eyes when he cut open the box made the purchase price of the laptop seem like a bargain. Richard slipped out the Styrofoam packing and offered his gift to her—though she still thought Interpol had bought it.

She removed the plastic wrap with her lips in an open smile. "Oh, Richard. I've seen the ads on this model. It's everything I could have wished for." Continuing her discovery like a kid on Christmas, she followed the easy set-up instructions and plugged it in. Laughter bubbled out when the sign-on screen lit up. "I should call Mr. Van Der Veen and tell him it arrived, and it's beautiful."

"At ten o'clock on a Sunday night? I don't think so." Klaas wouldn't know what she was talking about. Richard had mentioned her need for a computer a couple of times, but Klaas hadn't committed to Interpol's buying it.

"If I'm going to download programs and bring in files from my off-site stash, I'd better get a cord instead of using Wi-Fi. There isn't one here. I hope they have a loaner at the front desk."

"Keep working on your set-up. I'll go down and ask for one." Room service might take too long, and he wanted to help somehow.

When he returned with the thick yellow cord, she focused on the project with such excitement that her hands trembled.

Sometimes she mumbled, and at other times she directed indignant questions to the screen. "It's a touch screen. Also, it has a voice function. I can ask questions, and it scans the Internet for answers. Getting this computer in place of my old one is like thieves stealing a VW bug and having it replaced by a Ferrari."

She didn't need him for this process. He gave her space, moving to the sofa with the free newspaper that came under the door each morning. He wondered if she'd forgotten he was in the room until she swiveled and asked him if he wanted coffee.

"No, thanks. It's nearly midnight. I'll be driving tomorrow, so I'd better turn in."

"I'm going to stay up a while longer. This is a great connection, and I've had a lot of sleep this afternoon. I need to pull several files from my off-site storage, including my dissertation."

"Let's leave the hotel earlier than a stalker would expect. Breakfast at seven?"

"Sounds good. See you in the morning, packed and ready to eat breakfast and go." The computer claimed her attention with a beep.

Nothing like coming in second to a machine.

He reached for the handle, and she darted from her chair. "Good night, Richard. And thank you so much for whatever part you had in getting the laptop—and I know you did. It's exactly the tool we need to research the paintings we'll find in Austria, but Mr. Van Der Veen didn't come up with the idea by himself."

A smile grew from inside and rose to his face. Being appreciated felt good.

Another beep sounded, but she ignored it. "And thank you for staying with me at the hospital and while I slept the drug off this afternoon. I've never felt so helpless before." A glisten came to her hazel eyes.

He opened his arms to her, and she stepped into his embrace. "You're welcome. I didn't want to be anywhere else but watching over you," he said into her hair, which bore a sweet fragrance despite all she'd been through today. Then he backed up enough to touch her cheeks with his, aware that they needed to maintain a comfortable working relationship for the week to come. His earlier kiss had been a mistake in judgment.

Her face flushed, and she blinked shyly. At least he knew he hadn't offended her.

Perhaps before she flew home, he would share with her his developing feelings. But first, they had a job to do. Probably the most important job of his career.

ço∘ç

Kendra's two suitcases stood ready at seven a.m., one of them packed with artist materials and the other increasingly full of clothing. If she had to keep dressing like a professional, she'd need another suitcase. Her makeup fit in an outside zipper pocket, and only her toothbrush and paste remained to be tucked in after breakfast.

Richard's tap brought her to the door, her pulse setting up a rapid tap of its own. He looked vibrant and wide awake, like he'd risen early and worked out. She, in comparison, hadn't had any serious exercise for two days. "Good morning. I'm so glad you're in casual clothes. Me, too." She brushed a hand down her blouse and slacks. "Road trip, right?"

"Right." He stepped inside and closed the door, his finger across his lips in the sign for silence. "I want to say this without being heard by anyone else. There are two really neat towns on the way, if you're interested. The drive to Vienna will only take about two and a half hours. Győr, Hungary is halfway there, and if you want to deviate a few miles, Bratislava is another charming old town."

"Bratislava?"

"It's the capital of Slovakia, so you'd be adding another country to your summer experience. We can pass freely from one to the other. Three countries in one day: Hungary, Slovakia, and Austria. What do you think?" He smiled, his eyebrows raised in question.

"Amazing. This is the best summer of my life."

"To keep it that way, a technician will go over all our bags and persons to make sure we have no bugs hidden anywhere. Then we'll have a police escort out of the city. Once we're on the highway and they're sure no one is following, they'll turn back, and we'll continue on our road trip. If we feel the need of a guard in Austria, Interpol will make one available."

"That's super. I just hope we leave the stalkers behind." She touched the small bandage on her arm where she'd been stabbed with the anesthetic syringe. Once in a lifetime was too often. "Richard, I really feel bad about this whole situation. My joining you in Interpol made everything more difficult."

"If you hadn't joined me in Interpol, you wouldn't have armed guards. You'd have been plucked from Mrs. Graham's apartment house long before now."

She bent her head, unable to return his gaze. She'd never seen any danger in copying art until now. And her legal-but-ill-advised work had also compromised Richard. Finally making the kind of money she needed complicated both their lives.

And yet she wasn't ready to give it up yet. "I'm glad we're leaving Budapest. I'll be careful not to let anyone know our destination."

After breakfast with the policeman standing guard, the technician arrived with his equipment and accompanied them to their rooms. She had to open the bags, dump out her purse, and submit to a personal scan, but the sense of reassurance returned. For the sake of security, the policeman and Richard hauled the bags from the room rather than call a bellman. When she descended with Richard to the rented Mercedes he had arranged, she waltzed out with her head held high.

After a moment to set the GPS for Győr and conferring with their escort, Richard put the car in motion. "We have a lift-off."

She wanted to giggle like a little girl. What an adventure this day would be.

Sunlight streamed through the streets of the city, which had barely awakened before eight o'clock on a Sunday. Leaving the city was easy, and their escort turned back when Richard approached the M1 highway toll entry.

The modern, four-lane road rolled over hills and through green pastures. Her shoulders relaxed and relief spread over her mind. "I haven't been in the countryside since—I don't know, before leaving Texas. This is beautiful. I'm so glad you chose to drive instead of taking a bus or plane."

He returned her smile. "It's been too long for me, too. City noises, traffic—good to leave that behind." He rolled his neck and inhaled deeply. "Want to find us some music?"

She tackled the radio, trying to figure out the Mercedes's knobs. She'd never ridden in one before coming to Europe. After passing through energetic folk music and loud European rock, she found a classical station. Nimble fingers playing a sweet Chopin piano sonata fit her mood.

Richard stretched his arm over the back of the seat. "You like classical?"

"Great music to paint by. What passes as modern music tangles my brain waves."

He laughed. "Classical is my choice, too, but I didn't

know about you Texas girls. I doubt there's any country western music on Hungarian radio."

"That's fine with me. Don't believe the stereotypes. And don't you get a lot of honkytonk in Georgia?"

Richard sped around a large truck, of which there were quite a few. "Atlanta has excellent cultural opportunities. Museums, symphony, opera. My parents exposed us to all of it as we grew up."

"Fort Worth and Dallas both have the same." She looked his way, admiring his profile. If he fished for her cultural sophistication, she could play that game on her own economic level. "I usher at Bass Hall sometimes and see stars as well as the symphony. Fort Worth maintains its 'Cowtown' image, but its wealthy families support the arts and fine cultural events."

The highway stretched over verdant fields and across a river as Beethoven's strings accompanied their summer drive. She had rarely been so content. Her future seemed as bright as this clear day. While she had no interest in joining law enforcement, this week with Interpol added adventure and artistic accomplishment. She'd have so much to tell her roommate when she returned.

Onion-domed steeples signaled their entry into Györ, an ancient city of 128,000 people along the Rába River and near the Danube. Richard had never been off the road and into the tourist area before, so this would be new to him, too. He cruised past museums and churches, aware that these buildings were older than the United States.

The streets had few tourists this early, which made them more appealing to him. "Want to park and walk for a while? There's a wide pedestrian street right down the old city center."

"I'd love to."

Windows displayed fine Hungarian china and glistening cut crystal. Kendra oohed over their displays, but kept strolling.

Her artistic appreciation ranged further than framed canvases. "See something you want? We can go inside."

"No, thanks. I don't have any more suitcase space."

"They can ship it straight to your home address, insured and guaranteed." Even as he said that, he knew the expense would be prohibitive to her. If she indicated that she wanted a particular object, he would buy it for her. Or should he exercise caution there? He mustn't create a lop-sided relationship.

On the other hand, Taylor had come from great wealth, and her perspective on money seemed less healthy than Kendra's, who seemed to spend money after careful consideration. She bought a few postcards due to their perfectly lit, professional photographs, but no trinkets. And he thought she still ordered dinner from the right side of the menu, even though on an expense account.

"Maybe next time I come to Hungary, I'll shop for something beautiful and unnecessary," she said with a chuckle. "I must not let anything distract from paying my debts first."

"Then how about a cappuccino before this day heats up?" He pointed to a café a few yards farther. "There's a place with tables outside."

One other couple idled beneath a small tree, sipping coffee and munching something from the bakery.

"A lovely idea."

When he offered a sweet roll, she declined. "I'm not going to fit into the tourist class airplane seat this weekend. I was doing fine until you started feeding me three restaurant meals a day." She laughed, turning a complaint into pleasant chatter.

The more time he spent with this woman, the more he

wanted to be with her. A tingle ran along his spine, daring him to take her hand. Maybe he'd do that when the job ended, before he put her on the plane to Texas. Meanwhile, this day stood like an oasis between Budapest's fifteen paintings and Vienna's fifty, and no suspicious characters roamed the pedestrian street of Györ.

A square, four-pointed castle atop the highest hill announced their entry into Bratislava, the capital of Slovakia. As they drove through its streets, Kendra sensed a different feeling to the city. "It seems stark compared to Györ. Less quaint and homey."

"You see more of the German and post-war Soviet influence here. The tourist area has developed in the last decade. They have a pedestrian shopping street, too. The Main Square has a year-round Christmas market as well as crystal and fine china. Would you rather go there, or St. Martin's Cathedral?"

She chose the cathedral, having seen enough of beautiful items for sale, priced out of her reach. The cathedral, in contrast, lifted her mind to man's expression of devotion to God. The magnificent Gothic windows and complex, lofty ceiling reminded her of the many ways to worship.

She sat in a pew and drank in the spirit of this special place, and Richard joined her. He seemed comfortable with Christianity, but she knew nothing of his beliefs. If their friendship were to grow, a shared faith in God was essential. She dared to glance his way. The clean lines of his jaw and intelligence in his eyes told her nothing about what he felt in this house of God. Beams of colored light streaming from resplendent stained glass windows fell across and around them both.

He leaned toward her. "Are you Catholic?" His soft question did not disturb the silent sanctuary. The tourists may come later, but they enjoyed a moment of peace.

"No. I belong to a very large Bible church. And you?"

"Presbyterian. Our family has been for generations." He waved to the stained glass windows, gold-covered altars, and high ceilings. "What does this mean to you?"

She looked up, pausing for the right words. "An expression of worship. Creation of a place to honor God. I was reared in a church with almost no decoration—not even a cross behind the pulpit. But you read in the Old Testament how God planned his temple, with gold-covered poles and the Arc of the Testimony, and tapestries woven with gold thread. I think he would be pleased that people design glorious cathedrals to worship him in."

He nodded. "He gave us the need to express art. Such a sanctuary as this is like speaking to him in a language he understands."

He touched her hand, and it melded into his. She felt an unexpected bonding, holy and precious.

"I need to confess," he said.

Did he mean to go kneel at the altar, or here on the pew kneeler? Or did he intend to enter the confessional booth?

"When Maarten and I followed you and searched your room, we thought we'd found a fraud artist. We hoped you'd lead us to an organization that sold counterfeits. I was so wrong about you." He pulled her hand over and covered it with both of his, wrapping her in warmth.

Her heart melted at his apology. "You said you were sorry."

"Yes, but I still suspected you, to some degree or other, until these past days in Budapest. Now that I know you better, understand your motivations, I realize how wrong I was."

Her eyes stung, begging to wash her emotions in tears. "You couldn't have known." She squeezed back on his hands and chuckled. "I admit that I looked suspicious. And if you hadn't believed I was a criminal, we'd never have met. I wouldn't have been here, on the most wonderful trip of my life. Believe me, you are forgiven."

He withdrew his hands and gave her a side-ways hug, then abruptly stood. "We should get on with our drive, unless you want to walk through the old town. It's right around the corner from here."

She stood as well, giving the arches one last view. "Should we be visiting the Bratislava City Museum? It might help for what we're going to find in the next assignment."

"Not much. It contains a lot of historic items more than paintings. Perhaps in Vienna we'll carve out enough time to visit the Historical Art Museum. It's amazing."

"Then let's continue to our destination. Kings and queens of past centuries await us."

Chapter 20

Before leaving the city, they purchased the makings of a picnic to share during the second half of their trip. With that in mind, Richard chose a winding—but shorter—route along the Danube. Parks and picnic areas cushioned the river at every possible opportunity, with frequent wide, sandy spots where families swam and played together. He pulled off at a section where the river rushed around an outcropping of rocks. "How does this look?"

"Perfect. A picnic on the not-blue Danube. All we need is a waltz dipping and swirling in the background."

"Believe me, you'll hear plenty of that in Vienna." He raised the trunk, searching for something they could sit on. "Oh, good. There's a carpet covering the spare wheel pit." He pulled it out, and she carried the various bags of bread, cold cuts, and fruits.

"I hope we like what I bought for sandwiches," he said. "I didn't recognize the Hungarian names of the cheeses and cold cuts."

"The one with holes looks like a member of the Swiss cheese family, which is my favorite. I'm guessing that's ham, and the bread is crunchy fresh. Nothing can go wrong on a sunny picnic by the Danube."

As she spoke, a car angled off the road and parked. Seconds ticked by.

The bright reflection off the windshield prevented his

seeing the occupants. When a young couple and their toddler emerged wearing beach clothes, she breathed again.

Richard's attention also returned to their lunch, and the gleam of sunlight off her hair. "Pass the mustard, please. Don't worry. We're safe."

"I just … after that attack in the historic center of Budapest, surrounded by hundreds of people, it's hard to get danger off my mind."

"There's something you probably ought to know."

She halted the action of spreading dark mustard on the crisp bun.

"Van Der Veen loaned me a gun and got a license for me to carry it legally. It's like the Ruger I have at home, so I know how to use it."

"You normally carry a gun in the US?"

"It stays in my apartment. I never carry it on campus." He gave a one-shoulder shrug. "It'll probably be tucked away in its drawer when I get robbed on the street some night."

"I'd prefer not to believe the world is becoming that kind of place, but I suppose wealthy people have to be prepared. I, however, have nothing to protect."

"Except yourself. Hopefully, we've left behind us the threat against you."

She put the lid on her sandwich and lifted her eyes to his. "Would you mind if I said a blessing?"

"Not at all. Please do."

Her simple words blessed their food and asked for safety. They didn't rhyme and weren't memorized phrases. He considered her request to pray as a move to learn whether they had a spiritual connection, an essential component of a meaningful relationship. He felt the bond strengthening between them. Her forgiveness for his earlier blundering suspicions meant so much.

After eating, Kendra slipped off her tennis shoes and socks and rolled up the legs of her slacks. Laughing, she scampered to the river's edge.

"You're going in? Hey, wait a minute."

She dipped her toes into the water. "I just want to wade in—to say I've been in the Danube."

He ripped off his shoes and socks and joined her. "Whoa! It's cold."

She tipped her head toward the young family a few yards away, who now watched their antics. "They're swimming in it. Have you ever gone in?"

"No. Observing from a distance was always enough. Until now." He reached for her hand, and together they scooted their feet along the coarse sand.

His cell phone dinged, and he pulled it out of his pocket. "A message from my mother." He read it and then explained. "She says they arrived early this morning and have been napping. She wants me to have dinner with them tonight."

"That's good. You can see them before we go out to the caves, wherever that is."

"Want to come along? Meet my parents?"

The blood drained from her face.

He raised his brow. "Not to worry. They're nice people. You shouldn't be alone on your first night in Vienna."

"I don't want to intrude on your family time."

"It won't be a big deal. You're my friend and co-worker. They'd enjoy meeting you. They're always interested in my university friends." He had complete faith in her social abilities. She could handle this like meeting patrons at the museum. Like the cocktail party at the De Rooses' home in Amsterdam.

"Okay. Sure." Her lips moved, only in a whisper.

❦

Kendra had drifted asleep in the car for a few minutes since the picnic due to her almost-all-nighter on the new laptop. As she woke an hour later, gentle hills gave way to outlying portions of Vienna, or *Wien* in German. Continuing into the city by GPS directions, Richard drove them on the Ring Road lined with palaces, government buildings, and massive statues.

Kendra twisted to see the structures, wishing he could slow down. "This is amazing. Parks and statues everywhere, and these huge marble buildings." Vienna was the only city she'd ever seen that challenged Washington, D.C. for majesty, and D.C. didn't have centuries-old palaces.

"I wish you could stay longer. It would take a week just to see the best of the best." He turned off the Ring Road, down a few streets, and brought the car to a stop in front of a wooden canopy extending from a grey stone hotel.

Large green plants braced the canopy, and an array of national flags mounted above included the USA, England, and more European flags than she could name. The entry created a private courtyard effect.

"This isn't a five star hotel, but it's one my parents are fond of. They always reserve a corner suite, one that has sentimental significance to them. Our rooms will be less luxurious, but pleasant and adequate for our needs."

A bellman met the car and offered to take their luggage. Richard hopped out and explained which bags belonged to whom. "I'll check us both in before calling my parents."

He brought an actual brass key to her as she wandered through the lounge and peeked into the tea room. "Third floor. We'll go up the elevator, and the bags will meet us there."

Her watch said three. "When do we meet them?"

He accompanied her to the elevator. "They're coming down to the lounge in fifteen minutes. Just enough time for me to receive my bags in the room. I'll hang out with them and talk until time to leave at six. You could join us, but it will mainly be family talk. I haven't seen them since I left in May."

"If you don't mind, I'll crash for a couple of hours." As much as she wanted to see the city and its royal art collections, she could hardly hold her eyes open. "Shall I meet you in the lounge later?"

He touched the button for third floor. "Sounds good."

She didn't want to meet them before resting and freshening up. Not that it should matter.

The feather coverlet embraced her tired body, puffing about her in comforting softness. Then her phone rang. *Ugh!* Stefan Appelhof. She considered letting it go to voice mail, but she wanted to keep their communication open in case they could work out a safe way for her to ship paintings back to him from Texas.

"Hello, my dear," his voice rang with a forced cheerfulness. "I feared we'd lost contact. Are you well?"

"I'm fine. Just tired. I stayed up most of the night setting up a new computer. What's happening on your end?"

"All is well here, though I had to find another buyer for the Breitner floral. The Kimbell declined ... Would you know anything about that?"

Her call to Mrs. Odem cast doubts about its authenticity, for which she thanked Kendra. She hoped Stefan never found out. "The Kimbell declined? Such a pity. It was lovely." If he could pretend he didn't know it was a fraud, then so could she. What a strange duplicity had entered their conversation.

"Yes. Well, to the present situation, I was in hopes you would find the time to do more painting for me before flying away to the New World. Are you still in Budapest?"

In deference to Richard, who thought they should keep their location secret, she avoided his question. "I'm doing a brief assignment with Dr. Reed. Just a few days. There's no way I can set up my paints and easel until I get to Texas." She glanced around her luxurious room. They'd toss her in the street if she spread out her oils here.

"Alex is quite cross with you that you haven't yet signed his Vermeer copy. He's not a man to be trifled with, you know."

"He purchased a copy with no signature. I should have signed it with my own name, but he'd be twice as cross if I had. Tell him to get someone else to do it. Plenty of art students would be thrilled to have the job."

"You must understand, dear. Alex fosters world art by sharing copies of the masters. He is a generous and kind man who could sponsor your rise among successful artists. Why would you not accept his patronage? The system has been well respected in Europe for centuries."

"For originals, not fraudulent copies." The fact that no originals sprang from her brain onto canvas had only been addressed by Richard.

"But why should only a few privileged people own the finest paintings the world has ever known? You can duplicate them. Alex can underwrite your efforts here in Amsterdam—"

"I'm not going to argue with you about this, Stefan. I'm very tired, and I'm going to rest. Good day." She punched off the connection, aware that she had probably broken a very valuable connection for copies that would pay off the rest of her debt.

Richard relaxed a moment in the lounge, declining

refreshment until his parents arrived. Beethoven's Fifth played softly in the background, muffling the sound of ice rattling in glasses. He looked up when heard his mother's heels on the lobby tile, and he rose from the cushioned chair to greet his parents.

His mother looked fine, her hair perfectly in place though they'd flown overnight.

"Mom, Dad, how are you?" He hugged his mother and man-hugged his father. "It's so good to see you." He led them through the subdued setting to a cozy corner. When they were seated in the burgundy armchairs, they ordered drinks.

First came questions about his welfare, then about the summer's work.

"There's only so much I can tell you. Maybe in a few months when it hits the newspapers I can be more specific. But I'm enjoying the challenge, and we've done some important work." More would come after he and Kendra did the evaluations here, but they couldn't know the details.

His father crossed his legs and adjusted his suit jacket, perfectly matched for the color of his blue eyes and silver temples. "You said you're traveling with a woman from the Kimbell Art Museum? What's her part in the search for fraudulent paintings?"

"She has an uncanny ability to judge the veracity of paintings. I've watched her analyze canvases, and it's like she senses the truth and then finds facts to back up her determination. She also paints quite well and has developed formulae for the ancient oils, so she can spot a fake before looking at the provenance papers."

His mother clasped her hands in her lap. "I look forward to meeting her. Why didn't she join us?"

"She stayed awake most of the night setting up a new computer. Besides, I figured we'd mostly be talking about the family and personal things. My relationship with her is all business."

"Oh. I see. What did you say her name is?"

"Kendra Cooper."

"Hmm. Not a name I recognize. But there are so many oil millionaires in Texas, you know." She laughed and waved the subject away.

His mother too often assumed people in his art world had money. He hoped to avoid any embarrassment in that regard. "I take it that she's not from a wealthy family. She earned a master's degree and works at the Kimbell. She's not at all pretentious, so don't expect her to play the name game, or even the place game."

The surprised—perhaps offended—expression on Mother's face showed she hadn't taken his frivolous comment well. "You know I don't—"

"—Sorry. Of course not." He turned to his father. "How's the family corporation, Dad?"

"Ken's managing well. He seems to have a knack for securities, and has used his law degree in our favor repeatedly."

Kensington Reed, second son and bearer of their mother's maiden name, had rescued Richard from a career in business. Richard would always be grateful to his brother for the freedom to pursue a career in art.

"I do hope you'll join us in the fall family meeting," his father continued with a narrowing of the eyes. "If you ever want to finish that master's in business management, you know I'll cover the costs."

"Thanks, Dad. I really appreciate it. I promise to be there in November, and I do read everything you and Ken send me. Will Katheryn and James be able to come?"

"I doubt your sister can make it. The baby's due in October, you know, and her mind won't be on portfolios and investments. But James might come, or Ken's thinking about linking us all up on some kind of meeting program. We'll see."

"You're sure this art—career—is what you want to continue with, son?" His father's sharp features and the long chin, like his own, zeroed in on Richard.

How could he say it one more time so his parents understood? "Dad, I love what I do. It isn't just the art. It's the academic setting, interaction with the students … Emory is where I want to be." Time to talk about Ken's kids. His parents could always be redirected to the grandchildren.

At about five thirty, Richard's phone dinged one clear bell note indicating a text message. Expecting communication about the found art, he checked the screen. Instead, Kendra texted, "Tourist slacks or business suit?"

"Excuse me a moment. I have to take this." She stewed up there in her room wondering what to wear to dinner, probably concerned because they were going out with his parents. He typed rather than spoke his answer.

Chapter 21

Kendra smiled when she read his message. "The beige suit with the blouse that makes your hazel eyes turn blue-green." He must mean the aqua blouse with the draped neckline. Good thing she'd hand-washed it in the sink before leaving Budapest. After applying fresh makeup and twisting her long hair into a swirl the way she did for museum showings, she took her purse and went to the door.

With one trembling hand on the knob, she rested her forehead against the cool facing and prayed for the evening to go well. No reason for nervousness existed. Richard's parents just happened to be in Vienna. He was a working partner, not a boyfriend.

Yet.

At times when confidence escaped her, she pretended to be a person with confidence. As if an actress, she performed the role of Kendra Cooper of the Kimbell Museum. She lifted her chin and opened the door.

She entered the lounge, shoulders straight and imitating the easy walk that exuded self-assurance. Richard stood, drawing her attention to where they sat, and then the other man pushed up from his chair. This had to be his father. Almost as tall, and with the same slender but strong build. The lady remained seated.

Kendra smiled, weaving between the lounge groupings to their corner and praying she wouldn't trip on the carpet.

"May I introduce my father, Rick Reed, and my mother, Regina."

She bent to offer her hand first to Mrs. Reed, then she straightened to shake with his father. His clear blue eyes shined through rimless glasses, and his handshake extended his welcome. "It's a pleasure to meet you, Mr. and Mrs. Reed."

"Please just call us Rick and Regina." His voice, warm and casual, put her at ease. "Would you like a drink?"

The waiter had magically appeared.

"Thank you, but I'll wait until dinner." She accepted the upholstered chair Richard pushed from a nearby grouping. "So you men are both Richard, I take it."

"So is my father and his father," said Mr. Reed. "I took the nickname Rick, and Richard is known in the family as 'Zack.' He's actually the fourth Richard."

"Zack? Middle name Zachery?" She remembered his card gave his middle initial as "D."

His mother laughed. "No, Zack because his name is 'zackly the same."

She caught the joke and chuckled, too, but Richard tilted his head down and to the side, his lips pressed between his teeth. He didn't want to be teased about his name.

"It's a pleasure to meet you," cooed Regina. "Interesting. From his description, I expected you to be older."

"Kendra's a couple of years younger than I," said Richard. "But she's quite accomplished for her age."

How did he know her age? Oh, right. The bad Richard, back when they first met, had investigated her. And now he flattered her with pleasant cocktail compliments. "How lovely that you are able to meet Richard—Zach—while he's in Vienna." She glanced at him to see how he took her use of his family nickname. An amused smile indicated he wasn't upset, but she decided not to push it.

"Our travel dates synced perfectly," said his mother. "We'll only be here this week. After that, we'll be visiting friends near Paris.

The social banter continued until Richard suggested that they should leave in order to get to the restaurant on time.

Regina rose, smoothing out a chic black dress with a sequined top. Her golden blond hair, flipped in curls and waves, ranked as the best bottle job Kendra had ever seen, and her face had a regal smoothness. The smile, though, radiated warmth. "We have reservations at Steirereck. They offer a very creative menu."

The taxi delivered them to a gleaming modern one-story building in the Stadtpark area, all steel and black and glass, along a canal. A receptionist led them through the modern interior, past terrace exits to their table. Whatever this meal cost, she was glad she didn't have to pay for it. Richard seated her, and the waiter gave her a menu in English but with no prices. She began to study it, feeling required to order wearing a blindfold.

A white wine appeared at her plate which Regina declared her favorite in all Europe. The family toasted, and she knew enough to respond politely and take at least one sip. To refuse would be an insult.

One entrée, salsify, stumped her for a moment. She thought it was a root vegetable. Not what she had in mind. Barbequed sturgeon with kohlrabi, grilled venison, roast pigeon, grilled tubers … A creative menu indeed. "Cat-fish with Coconut, Farina, King Trumpet Mushrooms and Water Chestnut," she read aloud.

"You'd like the catfish?" said Mr. Reed.

"Oh, no. Sorry. I was just reading the menu. I didn't come all the way from Fort Worth to cat catfish. That and steaks and Mexican food are our default cuisine." They had the grace to chuckle. "Perhaps the mallard."

Slowly, she navigated the menu and chose foods she'd never ordered before, which arrived rather quickly. The very cold salad might have been prepared five minutes before its trip to the table. Steaming covered plates arrived in turn, each one a delight to the eye and then to the tongue. Char, ordered by Mrs. Reed, turned out to be a fish in the salmon family. She wouldn't have guessed.

A bit of iced lime served in a flute with a tiny spoon cleared their palates between courses. Finally, she accepted an air-filled confection, some sort of white foam with raspberry drizzle, for dessert. The preceding courses had all been small enough that finishing with the sweet foam didn't make her uncomfortable.

Mr. Reed slipped the waiter his credit card with no discussion from the others. Judging by the waiter's effusive good humor, he over-tipped.

In the taxi, Mrs. Reed announced that she had "hit the wall," which apparently meant she was jet-lagged.

Nearing the elevator, each one expressed their delight in the shared evening and how much they enjoyed meeting one another. Mrs. Reed, relaxed and sleepy, gave her two air-kisses, then Mr. Reed did the same. All four entered the elevator, and Kendra and Richard got off on the third floor.

"Good night, dear. Rest well," said Mrs. Reed. "Good night, son."

They waved and waited for the elevator to close on his parents, whose room was on the top floor.

"Your parents are delightful. Thank you for including me tonight."

"I thought you'd like them, and I knew they'd like you."

Richard walked her to her door. "Let's meet fairly early for breakfast. We'll have to drive about three and a half hours to the Five Fingers cave area. I've made reservations for us in Salzburg, which is much closer."

"We won't be returning here tomorrow night?" That meant she had to pack up everything again.

"Klaas Van Der Veen wants us to spend a couple of days with the paintings in the cave before they're moved. Then they'll be brought into Salzburg for packing and shipping to Vienna. Our more intensive workroom examination will be there.

He paused at her door while she fumbled with the brass key. "May I help you? These old locks seem a bit difficult."

She gave him the key and stepped aside. The empty hall held no bodyguard, no one observing every action. When he pushed the door open, she entered and turned to him. The door closed behind them.

"You made a good impression on my parents."

"They're nice people. I was nervous at first, but they're easy to talk to."

"You speak with intelligence on a wide range of subjects." He hesitated, then tipped his head to the side with eyes squinted. "Actually, you didn't talk much. You asked them questions, and *they* spoke on a wide range of subjects."

"You've found me out," she said with a shy smile. "I appear much more intelligent when not revealing my lack of knowledge."

He wrapped her in his arms and twisted her left and right. "You charming little lady. You know the secret of getting to anyone's heart." He bent and kissed her, and her heart flooded with emotion. She slipped her arms around his waist, and they stood looking at each other while her pulse raced.

"I wasn't going to do that until the day one of us flies away," he said. "I thought we should maintain a professional working relationship this week. But now let me go ahead and ask you, do you think we could see each other after we go back?"

"Pretty hard to do that from Atlanta to Texas."

"Could I call you?"

"Yes, you could call, and you could come see Fort Worth in the fall. Autumn and our two weeks of spring are the best times of the year."

He kissed her again, this time longer yet very gently. "Good night." He turned and reached for the door.

This didn't seem a good time to tell him about Stefan's last call.

૭∞✍

Richard tapped on her door at seven. When she answered it ready to go downstairs for breakfast, he glimpsed her suitcase standing near the door. In the years he'd known Taylor, she had never been on time for anything, preferring to be "fashionably late." Kendra respected his time and never made him wait.

"Good morning." He leaned close and gave her non-kisses in front of her ears. "You look lovely today."

"In my road clothes? I was wondering if your parents would be with us this morning."

"They'll probably sleep late, still trying to get over jet-lag. I don't expect to see them again until we're all home." He stuffed his hands into his pockets and frowned. "Klaas called this morning. The guy who cracked his skull in Hero's Square didn't make it."

"He died?"

Richard nodded. "Hemorrhaging led to a brain clot. He died during the night. Never woke up, so Interpol didn't have a chance to find out who he was working for."

"That's too bad. On at least two levels."

The unknown assailant's death dampened their mood as they went down to breakfast. Once they began the drive to Salzburg, Kendra found some Austrian folk music, which they tolerated well for a while. "I'm surprised that it takes us longer to get to Salzburg from Vienna than from Budapest to Vienna."

"Yes, but we can still drive from country to country in Europe faster than traveling almost any of the states of the US." Richard stretched his arm onto the seat back, totally relaxed as he drove through the green countryside. Mountain ranges stretched in the distance, mountains with caves in them. "Salzburg, I guess you know, is named for its salt mines."

She shook her head, wearing a smile as calm as he felt. "I've never studied German, so that went right over my head."

"Yep. Interesting that the Germans stored vast riches in the salt mines of Altaussee during World War Two, and this find also involves salt mines."

"Makes more sense than using the ice caves in this area. The humidity could ruin the masterpieces. And what if they had a big meltdown?"

He stole a glance her way, and found sunlight gleaming off her dark hair. He'd always been partial to blondes, but that was before Kendra's long, silky tendrils sashayed into his definition of beauty. "When Van Der Veen called this morning, he said part of the fifty items include *objets d'art* other than paintings. Fine ceramics, a couple of statues, and some gold candlesticks. Do you have any visceral inclinations about whether we'll find fakes among them?" He'd begun to wonder if she had psychic inclinations about art.

"No doubt some fakes were carried along with originals. You mean does this cache have recently painted frauds for the intent of deceiving the current market?"

"Yes. What's the chance this is a deliberate leak to

hoodwink collectors?"

"No guesses before we even see them. My first question would be, who owns the cave? Who made the discovery?"

"Klaas says two teenage boys found it while hiking. I assume he'll be interviewing them."

Traveling along the A1 highway, Richard noticed signs to a village in the foothills. A lake covered the valley, and the steeple of a church pointed straight into the blue sky. "Say, do you want to detour a few minutes? We could have lunch in Wels. It's just off the highway on the Traun River."

"Sure. I'm up for seeing as much as I can, and now I have a few—as yet undetermined—extra weeks of sabbatical. Mr. Van Der Veen is my new best friend."

After she agreed, Richard almost missed the exit. He took it at the last possible moment, swerving onto the ramp. The car behind him screeched brakes, slid on gravel, and almost hit the side barrier. They didn't make the turn, but the effort sent spiders of suspicion running down his spine. How could they have been followed? Who knew where they were? Just in case, he determined to be aware of a black Mercedes—in a nation full of them.

Kendra spotted an inviting café with outside tables under an awning. "How about that one? It's really warm today. The inside places might be stuffy."

"Looks good. Especially the ice cream signs on the front."

They passed a couple more shops and took seats in the shade. While they sipped cold drinks and waited for their sandwiches to arrive, she took a pencil from her purse and started sketching on her napkin. The shops along the lakefront backed by the tall steeple … She considered what paints she'd mix to capture the blues of water and sky.

"Nice." Richard twisted toward the napkin. "Thinking of painting a souvenir?"

"Maybe. What the world really needs is another schmaltzy European village scene."

"It wouldn't have to be schmaltzy. With your impressionistic abilities, it could be lovely."

Warmth rose to her cheeks. "I haven't painted anything in several days now. The itch for oils has returned." She laughed and pretended to scratch her neck. "What I need to paint is more good copies. A few more weeks like the past one and I'd be out of debt."

Their loaded ham and cheese buns arrived with their own pot of dark mustard. She paused and bowed her head a moment before crunching into the crusty bread. "Umm. This just came out of the oven. It's still warm."

"Delicious," he said, and bit down again, showering the small table with bits of broken crust.

She chewed her first mouthful and took another swig of Diet Coke. "The thing is, here I am trying to stop the circulation of fraudulent paintings, but attempting to paint well enough to pass for the originals. Why didn't I sign the two sold through Stefan? Because with my own signature, they had no value."

"Not *no* value, just not as much as if they'd passed as deceptions. Not everyone can buy a Rembrandt, but that doesn't mean they shouldn't enjoy a copy. Copies have value, too."

"But am I culpable if someone else signs my imitation as Rembrandt? If I leave the signature off, I'm participating in the trade of fakes. For that matter, if I sign as Kendra Cooper, someone else can overpaint the signature."

"You're not guilty if that happens. On the other hand, you've resisted the idea of creating original art, though I'm not surrendering that argument yet." He leveled a direct look at her. "Have you ever considered painting a pastiche of one of the masters you copy? Use the colors and even the same oil formulae as Vermeer, for example, but have the milkmaid on a stool milking the cow. Or in a simple, eighteenth century kitchen baking bread instead of pouring milk. Or paint a soldier in the style of Rembrandt's Night Guard, as if it were one he left out."

Her brain fired up with ideas. Anything was possible. She wouldn't be limited to exactly how the brush strokes lay on the canvas. Her excitement seemed to brighten the street scene before her, as if God had turned up the sunlight a notch.

The effect waned. "But who would buy them? I need paintings I can sell. Let's go choose some ice cream." She stood and walked inside the restaurant to the cold case with a variety of creamy colors. In this heat, it had to be the mint—but with chocolate bits.

The girl asked in accented English what size she wanted. Looking about for prices or some indication of scoop or cone size, Kendra floundered.

"Two mediums, please." Richard handed her the first cup of soft, swirled ice cream and a spoon and reached for his wallet. "I'll be right out as soon as I pay."

She wandered back to the table, dipping into light green heaven. It even smelled refreshing. The shaded area had filled with customers, driving the waiter to new speeds. The chatter noise level rose, and a little girl ran between the tables causing a waitress to dodge left to avoid being tripped. When she did that, Kendra found the long lens of a camera aimed directly at her from across the patio.

Chapter 22

Returning toward their table, Richard found wide-eyed panic in Kendra's expression. "What's wrong?"

"A man over there on the far side, behind you. He just took my picture. He's leaving now."

Richard twisted in his chair, but didn't see who she was talking about.

"He ducked around the side of the restaurant. He's gone. Do you think we're still being followed?"

The car on the highway that skidded and tried to take the same exit when they turned off here—it got his attention at the time, but he'd hoped it meant nothing. He'd left the Interpol gun in the glove compartment, having no way to conceal it without wearing a jacket. He should have gotten a nine millimeter in an ankle holster.

The noon crowd on the street gave them some cover, but also made it more difficult to pick out a pursuer. "Finish your ice cream, and we'll go back to the car. No one's going to grab you among these tourists and villagers. Meanwhile, I'll send a message to Klaas." He spoke a couple of sentences at his cell phone then sent the text with a whooshing sound. "I can't believe this is happening," he muttered.

Kendra had lost interest in her ice cream. She leaned close to Richard. "Let's browse in a shop with a back door and try to shake him off our tail."

"Okay. Sounds like a plan." He stood and escorted her

from the restaurant patio to the street of small tourist shops.

Strolling past several of them, she paused at a display of crocheted table runners. Holding out a lacy edge toward him, she smiled as if she had no cares in the world. "It's intricate. So detailed. And a breeze is coming through the back door."

He nodded. "Let's go inside and ask about their crafts."

She entered and posed questions about the handwork.

"I'd like to buy that one." He motioned toward an especially pretty piece. After he purchased it, the short, bald shopkeeper wrapped it in tissue paper and placed it in a plastic bag.

"Do you mind if we leave by the back door?" Kendra waved in that direction. "It would save us steps getting back to … the hotel."

He shrugged, a frown crossing his brow. She thanked him and, with a quick glance to confirm that no one watched from the front, they slipped into a narrow alley.

Walking quickly but not running, they completed that block and made several turns before heading downhill to where they had parked the rental car.

Breathless from rushing, Kendra stopped before opening the door. "What if they have a bug on the car?"

"We wouldn't find it without a signal-reading device." Still, he ran his hand over the bumpers and inspected the style lines where one might be hidden. "Let's get to Salzburg and turn in the car before we check into the hotel." Scanning the area again, he unlocked the car and Kendra scooted in without waiting for him to seat her. "What I can't understand is how they found us."

Before sitting in the driver's seat, he took his phone out of his pocket. "Kendra, turn off your cell phone. Shut it down completely, and I'll do the same. Before I left the US, I saw a TV program about apps that track people by their phones."

She did as he asked, but squinted at him. "I thought no one could find you without your permission."

"Ideally, it works that way. But it's possible to hack the location app. That must be what they're doing."

"But who, and why?"

"I'm guessing Alexander Holt is behind it, and you're his target."

The chill of raw fear permeated her core, and she rode with her eyes on the mirrors, checking every car without knowing whom she looked for.

Once on the highway again, Richard drove at the highest speed he deemed safe.

As they approached the city, Kendra pointed to the enormous castle overlooking the city. They'd made it without an obvious pursuer, and she just wanted to be a carefree tourist. "I wish we had time for sightseeing. Mozart's home town is beautiful." Built along the River Salzach, its houses and businesses climbed up the verdant hill and reflected in the water.

"Maybe next time," said Richard. "We won't be here long."

Taking a taxi from the car rental office to the Amadeo Hotel was a bother, but essential to their security. Richard handled their bags as if he didn't mind.

Kendra felt like an old hand at moving into another hotel. This one had none of the charm of the last. The functional German style dominated downstairs and in her room, but the hotel promised free breakfast and strong Wi-Fi. She just wished there were time to see the castle and Salzburg Cathedral. Richard could spout casually about "next time," but she didn't expect to ever be able to return.

The bellman dropped his bags off first, then Richard entered her room with her and tipped the guy. On the phone with Klaas now, he recounted the day's events and fumed about their continued security concerns. "No, I didn't see the car turn around and follow us into Wels, but Kendra is sure the guy was photographing her at the restaurant, and we're not talking about a cell phone picture. She said he had a big camera with a long lens ... I never saw him. She said he was medium height, wearing a faded blue T-shirt and jeans, just like any other tourist ... I realize that's possible, but what if they are still after us? What do they want?" He listened for a while and then said goodbye and turned his phone all the way off.

"Klaas isn't convinced that we were followed. He doesn't think anyone would be after me in this capacity. But from here on, there will be armed guards whenever we're with the art." He paced to the window then checked his watch. "We'll be taken to the cave tomorrow morning. It's less than thirty minutes from here. It's one thirty now. Would you like to see the cathedral? Or the castle?"

"Yes. Do we have time for the castle?"

At the hotel's front door, Richard signaled to a taxi which whisked them to the funicular railway right up the mountain to Fortress Hohensalzburg. At no point had Kendra observed anyone following them or making suspicious moves.

Entering the castle ramparts, they joined a smattering of tourists looking down onto the city. "What a magnificent view." Far below, the cathedral steeple pierced the sky, and rooftops cascaded down to the Salzach River. She snapped a few shots with her digital camera, hoping they would later remind her of what it really looked like. No photo could capture the span of beauty, the clear mountain air, and being here with Richard.

He stood behind her and rested a hand at her waist. She sighed and leaned back, enjoying this magic moment. He'd said he wanted to keep a professional working relationship. Now they had a brief time together added onto her vacation in Europe. Would all this end soon, or would he continue their new relationship once they'd flown to distant states?

He led her around to the back ramparts looking toward the Alps. A haze gathered in the valley, reminding her that being able to see forever also involved a layer of mystery.

While touring the castle's museum and vast rooms, he pointed out an advertisement for dinner and a concert that evening. "Want to hang around for this? A small orchestra, maybe a good meal. Then tomorrow we go to work."

The restaurant, a starkly modern area in the gothic fortress, offered a decent menu with excellent service. Their casual clothing fit in well with the other tourists. She decided not to fret about it.

They chatted over dinner about a smorgasbord of topics—his classes, Atlanta, her work at the Kimbell. She could hardly believe she was here, now, with this curly-haired man.

The concert was held in a large room with elaborate ceilings and walls, a setting known for its good acoustics. Selections of light classical music included solos by the flutist, which she particularly enjoyed. She knew just enough about playing the flute to appreciate its being done well.

As the applause died down, he ushered her out of the fortress and back to the funicular railway. They sat close and held hands as the car descended to the city. Their hotel lay a short taxi ride away. She didn't want the evening to end.

At the door of her hotel room, she fought the urge to invite him in, but recognized the danger there. These new feelings for Richard had flamed up over so few days.

Caution ruled. She opened her door, stepped inside, and turned around. He entered and let the door close. She wanted him to kiss her, but not out in the hallway. "This has been so fine. The drive, the fortress, the concert…one of the best days of my life." His smile warmed her insides, and tingles ran down her spine.

He pulled her into his embrace, kissing her forehead, her cheek, and then covering her lips with his. "I've enjoyed it, too. I wouldn't have had dinner up there, wouldn't have gone to the concert if you hadn't been with me." He kissed her once more, then opened the door and backed into the hallway. "See you in the morning. Breakfast at eight?"

"Tap on my door. I'll be ready."

"No need to pack up. We'll stay here again tomorrow night. We'll know more after we see … the stash." His voice lowered to a whisper at the end.

"Looking forward to it. Sweet dreams." She knew hers would be.

ভ∞ও

Richard knocked on Kendra's door in the morning and was rewarded by her wide smile. She wore light makeup, letting her healthy skin glow. "Good morning. Ready for an adventure?"

"You said hiking clothes and shoes to get to the cave. I've loaded my old denim bag with essentials. Let's go see us some art."

During breakfast, Werner Althaus found them and presented his Interpol ID. "Welcome to the team." A couple of inches shorter than Richard, he had a thin build but strong handshake. His energy spoke of an eagerness to get to the job, and his eyes darted about constantly, rarely looking directly to his. "We'll take a ride about thirty minutes to the Dachstein Alps, and up the funicular to the famous Five Finger salt caves." His accented English was easy to understand. "From there we hike on the mountain to the discovery about two miles." He nodded at Kendra. "I hope this is not a problem."

"No, not at all," she responded.

"That's good. We plan to move all the items after we perform basic forensics. We look now for indications of who put them there, and how. Because it could not have been easy. In their crates, they are heavy."

"How many paintings are we talking about?" He'd heard up to fifty, but then Van Der Veen said some of the items were menorahs and decorative objects.

"Fourteen highly significant paintings. Also some very good paintings by unknown or lesser-known artists, but we concentrate on the masters, eh? The oldest is a Dürer rabbit from the 1500s. A very dark Rembrandt, which an art expert in Vienna suggests needs the glaze cleaned. He didn't recognize the painting from known works, but there it is, the signature and the style of Rembrandt. To have an unknown painting surface, well, I cannot tell you how much it is worth." The excitement shined from his brown eyes.

"The photos I will show you in the vehicle. To spread them out here would be a great risk. We still run under the radar, as you say."

Richard nodded his understanding. Werner's contagious enthusiasm made him eager to get to the site. "Do we need to pack a lunch?"

"All that is provided. Two armed guards wait for us when you are ready."

He could hardly wait. Kendra looked excited, too, and had finished eating with nothing but crumbs left on her plate. He finished his coffee in two scalding swallows. "Let's get to it, then."

After introductions to Hermann and Dieter, who waited in the SUV, they buckled in and took off. Werner passed them several photos taken with artificial lighting in the cave. Three van Goghs, a Seurat, a Rembrandt soldier, one Manet. All quite interesting, but Richard couldn't make any judgments of their authenticity from a picture. He handed them, one by one, to Kendra, who studied them without comment.

The road wound through a valley with a foretaste of the Alps rising on both sides. Arriving at the Five Fingers salt caves, they found the parking area filling up with summer tourists. Hermann and Dieter hoisted bags of tools, food, and water and led to the funicular railway. At the top, the guards and Werner turned away from the crowd and headed onto a walking path to the north. Dieter shifted to the end of the party as Richard and Kendra began the hike, and Hermann remained in front. Both guards continually scanned the mountain above and below.

When they'd passed another cave with an obvious entry, the trail became rougher. More rocks and bushes along the wild animal path caused trickier footing, but the five trudged on.

An hour's hike brought them to a ledge, and Hermann halted before a thicket on their right. Holding aside the branches, he pointed to an opening. "You must take your bags off your shoulders and either bend far down or crawl in." Richard stared at the hole with dread. He hated dark, close places. He'd expected a wide-open cave like the salt mines he visited years ago.

"The crates are too large to get through here, so we think stones have been moved to close the opening. We'll make it wider when we move them out. We do not want anyone to know we work here."

Richard would have preferred that the guards go ahead

and clear out some of the rocks. Pushing down the quiver in his chest, he took a deep breath for courage and bent over. He had to duck-walk through the cave entrance, reassured by Werner's flashlight from inside. Then he looked back for Kendra, thinking late of protecting her from fear. "Can you make it? There's room to stand up once you get inside."

She had no difficulty managing the small aperture, and stood with her eyes wide and mouth parted in a smile. "Wow. This combines the best of *Monument Men* and *Raiders of the Lost Ark*. Are we the good guys?"

Chapter 23

Kendra followed Werner deeper into the cave, which widened and gave more headroom as they penetrated the mountain. News reports of miners trapped underground came to her mind. She pushed back fears of a collapse. A web—or maybe her own hair—brushed against her face, and she shivered and brushed wildly to get it off. Surely spiders didn't live in the rocky darkness of this dry salt cave.

A noisy roar and gas fumes of a generator reached her before the light it provided. Two men with guns drawn shouted out in German, and she snapped off her flashlight, hoping they couldn't see her. Werner halted and yelled a reply, then motioned the group forward. The men, backlit so that only their black silhouettes blocked the glow behind them, holstered their guns.

The passage opened into a large room full of wooden crates. Lit by bulbs strung onto rocky outcroppings, the cave danced with shadows as they moved about.

Richard touched her trembling hand. "You okay?"

She nodded, not wanting a squeaky high voice to give away her fear. No one else seemed jumpy. Inhaling deeply, she convinced her heartrate to slow down. Be calm. Act professional.

"There are more in another room of the cave. You go through there," Werner pointed, "and it's a few meters more."

Richard tested a board. "Have the crates been opened?"

Werner pointed to a crowbar on top of one of them. "*Ja*, most of them, but we put the canvases back inside."

Kendra moved among the aged wood. "Bare canvases? Frames often give us clues about the provenance of a painting."

"All are in frames, I think." He spoke to the guards who had been on duty when they arrived. He confirmed that the most important finds had frames. Then he dismissed those two, saying that Hermann and Dieter would be on duty all afternoon and that night.

Kendra halted where she had yanked on the end of a crate. She didn't want to be stuck here tonight. "Who will take us back to Salzburg?"

Werner chuckled. "Me. And probably bring you back tomorrow. We see how this goes."

She lifted a painting from its case, laid it on top, and unwrapped its protective cloths. She inhaled sharply. "The Rembrandt," she whispered. About two feet high by one and a half foot wide, it reminded her of the portrait of a soldier, *Man in a Gold Hat*. For that matter, it was also reminiscent of *Man in a Golden Helmet*, but this soldier had no helmet. The serious, mature face with texture and shadow across the skin resembled paintings of the master, though she didn't recognize the composition. She'd once considered doing a copy of *Man in a Gold Hat*—not a hat at all, but a golden military helmet with red and blue plumes—but the fatigue and world-weariness in his eyes has dissuaded her from the project. His would be an extremely hard face to paint well.

Moving into better light, she studied the background for the setting and noted the irony. Rock similar to this cave formed the dark surrounding. On the canvas back, several stamps and marks might yield valuable information. She searched the crate and wrappings, but no provenance papers accompanied the soldier's portrait.

"What have you got?" said Richard.

She took the painting to him. He held a van Gogh-style painting of the yellow house where the artist lived for several years. "The house in France. Do you happen to know how many he did of that subject?" Perhaps the professor had a ready number in mind.

"I've never seen a number, but he painted it in oil, watercolor, and also did some pencil sketches of it. His friends even painted it."

She surveyed the crates, stacked or leaning about the cave walls. "This is going to be quite a task. Without the provenance papers, we'll have to research each painting, identify it, and then determine if this specific one is the original or a copy." She felt her brief, negotiated sabbatical closing in on her.

Richard put down the apparent van Gogh and took the supposed Rembrandt from Kendra. "It's the man, but without the helmet. I wonder if he did a study with a model first."

"It's possible, but a study isn't usually executed in such detail. This is a finished portrait."

He rested that one on a crate also, and glanced about the room. "X-rays and dating tests could take months. I don't have that kind of time. We need to get these to a well-lit workroom and tentatively write notes on each one. Then we can fly off to our day jobs and leave the conundrum with European experts."

Several small pieces rested in a crate together, cushioned by cloths. Richard extracted one with great care and unwrapped a woman with a parasol. "Neo-impressionistic. Pointillist." He pointed to the bottom left. "P. Signác." Even in this gloom, the tiny dots of paint shimmered their combined colors.

Kendra's eyes danced around the small canvas. She breathed with her mouth open and a shiver running down her backbone. "What amazing patience it must have taken to do this. I never tried to reproduce anything in the Pointillist style—but I'd like to someday. Not a huge Monet, but maybe a simple subject on this scale."

"I want to get this under a magnifying glass, and then compare that to a known Paul Signác. Even so, we need the tests as hard evidence."

They'd ignored Werner, who ambled back from the other cave room during these discoveries. "What do you think about all this?" He waved an arm over the assembled jumble, a smile stretching his thin face.

"It's exciting," said Richard. "But we're limited as to what we can do here. The paintings have to be transported to a place where we can examine them in good light and start a file on the findings for each one. If they are what they appear to be, incredible millions of dollars—or Euros—sleep in this cave."

Werner nodded with enthusiasm. "It's the most significant find of the century. Want to see the other room?"

Richard touched Kendra's back and tipped his head toward the dark passage. "Let's go."

"Keep your flashlights on the cave floor," said Werner. "It drops off at the right. Might cause you to stumble."

Richard scanned their rocky, uneven path, using Werner's warning as an excuse to take Kendra's hand. This day would change his life. A history-making discovery in a black-as-night cave with his alluring colleague. It didn't get any better than this. His fear of dark, enclosed spaces receded in his eagerness to see more.

As they entered the room illuminated like the other one, golden menorahs reflected the light of the bulbs. On another crate stood delicate ceramic vases and cut lead crystal of the sort made in Hungary and Slovakia.

Kendra lifted one of the elaborate seven-branched candlesticks. "The menorahs indicate valuables were removed from Jewish homes. We could take a totally unjustified flying leap of imagination and assume all these objects and art were stolen from Jews."

Werner rubbed his chin with a fist. "That is our assumption."

She lifted the corner of a large piece of muslin cloth that had cocooned a painting. "While Interpol is testing for dates on the art, they should test the wooden crates and cloth wrappings as well."

Richard looked again at packing materials he hadn't thought to examine. "You're right. If these objects were taken in the 1940s, everything has to be that old."

Werner's face blanched and his mouth dropped open for a moment. "I doubt we have to pursue the question that far. If the paintings—"

"No, she's right. The fact is obvious and brilliant at the same time." This woman thought in unexpected ways. Richard would like to believe he would've come to the same conclusion, but she got there first.

She peered at a menorah and then lifted a deep blue cut crystal bowl to the yellowish light of a bulb. "I heard a couple of teenage boys found the cave and its contents while on a hike. Just a few days ago, wasn't it?"

"Exactly a week ago. The boys have already been interviewed, and Interpol has their contact information. Nothing suspicious there. Just a couple of local kids roaming the mountains." Werner crossed his arms and took a stance confirming his stronger voice.

"So the next thing I'd like to know," she said, "is who owns this land? And for that matter, when was it purchased? Would the contents of this cave belong to the owner of the land, or would they be taken into custody until the rightful owners or their heirs are found?"

In Richard's opinion, Werner's laugh sounded put-on. "Stick to validating the art, little lady. That's the only thing you're responsible for. Let us detectives investigate the land." He punched on his flashlight and left Richard and Kendra poking about.

"Little lady? I haven't heard that since I took my car to a local mechanic," she muttered.

"Don't let it chafe you. I understand Werner is a well-respected Interpol detective, but you're absolutely right. In fact, I'll mention the packaging to Klaas and see what he knows about the land ownership."

"Okay, so we have fourteen paintings expected to be of great value to focus on, not fifty." She pulled another board loose. "That's enough, considering that we only have a little over a week before you fly home."

At this moment, Richard would like to call the university and tell them he'd get there when he got there. A few more weeks in Austria with Kendra at his side …Who knew what they might discover?

"Hey, Werner," he called down the passageway.

"*Ja?*"

"Is there a list of what's where?"

Werner's shoes crunched on the cave rock as he returned from the front smelling of cigarettes.

Richard waited until he got closer. "We need to segregate the fourteen most valuable canvases to be hauled out of here. There's no need to waste time in poor lighting without the tools of our trade. Let's get the best of them into a lab setting."

"Not until forensics is finished with their study. I'm trying to rush them for you. Van Der Veen organizes armed guards and a helicopter, maybe two, and men to carry them to the nearest landing spot. It takes a day or two."

Then why are we out here on the mountain, Richard wondered. Impatience bubbled up as he feared he might not get to properly examine the treasures at all. "Come on, Kendra. Let's pull out the contents and mark the crates we want shipped back to Vienna."

"Not Salzburg?"

"Klaas says we'd have a much better setup and guards in Vienna. If these paintings are genuine, they're worth millions." Pulling a loose board off the end of a crate, he felt for a frame and found none. Moving to a large crate leaning against the rock wall, he tried again. "Besides, I'll need to fly out of Vienna in a week anyway." After gently sliding out a large wrapped frame, he laid it atop a makeshift table of other boxes and removed its protecting cloth layers. "Wow. Toulouse-Lautrec in all his decadence. One of his Moulin Rouge series."

As he admired his prize, Kendra came over. "Again, he did so many. I don't exactly remember this one, but it's his style. Haughty women strolling about the dance floor having what we would call a wardrobe malfunction. Seems a strange choice for a Jewish home."

"Did you ever paint any of Toulouse-Lautrec's designs?"

"Nope. Didn't care to. The perverted little drunk's subjects never appealed to me." She turned away from the semi-clothed woman. "Dürer's rabbit would be small, wouldn't it?"

"Yes, and very fragile. Anything that old may have been transferred to a new backing. We'll have to be extremely careful with it."

Their searching and finding continued for hours, interrupted only by a simple lunch of thin slices of meat and cheese encased in too much bread. To his surprise, the picnic included a bottle of red wine, which he gave to Werner.

Richard never drank wine while working. Two liter bottles of water had to suffice for the three of them.

Kendra spent the afternoon taking hundreds of photos from every angle and distance as Richard found and displayed the paintings. Then he rewrapped them and slid them back in their crates, this time with identification marked on the wood.

At the end of the day, Kendra requested that she be allowed to walk the long trail back to the car with the Rembrandt soldier.

Werner balked. "I'm not sure that's a good idea. What if you fall? And it wouldn't be safe in the hotel room. You couldn't even go to dinner and leave it unguarded."

She relented at last, and they agreed it was time to quit for the day. They proceeded single file past the ledge and around the mountain. Richard was concerned about her fatigue level after taking the trail twice and being on her feet most of the day. He put her in front of himself and watched to make sure she didn't stumble, but she kept pace with lighter steps than his.

On the half hour van drive to the hotel, though, she dozed. Her head rolled against his shoulder, and he relaxed and stretched out his tired legs. He was tempted to put his arm around her and pull her into a cuddle. Or maybe ease her head onto his lap. But that might be too much, especially with Werner and one guard up front and another guard in the third seat behind them.

As the vehicle came to a stop under the carport, he nudged her. "Wake up, Sleeping Beauty. We're home."

She jerked awake and rubbed her eyes. He exited quickly and went around to open her door. She took his hand and stood with difficulty. "My leg is cramped."

"Take it easy, and hang onto me." He offered his arm and escorted her up the few steps.

Entering the hotel, she dropped his arm and proceeded with stability to the elevator.

After such an exciting day, he hoped they could talk for a while alone. "Want to eat here at the hotel tonight?"

"Sure. I'll bring down my notebook. Just give me a few minutes to clean up and change."

ço◦ç

She tapped on his door in thirty minutes and tried not to overreact to how fresh he looked. "You clean up pretty well."

"As do you, my lady. No one would ever know we've been spelunking for art today."

Over a tourist-standard dinner of wiener schnitzel, they chatted quietly about their finds of the day.

She took another bite of the crisp breaded veal. Purple marinated cabbage and a hill of stir-fried potatoes held down the other end of the large, oval plate. Right now, she felt she could eat it all, but that would pass. The huge serving would feed a family of four.

After they'd had all they cared to eat, they pushed the dishes aside and spread out their notes. The waiter swooped in to clear the table for them.

"What do you think so far?" Richard said.

"I don't know. I wanted to bring back that small Rembrandt to compare it with everything I could find on line. It's like … It's his style, but not exactly any painting I remember. Like a pastiche. What do you think?"

"That's a possibility." He rubbed the backs of his fingers on his jaw. "I found myself becoming more skeptical as the day progressed. Are you going to stay up researching on your new computer tonight?"

She laughed. "I don't think I have that much starch left.

I'll probably bed down pretty early."

He seemed disappointed. "I thought I'd go to some of the sites I used to research the last paintings and see if I can place what we found today."

An unintentional smile crept out. She couldn't just go to sleep after a day like this. "Need some help from my super-duper whisper jet computer?"

"Working together, we can get half as much done in twice the time," he said. "I mean—"

"You probably got that right. How about if I come to your room? Would that be okay? Then I could leave when I'm ready to crash, and you can keep going all night."

His blue eyes twinkled in the candlelight. "Sounds like a plan."

Chapter 24

What was she thinking? Invite herself to a man's hotel room? This reminded her of a few study dates with fellow students in college which didn't stick to the curriculum.

Kendra jerked her computer's charging cord out of the socket on the desk and added all the peripheral items to the sleek black satchel it came in. She brushed her teeth, put fresh lipstick on, and gave herself a stern look in the mirror.

"Nothing's going to happen. We're professionals sharing information. He's going to show me some research websites I don't know about." She brushed her hair, though it still draped soft and shiny around her shoulders. The mirror continued its accusing glare. "If he doesn't respect me during our work session, maybe that's something I need to know."

She hoisted the computer, tucked her cell phone and key card in separate pockets of her slacks, and walked three doors down to tap on his door.

"Come in, come in. Welcome to my temporary abode." He stepped aside and waved her in. "Would you rather take the desk or the chair?" His room, like hers, had a comfortable upholstered chair and footstool in one corner.

"Oh, it doesn't matter. I may stay awake better at the desk."

"Fine. Let's get you set up and plugged in."

Kendra took care not to brush against him or give any long looks that might be interpreted as flirtatious. He reclined on the stuffed chair and footstool while she transferred all the photos from her camera to the computer. She set to organizing them by the numbers on Richard's list of fourteen.

"What's the first one we want to research?" He put his computer off his lap and came up behind her, leaning over her back.

Tense muscles bunched across her shoulders, and she held her breath.

"Okay, number one is Dürer. Then the Rembrandt and three van Goghs." He returned to his chair and pulled up a website on his computer.

Kendra released her breath and relaxed her shoulders. She wanted him to be attracted to her. At the same time, she had to trust him to honor her principles, though they'd never had that conversation.

Time to get to work. Focus on the bunny-rabbit, so realistically represented it could have sprung off the canvas. Dürer had led his contemporaries in painting subjects from nature.

"Watercolor and gouache," mumbled Richard from his corner, "painted by brush, 1502…such fine lines for watercolor. Amazingly detailed. Hey, the original is in the Albertina Museum in Vienna."

"That's great. When we get back, we can compare the hare from the cave to the known Dürer. But did he ever paint more than one?"

"No idea. Still searching." A moment passed. "Seems he did. Albrecht Dürer.org calls the one in the Albertina 'Young Hare I,' which indicates more than one was done."

"What's the address of that website?"

He spelled out the details, and they ran comparisons and shared observations. Her photos proved the "rabbit in the cave," as they started calling it, bore minor differences such as the tilt and twist of his ears.

Her time as an art librarian had taught her a few things. "We need a catalogue raissoné of every known work of Dürer. Surely someone has compiled one. Then we could figure out where this little guy fits."

They continued this way for two hours through the third item on the list, a van Gogh sunflower painting.

"He painted so many sunflowers in different media that I doubt anyone can authoritatively affirm every one is accounted for," Richard said.

Kendra stifled a yawn and rubbed her eyes. "The man only sold one painting in his life. But he gave away paintings to family and friends." The next yawn overtook her like a wave at sea. "I think I'm going to have to call it quits for tonight. It's only ten o'clock, but I've hit the wall, as your mother says."

"I'm not going to keep at this much longer, either. Pack up your laptop, and I'll walk you to your room."

She turned to look at him, surprised at his offer. "You don't have to. It's only three rooms down."

"I'm not doing it because I have to." His voice had softened. He approached the desk. "I want to." He lifted a strand of her hair that had fallen forward when she pulled out the cord.

She put a hand against his chest, ready to push if he became aggressive. Or maybe just because she wanted to touch him.

He reached for her laptop case and went to the door, opening it for her.

Together they made the few steps to her room, where he waited until she had successfully slid the card in the lock and opened the door. Then he handed her the case. "Good night. Sleep well."

She turned, appreciation for his gentlemanly care

swelling into a symphony in her mind. "Thank you. Don't stay up too late."

He bent and touched each of her cheeks in turn with his. "Don't forget to lock up. See you in the morning."

Kendra floated through her bedtime routine and slept with a smile on her face.

Richard tapped on Kendra's door at eight. When she opened, all ready to go to breakfast, he greeted her with double cheek kisses, keeping his true desires in check. "Good news. I've just talked to Werner, and a helicopter has been arranged to pick up the fourteen paintings we'll be working with. We'll fly to the cave today and assist with getting them safely here in Salzburg."

"Already? That's great."

"Klaas said they're making an effort to accommodate to our schedules. A professional trucker with the addition of armed guards will move them overnight to Vienna, and we should be able to unpack them inside Interpol headquarters as soon as Wednesday."

"We'll be back in Vienna tomorrow?" She scanned her room, probably thinking about packing again. Then she locked up, and they took the elevator to breakfast.

He enjoyed the view of Kendra both in person and in the mirror's reflection. "Can you stand another road trip so soon?"

"Definitely. The mountains are beautiful. Maybe we can picnic again."

"As you wish."

Werner entered the breakfast area as they finished eating. "Ready for a helicopter ride?"

Werner drove them to a heliport and walked them

through security. The vehicle of the hour stood high and mighty on the pad. Not a one-eyed mosquito, the six-passenger model had capacity for people and, later today, art and objects.

When they had buckled in, the pilot started the rotors turning and the noise began. By intercom he prepared them for lift-off, and they rose into the summer sky.

Kendra showed a curious combination of emotions, both excitement and anxiety on her face. "Have you ever been on a helicopter flight before?"

"Couple of times. Once just to get between airports in New York City, and in Hawaii flying over the active volcano on the Big Island. Seeing the molten lava and smoke right beneath us was disconcerting." He wanted to hold her hand, but not in front of Werner.

The flight took them to a landing place a short hike from the cave. Following Werner to its low opening, they passed two men from a shipping company carrying valuables to the helicopter. An armed guard ambled along behind.

In the cave, a team of four men wrapped paintings in multiple layers of protective material. The morning's work continued until the helicopter pilot sent back word that the bird was loaded. By that afternoon, nothing remained in the cave but empty crates and the original swaddling cloths.

Richard cornered Kendra in the deeper cave room. "Would you please keep an eye out for Werner or anyone else? His reaction to date-testing the packing concerned me. I want to collect some sample chips of the wood and fabric for dating, and I'd rather he not argue with me about it."

Her eyes spread wide, then she nodded. "Good idea. I'll go forward and make sure he doesn't walk back here for a few minutes. But be quick."

When the cave rooms yawned wide, empty of all the valuables, broken crates lay like bones after a ravenous feast.

Unaware that Richard spoke German, Werner ordered the guards to haul the packing materials out and burn them after they left. Directing them to be destroyed rather than save them for testing appeared suspicious in light of Kendra's suggestion yesterday. For that matter, were they rushing the transfer because Richard had so little time before leaving, or in order to cut short the examination of the cave and destroy the packing?

Though he wouldn't admit it to anyone else, he felt Interpol put too much credence in his ability to validate the paintings. His hasty examination might give them approval that would send them forward with his recommendation. If they were frauds, they would slip through the first gate on the path to authentication. Kendra's corroboration, as a Kimbell representative, would do the same.

Richard and Kendra walked the two mile trail to an Interpol car. Werner drove them and four guards to Salzburg, since the valuables occupied all of the helicopter space and weight allowance. The pockets of Richard's baggy cargo pants concealed a dozen samples of wood and cloth. He'd had no reason to distrust Werner except that one shock reaction when Kendra mentioned testing the packaging, but that threw up warning flags he couldn't ignore.

Now, compounded with the directive to destroy everything left in the cave, a cloud of guilt built up in his mind. He needed to talk to Klaas and maybe Maarten, his police buddy in Amsterdam.

With millions of dollars swaying in the breeze, he trusted those two couldn't be bought.

He'd lost faith in Werner.

The return to Vienna began on as lovely a day as they

could have ordered, but Kendra felt Richard's tension. He spoke less, smiled less, and maintained vigilance, always scanning the road behind them. She prayed for safety and, for the first time since arriving in Europe, looked forward to her departure.

Richard had requested a picnic lunch for the road, which sat on the floor behind them. "Keep an eye out for a pretty place to stop. We're close to the Danube, and the A1 highway is a prime tourist route. We'll see a good turn-out somewhere."

Kendra took a map from the glove compartment and found the town of Melk just off the road. Richard deviated a few miles to the river and soon found an uninhabited grassy spot.

Absolutely sure no one followed them, she noticed with concern that he loaded the Ruger in the picnic basket anyway. "What are you worried about?"

"Nothing. Just cautious." He gave a smile, which she felt was calculated to dismiss her fears, and lifted a container of German-style potato salad. Following that came a pretty plastic plate loaded with cheeses and fruit, and then another swirled with sandwich meats. Fresh breads and bottled water completed their meal.

"Are your parents still in Vienna?"

"Yes, they'll stay through the weekend. Mom mentioned that they have symphony tickets Saturday night." He loaded a sandwich, squirted on mustard from a miniature bottle, and bit into the crunchy bun. "Would you like to go? That is, if we can get tickets? It's a program of Mozart compositions."

"I'd love to. But … are you afraid of giving them the wrong idea about us?"

An almost mischievous grin covered his face. "That we're dating? Not a bad idea. Just a few months ago, Mom was gearing up for a huge society wedding." He took a long drink of water. "I broke off an engagement with a girl—woman—whose family circulated in the same Atlanta social group as my parents. She graduated from my high school, but was two years younger, so I didn't date her until about the time I began my doctorate."

She savored a slice of nutty Emmenthaler cheese, daring herself to ask why he didn't marry her.

"Her brother and I did a lot of camping and hiking together. He set us up." He took another bite and chewed, watching a motorboat chug upstream. "Hope we're still friends. The breakup happened just before I came here the end of May, so I guess I'll find out soon."

"Okay, so what went wrong?"

"I don't know. I didn't feel right about it. I was ready to settle down, you know, be married. I'd looked for the right person and found a beautiful woman who wanted to marry me. But it seemed we had different expectations of what our marriage would be like. Finally I felt like I'd made a mistake and needed to get out of it."

He put down his sandwich and selected a ripe apricot. "Okay, so I prayed a lot about it. Kind of after the fact, but we weren't married yet. She's beautiful—I said that already, but really. I mean, she's blonde, tall and slender, and totally into social life. Graduated college in English and spends her day blogging and Tweeting. Never got a job. She moved into an apartment on her dad's dime and spent a fortune decorating it, then hired a maid to keep it clean." He gave a sad laugh. "I couldn't see living in a house with a woman who can't cook and doesn't pick up her own clothes."

He took a long drink of bottled water. "I guess that sounded frivolous. There were more serious issues, too."

Richard stretched out his legs, leaned back, and propped with an elbow in the sand. "I asked our pastor—the one who was going to marry us—how do you know when you're in love? He said if you have to ask, you probably aren't."

Kendra nodded. "Sounds wise."

"Anyway, my mom's pressuring me to grow up, find the right girl, and get married. I'm just not sure her definition of 'the right girl' is the same as mine."

Lounging on the beach before her, he epitomized the description of a good catch: intelligent, employed, good looking, and wealthy.

It was increasingly difficult for her to work side-by-side with him and share every meal with him and not fall for his charm. In ten days, he'd fly to Atlanta, and soon after, she'd fly to Texas.

That separation already hurt.

Chapter 25

Setting up in the Interpol workspace in Vienna, Richard fell into his usual pattern with Kendra. They studied a painting together, took notes of any evidence on the back as to its history of ownership, made notes on the frame, and shot exhaustive photos with a good camera. Then they got serious.

"Paintings this old have to have damage. Most have overpainting of troubled or injured areas." Scrutinizing the Dürer rabbit with a magnifying glass, he found less artifact of age than expected. "It's in nearly perfect condition, except for this background in the middle left."

"Very fortunate," she suggested, "or else a fraudulent artist couldn't bear to damage the rabbit's body."

"You think it's a fake?" he murmured. With their faces so close, he was distracted by the warmth of her cheek near his. The fragrance of her shampoo. Her dark brunette hair tumbling over her shoulder. Determined to concentrate, he straightened up and took a more distant view.

"Fake? Or a pastiche. We've found no details on a series of rabbits, and yet this little fellow's ears listen to the sounds from a different direction." She pulled up a photo of the original rabbit and enlarged it. "I really do want to visit this one in the Albertina Museum. Seeing it in person, we could get a better feel for its condition."

"It would be cleaned of its ancient varnish and brought into premium form."

"That's just it. Our cave rabbit is in perfect state, even after supposedly being crated in a cave for some seventy-five years. Too perfect."

Richard rubbed the back of his neck. "My time in Europe is coming to an end. I've found a lot of fraudulent art, but not fraudulent artists. I'd hoped my work would lead to a network of painters and people who leak them into the world market."

As the day wore on, more of the canvases were relegated to their suspicious list.

Richard's eyes wearied and fought his constant demand for focus by the end of day. A tap on the door preceded Werner opening it and sauntering inside. "How goes it?"

They greeted one another, all agreeing that the "master-pieces" could be much better evaluated here than in the cave.

"Aren't they marvelous?" Werner waxed euphoric as he wandered from painting to painting. "Imagine our good fortune in finding them. This represents enormous wealth—"

"But they'll be returned to their owners or heirs, won't they?" Kendra twisted from her study of a van Gogh. Or another faux van Gogh.

Kendra's question seemed to yank Werner back from his jubilation. "Of course." He moved to the next table bearing an Éduard Manet—or its copy—and praised it to the heavens.

Richard thought less of it. "The heavy varnish must be removed before we know about that one. It's almost as if the artist double-coated it." And that was a copyist's technique for creating the appearance of age.

"What are your conclusions so far? Are we ready to pass them on for Interpol to locate their owners?"

Kendra flashed Richard a look. When he didn't speak, she shook her head slowly. "We're not convinced they're originals," she said. "They're in such good—"

"We'll know more after the X-rays are done," he

interrupted. Having his faith in Werner already, he didn't want to arouse conflict which might lead to danger. If this were a giant scam effort, a lot of money and power sponsored it.

The following afternoon, Werner entered with two men he introduced as distinguished authorities on classical art, Drs. Hirsch and Fischer. The elder gentlemen wore visitors' badges on the lapels of their dark suits and moved through the room elated at what they found. A gut reaction pled for his attention, that these "authorities" came to praise the paintings and sway his judgment in their favor.

He decided to play along and hope to learn more. "Come look at Dürer's rabbit." He motioned them to the table where it lay. "I think we have some overpainting in this area."

"Hmm, yes," said Dr. Hirsch, bending over the painting. "Covering a spot of damage in the past centuries. Could be cleaned up. No doubt they all need a bit of restoring."

Dr. Fischer continued to laud each item, even those Richard had convinced himself were recent creations. "Ahh, this soldier by Rembrandt. I've never seen this one of the series. He wears no golden helmet, but has the same battle fatigue in his face. Marvelous, don't you think?"

Kendra stood next to the man and picked up the painting, tilting it to the light. "An excellent painting in Rembrandt's style, but is it really by the master himself?"

"It bears his signature … It's entirely in the style of his hand. There's a whole history of stamps and seals on the back. Why would you doubt it, my dear?"

"It's hard to explain. Somehow, it doesn't feel just right. If you compare the face to the original—see here, on my computer? The width of the face, the shadows on his jaw … As if it's the same man seen through different eyes. And the Dürer—it could have been painted this year. It just doesn't look old enough. I'm afraid we won't be able to verify these paintings."

Werner interrupted her evaluation to suggest they all go to dinner together and discuss the fortuitous find. Richard and Kendra accepted, and were treated to an excellent meal and fine wines, which the visitors insisted on hosting.

He would rather have had dinner with his parents and Kendra again, though his mom and dad were guests of long-time friends tonight. They'd bought two extra tickets for the concert tomorrow night, so all six of them would go.

Richard and Kendra returned to the hotel sometime after ten p.m., his dry eyes blinking away fatigue. Having talked for hours, they crossed the entry area and rose in the elevator without speaking. He waited at her door while she ran her key card through the lock.

She motioned him inside, then closed the door behind him. "What was that all about?"

"They worked so hard to convince us the paintings were originals." He kept his voice low, his faith in Werner so destroyed that he only hoped the room wasn't bugged. "The entire exercise became rather silly, don't you think?"

"I agree, but whom can we tell? Werner is obviously in their camp."

"Van Der Veen, and maybe Maarten. I don't trust anyone else."

"Maarten Alders? You're thinking of reporting to the Amsterdam police?"

"Maarten is honest. He can do what he wishes with the information. I just want ... " He ran his fingers through his hair. "I just want someone else in on this."

She went deeper into the room and tossed her purse on the bed.

He followed her, pacing toward the window and back. "I mean, really. An amateur could see the paintings simply didn't show the age originals would have been. How gullible do they think we are?"

Plopping on the sofa, she checked her watch. "I guess it's too late to call."

"No need to bother them tonight. How about if I come by a half hour early in the morning and we call before breakfast?"

"Sure. We can speak freely from here. I hope."

"I suggest that we not share our opinions and reasons with anyone in Vienna, not even Interpol officers. We could be in danger if we don't play along with the scam."

ഇൈ

A phone call woke Kendra in the middle of the night. Her first thought, that either Appelhof or Dr. Holt harassed her about Vermeer's signature, proved false.

"Kendra, this is your Aunt Marilyn. Your father is in the hospital, and I thought you should know."

She shook the cobwebs of sleep from her brain enough to switch on the bedtable lamp. "Dad? In the hospital? What's wrong?"

"He had a heart attack while he was working up in someone's attic. This heat has been over a hundred every day. They've already done a heart catheterization, but the cardiologist says he needs a triple bypass. I knew you'd want to come home."

"When's the surgery going to be done?"

"Probably tomorrow, Friday. The doctor doesn't want to wait all weekend."

Kendra swung her feet to the floor, fully awake now. "There's no way I can get there so soon. I'm in Vienna now, and I've extended my stay to work on something important."

"How important can an art job be? This is your father we're talking about."

Guilt trips came natural to Aunt Marilyn. "Tell him I'll try to get home as soon as I can. I'll call his cell phone."

"They don't allow cell phones in the cardiac ICU." She gave the hospital room number with a warning that it might change. "And you know my number. I'll let you know what's happening."

After ending the call, Kendra checked the time. Four a.m., with no chance of sleep. She sunk to her knees beside the bed and tried to pray, but didn't know what to say after asking for her father's healing and successful surgery.

The Bible had a verse about the Holy Spirit interceding when you didn't know how to pray. She claimed that promise now. She knelt on the plush carpet and meditated until her mind wandered back to art quandaries and the present endeavor to validate or discredit the fourteen canvases.

She woke up her computer and searched for anything about Dürer's rabbit until time to dress for the day. Richard knocked at precisely seven thirty.

Opening the door, she greeted him with air kisses and invited him in. "My aunt called during the night. Dad's had a heart attack and will have surgery today. She wants me to come home."

Richard turned, his brow tense with lines. "What are you going to do?"

"I don't know. I can't get there in time for the surgery, and he'll be cared for in the hospital for several days. I've been praying about it, and don't feel I need to rush to Texas. Aunt Marilyn will take care of him, or maybe he'll have home nursing care."

He grasped both her shoulders and looked straight into her eyes. "Do whatever you need to do. We'll work this out ... or not. I've only got another week, and then we'll turn the whole can of worms over to other art experts anyway. If you need to leave, Van Der Veen will understand."

Her eyes stung and her lips trembled. "Why should I drop everything and run back? If the positions were reversed—if he were at some plumbers' convention in Vienna and I were sick in Texas, he wouldn't come running to me." She took a step closer, and his arms dropped around her and held her in a firm hug. The tears began, and she broke away to snatch tissues from the bathroom box.

"What is it between you and your father? With both your mother and brother gone, why aren't you close?"

"I guess I feel guilty at being alive." She sobbed out the words and sunk to a corner of the bed.

"You know that isn't reasonable, Kendra. Your father—"

"But it is. He told my mother … " Her sobbing interrupted her ability to speak. "I was returning to college a few months after Bry's death and needed money for tuition, before Mom got sick. I heard him in the kitchen ranting about my useless major, and then he told her, 'The wrong one died.'" She tried to smother her sobs and ran for more tissues.

When she returned, Richard stood with his eyes wide and mouth open. "That isn't … I've never heard anything … Oh, Kendra, I'm so sorry." He enveloped her in his embrace and held her until her crying ceased. "Sweet Kendra, you didn't deserve that. You're so precious."

She backed up and looked to his face, hoping to see sincerity there.

Pain showed in his squinted eyes and twisted mouth. "I'm glad you're alive. What happened to your brother was tragic. Teenagers drinking and driving—careless actions by kids who thought they were immortal. But you didn't do that. You lived, and you validated the life you were given."

She nodded, then took advantage of this moment to be surrounded by his arms again. Such comfort she stole there, surrounded by his fragrance and warmth. She inhaled deeply, capturing the moment and relishing the feel of his cotton shirt against her cheek.

"Oh, I hope I didn't mess up your shirt."

He made a show of checking and pronounced it clean. "You wear so little makeup. It's fine."

She shouldn't have told him about her father's rejection, the greatest pain of her life. He probably felt sorry for her, if he could relate at all. She splashed cold water on her eyes and snuffed up the dribble caused by crying. When she came out of the bathroom, she tried to put her emotional outbreak behind her. "We'd better make those calls to Mr. Van Der Veen and Maarten and get down to breakfast."

ও০০

Richard took Kendra to the Albertina Museum on Saturday, especially for the purpose of seeing Dürer's *Young Hare*. Housed in the Habsburg Palace, the museum also offered tours of the state rooms, which he was sure she would want to see.

She exhaled a long *ahhh* as they approached the regal structure of light-colored stone. Together they drank in the beauty of *House Among the Roses* by Claude Monet, Leonardo da Vinci's somber ink study for *The Last Supper*, and made their way to Dürer's *Young Hare*. The crowd hadn't arrived to flood the museum yet, so they were able to stand before the ancient watercolor a long time.

Kendra snapped a dozen photos without using the flash— photos emphasizing the ears and delicate lines of the fur. "It's in excellent condition, and yet the one from the cave seems newer somehow. Fresher, without any tiny impressions of being handled over the centuries." She spoke close to his ear.

"Whoever painted the one from the cave was excellent. The only thing different is that this one has more gradations of brown tones in the fur." She shook her head slowly. "And this one radiates its age. Can you feel it?"

Her puzzling expression took Richard by surprise. He leaned as close to the painting as allowed. "Feel what?"

"Its age. Its veracity. I wish we could view its provenance, whatever may have survived of its paper trail. But in here … " She patted her stomach. "… I know Dürer's hands brushed this rabbit into existence."

He found it odd that Kendra sensed an emotional tie to the veracity of the painting. Another man, young and well built, dressed in worn slacks and a black knit shirt, eased toward the hare. He looked from it to Kendra and probably heard what she said. Any vibrations Richard may have felt from the painting were quenched by that fellow. The scar on his jawline and evidence of a broken nose in his past made him think this wasn't the ordinary art connoisseur.

Richard touched her elbow and led her into the next gallery room. "How is your father doing?"

"He came through the surgery well. The hospital will probably move him out of the cardiac ICU, and he'll stay a few more days. There's very little heart damage. He got to the hospital in time."

"That's great news." They wandered toward a display of later impressionists. "So are you thinking of flying home for a few days? Or returning early?"

"He'll do fine with Aunt Marilyn's help. He has good health insurance which provides for in-home nursing and physical therapy and everything. He doesn't need me."

❧

Kendra had never before seen any palace so magnificent as the Shönebrunn. Austrian tourist brochures featured its history and grandeur, and she was delighted when Richard suggested they could spend the afternoon on the tour. They'd have plenty of time to return to the hotel and freshen up for the Mozart concert with his parents and their friends.

The former imperial summer residence of Maximilian II, with over 1,400 rooms, kept her awe-struck for the entire afternoon. An English-language tape pointed out major items and gave interesting history of the dwelling and its residents.

Within a couple of hours, her relatively new shoes rubbed a painful blister on her heels, and she began to limp. She'd been awake since four o'clock and felt so tired.

"Would you like some ice cream? There's a patio restaurant just off the front square. The chocolate mint is especially good." He winked at her as they went down the front steps of the palace.

"If it involves sitting down, I accept." She returned his smile and straightened her shoulders.

Chatting about his work as a college professor, she savored her ice cream and tried to imagine sitting in class with Richard teaching. She'd bet some of his young female students had difficulty keeping their minds on Renaissance art.

When he excused himself to find the men's room, she pulled a charcoal pencil and note paper from her bag and began sketching an outline of the ice cream shop, which had been renovated from one of the castle's workshops. After his return, she flipped the page and drew the general shape of his face.

"So you *can* think creatively. Is my chin really that long?"

"Yep. It gives you a look of importance. Authority." She gave the illustration curly hair on top, close on the sides. "As for being a copyist, it takes a lot of creativity to precisely imitate another artist. You'd be surprised at the techniques and paint formulae I've had to devise."

She made a few more strokes of the pencil. "There. Your dimples that only come when you smile. I made you happy."

He leaned close and brushed her temple with a kiss. "I am happy."

After a glance at her watch, she put away her sketch pad and pencil. "We'd better get back to the hotel and dress for our gala evening at the symphony." She slipped her shoes on her feet, which had enjoyed a few minutes being bare. As they walked to the main gate, she tried not to limp.

When they reached the front gate where buses and cars churned along the busy street, Richard suggested that she wait on a bench there while he walked the block back to the parking area. "When you see me coming, cross the street and hop in."

She resisted only a moment before giving in, grateful to be with such a gentleman. Taking a seat, she watched him lope on his long legs, much faster than she could have gone.

When a car approached that was probably his rental car, she stepped to the crosswalk and waited for the light to change.

A black Mercedes rolled to the curb. A man stepped from the back door and called her name. "Miss Cooper, please come with us. Interpol needs you to come back to the office."

Caught off guard, she hesitated. The guy, who didn't wear the typical dark suit of an agent, had a familiar strong build. She'd seen him somewhere before. He reached an arm around her waist and pulled her toward the open door.

"Excuse me. I'm waiting on a friend—"

"Dr. Reed will be along in his car. Please come with us." The man wore an intense scowl.

"No, please, I have to—"

He lifted her off her feet and stuffed her in the back seat then followed, shoving her legs out of the way. She scrambled to open the door on the far side, but he swept her hand down with a strong blow. The car jerked into motion and sped up, pushing her against the back seat. Throwing a heavy leg over her lap, he reached for a white cloth being handed back by a woman in front and pressed it to her face.

She struggled to get away from the pungent cloth without inhaling. A car honked long and loud. If she could just scream … could just unlock the door and jump out … get away from this brute holding her down …

Chapter 26

Richard saw the abduction from his car about twenty yards away. The Mercedes raced toward him in the opposite lane. Terror froze him. He hunched over and gripped the steering wheel for an awful second. Then he turned his car sharply and hit the side front of the car, shoving it to the sidewalk but not stopping its forward motion. Pedestrians screamed and jumped out of the way. The Mercedes roared forward and continued its mad dash.

In the rented Fiat, he whipped a U-turn in the middle of the street, buying time from the startled driver whose passage he blocked. The Fiat responded poorly to his demand for speed. He'd only gone a block when the tire on the injured side gave up. He'd never catch the Mercedes on three tires.

With trembling fingers, he punched a series of keys to reach Werner's cell phone, which rang and went to voice mail. Never mind. Policemen, hands on their guns, stood at his windows.

"That car! Someone kidnapped a woman. An American. They grabbed her off the street. I went to get my car, and they—"

One of the policemen stepped forward. "Excuse me, sir. You said 'kidnapped?'"

"Please follow them. They just—" Trying to clear his brain enough to speak coherently, he pulled out his Interpol ID. "We're both here working with Interpol. Someone just abducted my partner." He got out of his Fiat and urgently pointed down the street.

By then his hopes of pursuit dwindled like a candle out of wax. The officers, on foot, waved to a police car with its lights blinking and swirling. The policeman who had spoken to him in English bent to the window and pointed down the street.

"What kind of car was it?"

Richard thought. Was he sure? "A black Mercedes."

"Did you get the tag number?"

"No, I was too busy trying to stop him." His ears rang, and spots danced before his eyes. He bent over his car for a moment, slowing his breathing in an attempt to quiet his heart and clear his head. Macho guys didn't faint.

The officer spoke at the window of the police car again, and the driver nodded and took off. Richard knew it wouldn't do any good now. He hadn't even told the guy that the Mercedes turned left after a couple of blocks. He only hoped he'd done some damage which would slow them down.

The cops asked him to move his vehicle off the street as much as possible, and they began to direct traffic past the area.

After leaving a message on Werner's phone, he called Van Der Veen, who promised to instigate an investigation with both the police and Interpol.

In the aftermath, Richard's head pounded. He sat in the Fiat and leaned his forehead against the steering wheel and closed his eyes.

"Sir, are you all right?" One of the officers spoke at the window.

He raised his head and pushed back against the seat. "I'm not physically injured." But he definitely wasn't all right. Someone had snatched Kendra off the street the one moment he left her alone. He didn't know who, and he didn't know why.

❦

Kendra curled up in the bed, but couldn't escape the nausea. A putrid taste in her mouth didn't help. She roused from her position when she knew she was going to vomit. The strange bedroom, lovely but completely unfamiliar, caused further confusion. She belched with the first heave, and a young woman dressed in black with a white apron rushed to her with a pan.

The taste of chocolate mint ice cream mixed with stomach acid flushed from her system, and she relaxed on the bed again. Her helper took away the pan and brought a cool cloth from a bathroom within the bedroom. Speaking in a foreign language, probably German, she attended Kendra with kindness.

She slept again. When she stirred, the woman sat by the wide window knitting. Burgundy curtains hung to the side, and sheer curtains let in late afternoon light. The next time she woke, the woman had gone but left a lamp glowing softly at a pretty little desk against the wall to Kendra's back. Her stomach growled. The nausea had left.

A tap on the door snapped her attention. "Yes?"

An older woman in the same kind of uniform entered bearing a tray of soup, bread, and a glass. Apparently she spoke no English either, but her voice came in gentle, motherly tones. She turned on the ceiling light, motioned to the desk, and asked a question. Then to Kendra in the bed, and another question.

Kendra made a wild guess and pointed to the desk, and the woman placed the tray there. She rose from the bed, still wearing slacks and a blouse. How she got here was a mystery. Ice cream with Richard—then she woke up sick, in bed. The situation resembled the time she'd had an appendectomy. One minute she hurt, and then she woke up in a hospital room with a bandage on her abdomen. Her mother had been there.

Where was Richard?

"Where am I?" Her question came in a dry croak.

The woman shrugged and shook her head. She pointed to herself and said, "Inge." Then she pointed to the tray and made a drinking motion.

"Water. Just water." She went to the desk and sniffed the steaming tomato soup. "Thank you." One spoon of the savory soup flooded her mouth with flavors. She sat at the desk and pulled the bowl closer.

The woman pointed to a bell pull like one might find in a *Wuthering Heights* movie, then pointed to herself. She left the bedroom, but Kendra distinctly heard her lock the door.

When she had finished her light supper, she went to the window and opened the sheer curtains. Far below, lights illuminated a patio and the near edge of a green lawn. Bars prevented her from leaning out to see more. This appeared to be the side or back of a huge house, and she guessed she was on about the third floor.

The bathroom, long and narrow, appeared to be a retro-fit to the old home. The modern, low tub and shower apparatus with plastic curtain fit at the end. A toilet and sink occupied little space. Kendra turned on the lights around the mirror and found her make-up bag hanging from a hook near the sink. Strange. This was neither a hospital nor a hotel. The woman had locked her in, and bars on the window reinforced that. Next she tried the hall door, and found it locked as expected.

Her heart pounded and she breathed rapidly, making her light-headed. This must be what her former roommate called a panic attack, something she'd never experienced before. She returned to the bathroom, grabbed a towel off its rung, held it over her face, and sat in the upholstered floral chair. Bending forward, she braced her head in her hands. Forcing herself to calm down, she remained still for a long time.

With no idea how she got here, she wracked her brain for the last thing she could remember. From the cottony past, she pulled out the castle tour with Richard. The ice cream, which she tasted again after her arrival here. She'd been drugged, or maybe anesthetized. That's what her stalkers had tried before in Hero's Square in Budapest, but unlike today, she'd remembered the event when she woke up.

As for the loss of memory, she'd heard of a drug given to surgery patients so they would forget any fear or pain they may have experienced. Versed, she thought it was called.

Okay, someone had drugged her and brought her here. She was locked in and the window barred. The only person who had threatened her, who in fact insisted she obey him, was Alexander Holt.

Was Richard also here? Was she, or were they both, in danger? She prayed for clarity and wisdom.

Another door on the near wall, opposite the desk, invited her curiosity. Being as quiet as possible, she turned the crystal knob. It responded. She peeked into the dark room. Then she opened the door wide and stepped inside. By its exit door, she assumed, an old fashioned button switch turned on the light.

Propped on a large easel, her copy of Vermeer's *Milkmaid* rested in all its gentle beauty. Kendra gasped. Showing no damage, the painting's lower right corner remained blank of any signature. Near the easel stood a wooden work table holding a palette—no, *her* palette. And her own paints from her suitcase that should be at the hotel. Stacked in the corner were her two suitcases. Her new laptop case rested against them.

One more item rested on the table. Her old computer.

Richard could not be still. He paced the Interpol area dedicated to finding Kendra until his feet hurt. When Werner suggested they go eat some dinner together, he accepted but stared at his food without interest.

"Have a beer," said Werner. "Loosen up. It does her no good to starve yourself."

"I can't figure it out. We know Holt wants her to sign the copy she painted of a Vermeer, but any art student could do that. It's not worth kidnapping her for."

"No, that makes no sense." He took a long drink from his beer. "Besides, I've met the man in Amsterdam once. A fine gentleman. He would not do this thing."

Werner didn't ask questions about Kendra's painting. Perhaps Van Der Veen had mentioned the need for guards and how she'd been stalked this past week.

After buttering a roll and crunching down on it, Werner chewed with a faraway glance. "She's a lovely woman. I hate to say it, but there's a lot of human trafficking going on in Europe. Usually younger, though."

What a horrible thought. Sweet, naïve Kendra in an abusive situation. Richard squirmed in his chair.

Everything about Werner's manner, his inability to look Richard in the eyes, gave off vibes that he lied. Richard trusted him so little already that a glowing halo around his head wouldn't be sufficient to believe him. The main reason he agreed to eat dinner with him was to pry for information. "Did Interpol ever discover who owns the land with the cave?"

"Oh, some business consortium hoping to develop another attraction for tourists like the Five Fingers." His tone of voice seemed indefinite for a man who usually spoke with firmness.

"It should be easy enough for Interpol to learn who."

"Doesn't matter. Some of them are Jews who will hire

investigators to return the art to the correct families."

Richard stirred his plate of spaghetti and took a taste of a meatball, cooling in a puddle of oily sauce. The best Italian food, in his opinion, was in the US. "Is Holt Jewish?"

Werner's startled look reminded him of when Kendra said the crates and protective cloths should be date-tested. A stunned expression, mouth open and eyes wide. "Not that I know of. The dealer she sold *The Milkmaid* through, Stefan Appelhof, is Jewish." He munched on a hard roll, dropping flax seeds on his plate. He chuckled, but the humor didn't reach his eyes. "Someone who reads legal documents is working on that. Leave it to them."

So he did know about the painting and its sale in Amsterdam. Interesting.

Van Der Veen should arrive tonight. Richard wondered if he would have more details about the land ownership.

Despite having slept so much already, Kendra felt drowsy. She opened the wardrobe to see what she could sleep in, and found all her own clothes folded and put away in its drawers. Her suits hung in the other side. She selected her knit sleeping shorts and shirt. Feeling unusually drowsy, she showered, dressed, and went to bed again.

Early morning light through the thin curtains woke her. Maybe there had been something in the soup.

The older woman returned with three pretty summer dresses. She spoke in German, her hand signals indicating that Kendra should put on one of them and leave the room to eat. When the woman left, she did not lock the door, nor did Kendra hear her footsteps retreating.

The dresses were light and lovely. Her usual casual

clothes were slacks and knits. She'd brought so few things that she tired of them, and chose a blue floral dress from those brought by the woman.

After entering the bathroom, she dressed and brushed her hair and teeth with her own items from her makeup bag. Sure enough, the woman waited for her in the wide hallway outside her room. She followed her to a stairwell, wooden and worn by many feet, and descended two long flights.

Alexander Holt, all slender six feet of him, turned to meet her in the dining room. She recognized him primarily by his neatly-trimmed gray Vandyke beard. "Good morning, Ms. Cooper. May I call you Kendra? Thank you for accepting my hospitality. I hope you will be very comfortable here."

His voice assured her this was the man who'd called her about *The Milkmaid*. "Really, Mr. Holt? How could a signature be so important to you?" She endeavored to sound cool and unafraid while her empty stomach flipped.

"The pleasure of your company is important to me. The signature is merely a request while you're in residence."

"And how long do you intend to keep me? I have a job, you know. I have things to do and places to be."

He waved away her protest. "A job that barely supports you. I hope to convince you to share your talents with the world and be handsomely recompensed. But first, let's serve ourselves from the buffet." He stepped to the long, high table and offered her a plate. Over a white embroidered runner lay dishes of bread, butter, jam, soft-boiled eggs, and ham slices.

Though hunger hit hard, she feared eating the food. "Will I find myself becoming very sleepy after breakfast?"

"Not at all. I wouldn't want you to waste such a beautiful day. I shall eat with you, my dear. Do you take coffee or tea?"

"Coffee, no cream."

He poured coffee for her into a china cup at one place

setting on a large dinner table. Then, from the same silver pot, he poured at the other place. Only after she saw him drink from his cup did she taste her own. Rich and strong, the coffee bolstered her and filled gnawing spaces in her middle.

"Have you explored your suite?"

She deliberately kept her head bowed in silent prayer. When she opened her eyes, his smile seemed patronizing.

"I say, have you discovered your studio?"

"Yes, and my computer. You must have been terribly bored with what you found on it."

A silver knife rested in his hand, poised to apply butter to his roll. "The boy shouldn't have taken it. He was ... severely disciplined."

A twinge of pain slid through her mind for the criminal she never met. No telling what Holt had done. He was not a man to be trifled with.

He must have caught an expression on her face.

"You have nothing to fear from me, dear Kendra. I've been unable to convince you by phone of the vast advantages of partnering with me, so I found it necessary to bring you to my country retreat." He drained his cup and poured another. "First, let me lay down a few house rules. Your computer works, but is not connected to Wi-Fi. You will never, ever guess the password, so don't even try. I will tell you that it has a daunting number of numbers, letters and symbols. Don't waste your time."

She digested that for a moment along with the exceptionally fresh apricot jam on a crusty roll.

"This country home," he continued, "has been in my family for a century. No neighbors live within miles. There is truly nowhere to run. Please relax and enjoy your time here. Doesn't every artist long for peace, plenty of materials, no pressure, and plenty of income? All I ask is that you cooperate in my endeavor to share art and its appreciation with the world … for a tidy sum."

He rang a silver bell, and a waiter appeared and removed his plate. She indicated with a nod that he could take hers as well.

"Remember that all the employees work for me. They cannot be bribed or coerced to work against me. There are armed guards, and the house and grounds are under surveillance. They've been told that you are the daughter of a friend who, unfortunately, became an addict. You are here for a voluntary detox and have frequent hallucinations."

She rolled her lips inward and pressed hard, holding back angry words and threats she had no way of backing up.

"Today I ask that you sign the Vermeer—"

"—copy," she interjected.

"—and this evening, I shall pay you one thousand dollars for your effort. Or the equivalent in Euros, if you wish. It's my desire to make you so comfortable that you will remain in Europe."

"Don't count on it."

Chapter 27

Richard met with Klaas Van Der Veen as soon as the Interpol handler arrived in Vienna. He wanted to grab hold of the man and pour out his agony over Kendra's kidnapping, but that wouldn't speed her return. Instead, he tried to deny his anguish and act with a reasonable degree of sophistication.

After handshakes in the Interpol tactical room dedicated to finding her, Klaas turned a sharp eye on him. "You're taking this hard, I see."

Richard turned his head to the side. "Can't sleep. If I just hadn't left her alone on the sidewalk …"

"It isn't your fault. You know that. What we don't understand is who and why. Want to sit in on the session this morning?"

"Yes, please. First, are you discarding the idea that Alexander Holt is involved? Or Stefan Appelhof? They've both called and texted her about illegal art activities."

"That's all in the file we'll start with today. Have some coffee and pull yourself together. The two people assigned to the case, Agents Bader and Hahn, will be here any minute."

"Is Werner, the guy who took us out to the cave, one of them? I really don't trust him."

"You were explicit in your phone call yesterday, so he'll stay on the cave investigation. If he's linked in any way to her abduction, he must not know what we're planning."

"He was evasive about the ownership of the land where

the cave is. Said a Jewish consortium had bought it for tourist development, but didn't want to talk about who the owners are."

"With good reason. It's not so much a Jewish consortium as a group of investors—including Alexander Holt, by the way. And the group has no direct ties to any reputable organization for restoring valuables to their owners such as the Jewish National Fund. We must consider the likelihood that the owners of the cave either knew about the hidden art before buying the land, or they placed it there themselves. It's possible that the 'discovery' only seeks to put fraudulent art into the world market."

"But how can they profit from this? A painting in the style of a master but without provenance has little value."

"Have you ever read what John Drewe and the fraud artist John Myatt did in the 1990s? Drewe stole, copied, and created his own provenance for Myatt's paintings. They made a lot of money until the house of cards collapsed."

Time to reread that book, which he'd scanned in grad school. Richard mentally reviewed the fourteen paintings they'd examined for most of a week. He and Kendra had staked their professional reputation on the precursory judgment that they were all fakes. "Where are we on the dating of the art, crate wood, and cloths? Anything coming back yet?"

"Not yet. The samples went to Amsterdam, where I can keep better control of the information."

Richard shoved his hands in his pockets, feeling as if a heavy weight bent his frame. "I keep thinking … Where is she? What are they doing to her?"

Kendra stood before the *Milkmaid* copy, a fine brush in

hand and the old computer displaying an enlargement of Vermeer's signature on the original. If she did this, would Holt release her? Fat chance. First he'd want her to finish the van Gogh taken from her apartment. It now leaned against the far wall. Finish it and sign that one, too. Never mind that the original hung in the Amsterdam's Van Gogh Museum. What then? The other two paintings which she'd barely begun?

The bitter truth was that she had seen and talked—even eaten—with Holt in his family mansion. He couldn't allow her to leave. He had to either turn her or kill her.

She rested the brush and stepped away from the painting she loved more than any she'd ever done. Simply refusing to add the signature meant that, eventually, someone else would. She'd worked for weeks to get the lighting perfect, the way the softened sun came in the window and graced the milkmaid's face and the folds of her clothing. The exact blue of her apron.

Kendra picked up a palette knife and raised it high to strike the painting, to slash it to irreparable trash. Her creation, her child, waited for the blow. She might as well stab herself in the heart.

A key rattled in the door to the hallway and Inge lunged inside, shouting in German. Kendra whirled around, gasping at the sudden intrusion. Inge grabbed her wrist. The much older and heavier woman had arms of steel and quickly twisted the knife from her hand.

Caught off guard, Kendra didn't resist. She didn't want to destroy the painting, and Inge had given her that reprieve. She crumpled onto the stiff wooden work chair and sobbed. After a moment, Inge took her arm and led her through the connecting doorway into the bedroom, making cooing, comforting sounds.

Remaining in the room, Inge pulled the bell cord and the younger maid appeared. Inge ordered tca.

When it arrived, with cookies on the side, Kendra

declined it. "I don't want to sleep again."

Perhaps Inge understood her suspicion, if not her English. She urged Kendra but didn't force her.

ᖗᕉᕉ

"Did Ms. Cooper have a cell phone with her when she was abducted?"

Klaas's question brought Richard back to the discussion with two agents working on her case. "I assume so. She usually carried it."

"Do you know if she had activated a phone location alert, or a map program permitting use of her current location?"

He considered the question for a moment. "That's possible. She may have looked up the cave once. I don't know."

"Have you tried to call her since the kidnapping?"

"No. If she has the phone and it's in service, I didn't want to give away her secret. I was hoping she would call us."

"Good reasoning. She has now been gone for nearly twenty-four hours. If she doesn't attempt to call by tomorrow, we'll set up tracing technology and try to contact her. She doesn't have a computer anymore, does she?"

"Well, uh, yes. She bought … That is, I bought her one. But she thinks it came from Interpol as a replacement for the one that was stolen." Richard's face warmed at the admission of his gift.

"Um. Generous of us. It's at the hotel?"

"Yes. She wouldn't have taken it on our visit of Shönebrunn yesterday." They'd planned a fun tourist day checking out the sights of Vienna before dinner and a concert. How wrong that had gone. This morning, his parents had flown to Paris, his mother in a tizzy, extracting promises that he call whatever happened.

Today was Sunday, and he'd had expectations of sharing this amazing city with her.

"By the way, have her checked out of the hotel and bring her suitcases and personal items here. I don't expect to find anything useful to the investigation, but we have to look under every rock."

The meeting came to a close before lunch, and each person set off to a specific task related to finding Kendra. Though Richard had no police training, Klaas allowed him to hang with the team for at least today. On Monday he was expected to continue investigations of art from the cave. With such distrust of Werner, working with him would be difficult.

The rental car had been impounded for Interpol to analyze paint scraped off the kidnappers' car, and Klaas insisted that Richard not take a taxi. Instead, a Viennese policeman delivered him to the hotel and would bring her suitcases back.

After he presented identification at the reception desk and asked to collect her belongings, the attendant checked his screen. "I'm sorry, sir. Ms. Cooper checked out yesterday."

"What? She was kidnapped yesterday. She couldn't have."

After a surprise reaction, he frowned and tapped more keys. "She checked out at three o'clock."

"That's impossible. She was with me at the Shönebrunn Palace at three o'clock."

The attendant blinked rapidly. "I don't actually know who checked her out, but the room is vacant."

"May we go up and see it?"

"That's highly irregular, sir, but since you have an officer with you … I'll ask our bell staff chief."

After conferencing with the hotel manager, Richard

received permission to inspect the room. The senior bellman, a large, balding man in a black suit, opened the door and stepped back. Richard found no clothes, no toiletries, no personal items. The suitcases were gone. Not a deodorant or toothbrush in the bathroom. "Was anything removed by the staff, perhaps put in storage?"

"No, sir. I remember the lady because she had misplaced her key card. She came at a very busy time, and brought her own bags down a few minutes later."

It was amazing how some criminals managed to jump over barricades. "So someone let her in the room?"

The bellman gave a slight sniff and raised his chin. "The front desk assisted her."

"What did she look like?"

"She was of a certain age, not particularly notable in appearance. Short hair, touch of gray."

Heads turned when Kendra entered a room even if her long, brunette hair swung in a ponytail. Someone else had cleared out her belongings. A woman had been in the front seat of the car when she was kidnapped.

The policeman turned to the bellman. "This room is a crime scene. It must not be occupied until our team has cleared it."

Someone tapped on Kendra's door and opened it. Mr. Holt waltzed into her bedroom as if he owned it. And he did. "Kendra, my dear, why do you fight so hard when I'm trying to help you?"

It didn't escape her that he or his hirelings had been watching through a hidden camera when she attempted to cut the painting. She gave him no answer, but continued sitting in the comfortably upholstered Queen Anne chair. He bent over her and lifted her chin. "Why do you stubbornly resist the life of luxury I offer you?"

He tried to kiss her, but she twisted away. "You came to the De Rooses' home with one of the most elegant women at the reception. Does she know I'm a guest in your family home?"

A bitter expression twisted his lips. "I do not bother my wife with details that neither involve nor interest her." He paced to the window. "She never appreciated this magnificent castle. Never comes here." Turning back to her, he smiled. "So it is all ours. Your studio, the servants, the hills and grasslands. You can paint to your heart's content."

"I have a job ... and obligations. I can't remain in Europe."

"Your job barely makes enough to live in a one-bedroom apartment. As for your obligations, I have already taken care of your debt."

"You ... what?"

"It has been paid off." He approached, lifted her hand from the armchair, and gave it a feather-light kiss. "All of it."

She retrieved her hand, aware that her mouth hung open. "How did you know?"

"Your cell phone, FaceBook, so many sources of information you put out there. Stefan told me you were selling *The Milkmaid* to cover your educational debt. I called your roommate, who's listed as such on your cell phone, and told her you would be staying longer than originally planned and were concerned about your next payment. She found papers in your file for what I needed to know."

He recaptured her hand in his soft palm, this time giving a pull. "Come. We have work to do. Don't you think you owe me at least a little? No one will be fooled by copies when the originals are on public display. Your resistance is needless."

"There's something else—terribly important. My aunt called Thursday to say that my father had a heart attack. He had a triple by-pass surgery the next day. Aunt Marilyn wanted me to come home right away."

"What did you tell her?"

"That I couldn't get there in time anyway. But I've been calling her every day. If she doesn't hear from me and can't call me, she'll worry. Could I please call home?"

"Let me think about that." He led her into the studio. "Have a seat there on your stool. I'll have a chair brought close to watch." He stepped into the hall and summoned an armed guard, who brought the Queen Anne chair over from her bedroom.

She lifted the brush thinking she would be safe if she appeased him. If she gained his confidence, she might eventually find a way of escape. After waking her old computer, which showed a close-up of Vermeer's signature, she lifted the fine brush.

Nearly a half hour later, during which he watched her every move, it was done. She had just fraudulently signed the great master's name to a copy.

He rose from the chair, lifted the painting, and placed one thousand dollars in hundred dollar bills on the support ledge of the easel. "There, my love. That wasn't so hard."

Richard hit the bed exhausted, having slept little last night. This morning's revelation that someone had checked Kendra out of the hotel and taken her belongings had troubled him all day. What if she allowed that to happen, or the person worked at her request?

No, she hadn't given her key, and she'd been with him at three o'clock. She wasn't complicit. He struggled to believe that all the money she could make as an artist of frauds hadn't turned her from the sweet, innocent woman he knew.

He rolled over and threw up a prayer for her safety. Sleep dampened his thoughts, and he almost made it to the never-world of blessed unconsciousness, when a vision of Kendra came to his mind's eye. She stood on a green hill. A gentle breeze blew her long, dark hair in swirls about her face. "Richard, come get me. Bring me home."

His eyes sprang open. She seemed so real. He tumbled out of bed onto his knees and pleaded with God to keep her safe. "Help us find her, Lord. You know where she is. Lead us to her."

When he ran out of words, he dragged himself to a chair and sat with his head in his hands. He'd been so cautious about showing her how much he cared. Now he might never have another chance.

He shouldn't think like that. He could either pray or worry, but it made no sense to do both. He chose to pray, something he hadn't done enough of lately.

The younger maid, Matilda, motioned for Kendra to follow her. In the hallway a burly man wearing a gun over his khaki pants and shirt joined them. She did a second glance at him, wondering if he was the man who abducted her. She panicked and bolted down a flight of stairs, where another armed man stretched out his arms and yelled for her to stop.

Holding onto her upper arm, he walked her out through the dining room and double doors onto the outside patio she'd seen from her window.

The armed man released her slowly, as if ready to grab her again if she ran. He pushed at the air in the international symbol for "slow down," and shot her a warning look.

She turned away, commanding her breathing to calm. Resting a hand over her heart, she felt how cold her fingers were for a summer day.

Looking up toward the third floor, she noticed that only two rooms had bars—no doubt her bedroom and studio. Did her host capture unwilling guests often?

Two places had been set for lunch. Mr. Holt strolled out and dismissed the guards. "Don't be concerned. I would kill them if they hurt you." He brushed an air-kiss on one cheek before she turned away.

She breathed easier when the guys with guns went inside. Since Holt pretended this was a social occasion, she'd do better to play along and keep the goons away. Hoping to gain his confidence, she might be able to establish a more peaceful relationship. Surely he would have to return to Amsterdam eventually, and she'd have her chance to escape.

"I thought you'd like the blue floral dress best. I chose them myself, just yesterday. Ladies look so much nicer in dresses."

She hated that she'd worn the dress he expected her to. That he even knew her size. A thing like that was too personal.

Matilda served them pan-fried trout with fruit and cheese, a light meal shaded from the summer sun by a giant tan umbrella. Kendra sensed that the young maid didn't understand the situation, and wished she'd elected German in college rather than French.

"Mr. Holt, you must realize I have a contract with Interpol. They'll search for me."

"Please call me Alex. And tell me, on what basis did you determine the cave art was fraudulent?"

The question surprised her. They hadn't turned in any reports, and only spoke their doubts to Klaas Van Der Veen, though she suspected Werner also knew. Oh, and the two elderly "experts" who visited the workroom. "Is it fraudulent? We weren't sure."

A sudden cloud came over his face. "Do you realize how much damage you've done? You and that American professor." He slammed his fist down on the table, rocking it and the stemmed wine glasses.

She jerked back, unprepared for the sudden outburst.

"Your little summer holiday in Europe may have cost me millions. Those works were beautiful. Every one of them." Fire shot from his eyes, and his face flushed around the gray beard. "How dare you judge any one of them by the way they made you *feel?* Who made you the expert?"

"Were the two Austrians who came to see them in the Interpol art lab on your payroll?"

He glared at her. "They didn't have to be. The industry-recognized authorities on art were thrilled to see works of such brilliance."

"But no papers of provenance came with the paintings." She tried to keep her voice low and level to gain as much information as possible without riling him. "They needed validation."

"The provenance will be provided eventually. It's all part of the plan."

"Pastiches instead of copies were brilliant." She hoped praise would mollify his anger. "You don't have to prove they are particular paintings, only paintings in the style of a particular artist."

"Yes, and with you off the case, we may be able to convince all the right people they are genuine ... so long as Mr. Reed leaves on Saturday."

His tone had become more placid until this last comment. Was he bipolar?

She'd better skim above sensitive subjects with this guy.

Chapter 28

Kendra took the last bite of a succulent peach and dabbed her lips with a napkin. Looking downhill and across a valley to the Austrian Alps, she longed for freedom. "Would it be possible for me to take a walk? It's my favorite form of exercise, and I've had none for days."

Holt studied her face. "Maybe later. Why don't you take the afternoon to complete the van Gogh? I've had it placed in the studio for your convenience."

Her convenience. Right. Just as she expected, he wanted that one done and signed as well.

"Don't you think you owe me that much?" he continued. "I should think the twenty-three thousand dollars for your debt is worth more. Stefan confessed that he paid you six for *The Milkmaid*, though he added a tidy profit when he framed it and sold it to me. I know because of the provenance details—as a copy, not an original, of course. Stefan can be a real Boy Scout about the rules."

She wanted to believe Stefan wouldn't allow her to be captured or forced to sign a fraud, but he had passed Holt information about her which resulted in the kidnapping.

Stefan had flirted with her. What would he think of Holt's advances if he knew?

"He pleaded your cause to me. He urged me to sign *The Milkmaid* and gave all the reasons it shouldn't bother me to do so." She lifted the lemonade to her lips, eyeing her adversary over the rim of her glass. "Remember the night we met at the De Roos reception? Did you have anything to do with the theft of the van Gogh by putting a copy in its place?"

His eyebrows shot up, and he raised his head. "Certainly not. Luuk and Katrina are friends of ours."

She stuffed down a chuckle at his implication that he only stole from people outside his social circle.

"Nothing to do with me," he continued. "But the way Stefan told the story, it was you and you alone who discovered the theft during the reception. Someone somewhere was very unhappy with you that night."

"Surely the switch would have been discovered eventually. Anyone who really knows van Gogh's style could have recognized it."

He leaned forward and touched her hand, which she moved to her lap. "But it was you. If not for you, the thief might have gotten away." He dismissed the subject with a flip of his hand. "It doesn't matter. Stefan reports that your friends of the Amsterdam police have arrested someone."

"So he stays in touch with you?"

"We both are intimately concerned with art in Europe. Our professional relationship will also be beneficial to you, my dear. All of this will play very well. You will see."

He stood and gestured widely with his arm. "This view is yours to enjoy. I put my home at your disposal." He paced a few steps, then stopped and drank from his wine glass. "You are well versed in art history. Which of the masters would not have given their firstborn child for the patronage I offer you?"

She ignored the question. "When I finish the van Gogh, may I walk around outside? You could dispatch Inge the Strong to go with me."

He sat and took a final sip of his wine. "Perhaps we could walk together, if I get my paperwork finished before dark."

Not at all what she'd hoped for. Maybe she could head this cowboy off at the pass. "You're a married man. I could not be interested in a romantic relationship with you. I hope you understand that."

He touched her fingers as she held her glass. "Then we must be friends. My desire is to have a long working relationship with you, to the advantage of us both."

His sly grin chilled her. She glanced again to the mountains.

Alone in her studio later, she set up her copy of van Gogh's *Wheatfield with Crows*. More than twice as wide as it was tall, the painting balanced on the easel. She'd have to be careful.

The sky needed more black, and the dirt trails lacked the artist's swirls and dashes. Referring several times to her computer photos, she dabbed at the earth without satisfaction. What had been an exciting project a couple of weeks ago, when it was her own idea, no longer transferred the charge of energy and challenge.

She overpainted something she didn't like in the sky and stood back to absorb the overall effect. The yellow wheat glowed too bright, and the blowing grass wasn't bright enough. Mixing paints, she tried again. What had the mad painter tried to convey? This work came from his more-than-a-painting-a-day phase, and his frustration cried out to her and blended with her own.

She couldn't do this. "Alex, can you hear me? Alex, I need more canvas."

She wandered to the window and tried to lift it, but the facing stuck to the frame with old paint. Resting her forehead against the wavy glass, she allowed tears to fall. What was the chance that Richard had allowed her kidnapping in order to follow a trail into the network he so desperately desired to discover? If she could only speak to him for a moment. She wanted to believe his tender, almost shy kisses came from an openness to discover a relationship between them.

Reflecting on how Alex Holt kept touching her caused waves of repulsion to wash over her skin. He expected—almost demanded—that she be attracted to him because of his wealth and all he could do as her sponsor. But nothing could make her lie down in that bed. After keeping herself pure for this many years, she'd rather die.

If she continued to reject Alex's domination, that possibility existed.

Inge knocked and entered, but communication attempts failed. Kendra wiped away her tears of exasperation and pointed to the canvas. The sturdy woman left, not giving her any satisfaction.

Alex strode in next, an impatient twist to his mouth. "I was told you called for me. What is it that you want?"

"More canvas. I can stretch it myself … if you have stretchers, that is."

"What do you need it for?"

"More paintings. *Other* paintings. I can't work with this one right now. Maybe tomorrow, but my van Gogh muse is gone. Please?"

He stalked to the easel and stared at her attempts. "The same size?"

"I'll do it—"

"I can't trust you with sharp objects yet. What size do you want?"

"Maybe …" She looked through the bars to the mountains. "…two feet by three feet, for starters. Just something to get the paint flowing again."

Within an hour, Inge returned with a canvas stretched by someone who didn't get the task quite right. Somewhat warped at one corner, it would have to do. She thanked the woman, moved the easel to the window, and placed the canvas on its platform.

Hours passed. The light changed on the mountain. From that point she painted by memory and inspiration. Colors blended, but she kept the dashes and fervent energy of her mad mentor. The painting lacked a focus. It needed something like the reaper in van Gogh's other wheat field. Stepping back, she perceived that wind whipped the scene from the north, an attribute she hadn't planned, yet it appeared. A modern woman, some distance deep into the left side of the composition, light dress blowing in that wind, took her place.

The oils blended too much. The time had come to stop. The joy of creation swept over Kendra. She'd done it. A new piece, all her own. One which used the paints and the strokes of the master artist, but with a contemporary feel.

Technicians assembled with their equipment ready to trace Richard's call to Kendra. His anticipation built up to the screaming point before Van Der Veen and the Viennese police gave the go-ahead signal.

He silently but fervently prayed before he touched her number on his cell phone. It never even returned a dial tone. All that hope packed into one chance at reaching her, and it was over.

Everyone in the tiny room drooped. "It has been turned off. Or it's broken, completely out of commission," said the female technician. "There's nothing more we can do here unless her phone works. Sorry."

He and Van Der Veen thanked her for trying and slumped out. They said nothing in the hall and headed back to the investigation area where the two other agents, Bader and Hahn, waited for good news. Bader, in a dark suit, white shirt, and tie like a stereotypical FBI agent, stirred his coffee. Hahn, the young techie working on the case, glanced up from a computer. The faces of both men fell when Richard and Klaas returned in so few minutes, posture bent with failure.

"What now?" said Richard. "Do we have any other leads?"

Van Der Veen dropped into a desk chair. "The car paint analysis only indicated what we already know—that the kidnappers drove a black Mercedes. Cameras at the hotel show us a strongly-built middle age woman, but facial recognition turns up nothing in all of Europe."

Richard fingered his phone. "Has Maarten Alders called back about the questions we raised?"

Bader shook his head. Hahn consulted his computer. "Nothing here."

"Might be time to give him a call." He touched the numbers for his Dutch friend, wishing they were working together as they had back when they found Kendra, a lithe and lovely tourist in the Amsterdam museums. After greeting the policeman, Richard told him who was in the room and that he'd put the phone on speaker.

Maarten's strong voice filled the room. "Katrina Holt, the wife of Alexander Holt, says she does not know where her husband is. She suggested he had business in Rome this week, but we did not find his name on airline records to Italy. We did discover, however, that he flew to Vienna on Monday, August first—six days ago."

"He's here now?"

"There's no record of him on a flight since. Then I visited the gallery of Stefan Appelhof, because you said he'd been in contact with Kendra. He said he last spoke with her several days ago, and did not know about the abduction. He seemed upset in earnest."

Richard drank in the tidbits of data, trying to connect and interpolate them.

"When I asked if he knew where Mr. Holt was this week," Maarten continued, "he stammered as if he did not want to share information. A veiled threat about selling fraudulent art through his gallery softened him up a bit. He says he thinks Holt is in Vienna and hoped to bring back some interesting paintings, but Appelhof didn't know what paintings he meant."

"Any idea where Holt stays when he's in Vienna? Some favorite hotel, or—"

"Appelhof says the family of Holt is originally from Austria, and left before World War Two. He has heard Alex talk about some grand estate, but he doesn't have any details. I go back to Mrs. Holt this afternoon and call you again."

"Good work, Maarten. You might be on to something." Van Der Veen's voice boomed from a couple of yards away.

Richard closed his eyes after ending the conversation. "I do hope so."

Kendra freshened up and descended for dinner in a much better frame of mind.

Alex, however, spoke with a testy edge to his greeting. He seated her without his usual flair. Matilda swooped out with their salads, hers doused in a dressing he knew she didn't care for. "Do you feel better after wasting the afternoon and a clean canvas on your whim of the moment?"

She absorbed the insult and chose not to argue. "Yes, I do. I rarely paint anything that could be called original, but this afternoon was an adventure for me. I incorporated some of van

Gogh's strokes and techniques and the beauty of the Alps out my window. Then I added a woman in modern attire. A blonde. If you like it, you may keep it as a memento."

His nod to the doorway produced their dinner plates. "Are you now in the mood to finish the wheat field and crows?"

"Perhaps tomorrow when the light is good. Would that be all right with you? I don't expect it to take much longer … unless I mess it up." She looked away, insecurity surging over her like a wave.

"There must be no mistakes. Copying art is a discipline. You must practice to be perfect." He sipped his red wine and sliced into the thin steak. "After this, I have another challenge for you."

"What's that?"

"Paint for me a Monet-inspired pastiche. Perhaps a lily pond."

A mouthful of potatoes turned dry in her mouth, and she struggled to swallow without choking. "A lily pond, like the wall-sized masterpieces?"

"Oh, no. Nothing that large. I was thinking more like a meter high and two-thirds as wide."

"He's my favorite artist, but … It's like loving a certain fine restaurant and going back over and over because you can't duplicate the food at home. Copying all his tiny impressionist dots would require massive patience."

"And time, of which you now have plenty. I have provided everything for you. You don't have to cook or clean or study or go to a dead-end job." He leaned close and murmured with a placid smile. "Take hold of this gift. View it as your opportunity for greatness. You have the time and materials to study and duplicate all the masters."

But her experiences this summer had shifted her

direction. Coals of imagination glowed deep within, and Richard had thrown kindling on that heat. A yearning to paint her own visions had begun.

The following morning she descended to the patio and approached Alex about calling home.

"I've been thinking about it, and decided that it would be permissible if you use my phone." His cool, thin smile gave him a haughty appearance.

"But her number is on mine. At least let me find her last call to me, or my call to her." She fought to remain cool while her heart pounded. Getting the phone in hand—or at least turned on and linked to the server—would make it possible for Richard to find her. She desperately hoped he was trying.

He peered at her through a squint, as if trying to see past her ploy. "Don't you have it on your computer?"

"Probably not. I rarely call her." In fact, she did have a spreadsheet of family information. Since she was not experienced at lying, he probably observed her deception.

"We'll go to my office after breakfast. I'm sure we can work something out." He checked his watch. "It's too early to call the US yet."

She couldn't sit still for a languishing second cup of coffee. After finishing her bread and cheese, she feigned an eagerness to work on the painting. "But I must find out about my father first. He expects me to be flying home and doesn't know why I'm not calling."

His office occupied a large room on the ground floor. Both goons stood in the hallway. An elaborately carved desk large enough to serve dinner for a family held his laptop, scattered papers—and her white iPhone.

"Your phone is not connected to the server. Turn it on and find the numbers you need for your father and aunt." He pushed a note pad and pen to her. "Sit down and relax. Your call must assure them that you are well."

She retrieved the information, and then he tapped her father's mobile number into his phone. It went to voice mail immediately, and he tried the other number.

"I could have left a message—"

He handed her the phone with a stern glare. "Be careful what you say. It will be on speaker."

She nodded, realizing that he gave her no chance to send out a cry for help. Not that it would help. Her father and his sister in Texas couldn't rescue her.

Her aunt fumbled the phone. "Hello?"

"Aunt Marilyn, this is Kendra. I hope I didn't wake you."

She huffed and made a noise like she was pulling out of bed. "That's okay. I was about to get up anyway."

"How's my dad?"

"You know he had the surgery Friday. Aren't you coming home to take care of him?"

As usual, Aunt Marilyn took the most direct line to a guilt trip. "No, I can't come." She glanced at Alex. "Not at this time. Is he still in the hospital?"

"He can't go home alone, you know. He's disappointed that you're staying over there in Europe when he needs you here."

Kendra's mind spun with clues she might drop. She might use Texan slang and say someone had a-holt of her, but Holt would just grab the phone. Besides, Aunt Marilyn's head lodged firmly in her own world. She'd never realize Kendra needed to be rescued.

"I don't really have a choice." She glanced at Alex, whose warning hit its mark. "Tell me about Dad."

"He's been cut right down the middle, so he hurts a lot. He cain't sleep and doesn't like the hard bed, but they let him give himself doses of pain killer. He just don't use it enough. Says he don't want to get hooked. I tell him they won't let that happen, but you know him. He's worried about the bizness and bunches of contracts he's got to do."

Alex pulled his finger across his neck, which she took as indication that she had to cut off the conversation.

"Tell him I'm thinking about him and praying for him, okay? I'll call again when I can."

Alex took his phone from her. "There. Satisfied? He's going to be fine. Thousands of those surgeries are done every day."

"Yes, but not to my father."

Kendra wondered why it mattered so much to her. Their relationship had been so strained since her brother's death, even more since her mother's death, and refusing any interest in her dad's plumbing business widened the chasm. He no longer even hinted about her marrying a man who would take it over.

"Now are you ready to paint?"

She nodded. "Thank you. I'm relieved he pulled through the by-passes."

If he lived long enough, a chance for a better relationship existed. She ought to pray about that this week, too.

Chapter 29

Richard slept through his alarm. No surprise, since he'd lain awake until the wee hours. Detouring through the hotel restaurant on the way to the police car pick-up, he skimmed the buffet for rolls, cheese, and an apple.

Getting the food through the security scanner at the police department cost him another couple of minutes, so he burst into the room where Klaas Van Der Veen, Bader, and Hahn chatted and drank coffee. He zoned in on the pot. "I'll take some of that."

"Good morning to you, too," said Klaas, who gave him the once-over twice. "Having a rough morning already?"

"Couldn't sleep last night. Overslept this morning." He held out his handkerchief cache of breads. "Have a roll?"

Klaas took a small sweet one and the other two declined. "What kept you awake? It's a nice hotel, isn't it?"

"Hotel's fine." He drank hot coffee from the Styrofoam cup, scalding his tongue. "Kept thinking about Kendra. Where she is, how they're treating her." He shook his head and plopped on a chair. "Whether she's still alive," he muttered.

"You can't do that, Reed. It gets in the way of trying to find her. Remember our supposition: Someone captured her for what she knows and how she can paint. Killing her would not be part of the plan."

"Unless she refuses to obey. I haven't known her for very long, but I can tell you she's persistent to the point of being bull-headed. And in a lot of ways, she's naïve. She has no bag of dirty tricks."

Van Der Veen took the rest of the sweet roll in his mouth and drank coffee on top of it. He gave it a couple of chomps and a swallow. "Okay, do we call her father now and risk scaring him in the middle of the night, or wait until after two or three this afternoon?"

"My gut says call now, because we have nothing else to try. We can't waste a day waiting to be nice." Richard had tried to occupy his mind with the art upstairs, but just couldn't stand another day working on the paintings without Kendra. He'd just about decided they were all contemporary frauds anyway, and was in no frame of mind to give them a decent evaluation.

"Then you place the call. Your English will be less likely to frighten him." Klaas picked up a page with scratchy notes. "We have both home, business, and mobile numbers for her father. Fort Worth police called Cooper Plumbing while we were sleeping, and the secretary there knew the name of his sister, Marilyn Harrington, and her number. We can go to Hahn's desk and use the Interpol phone."

"Just give me the number. I'll dial it, and that will give Mrs. Harrington my number in case she needs to call back."

Richard held his breath and listened to the dial tone. One ring ... second ring … third ring … Someone picked up on the sixth ring.

"Harrington residence." The woman's garbled speech indicated she slept with some sort of appliance in her mouth. Or maybe without her teeth.

"Mrs. Harrington, please forgive me for calling so late. This is Richard Reed, in Vienna, Austria." He chose not to use his 'doctor' title, since that might confuse her further. "We have a situation here and need to speak with you or Kendra Cooper's father."

"Wha—? Jus' a minute … There now. Is Kendra okay?"

"We don't know. She was abducted this past Saturday. I'm working with Interpol to try to find her. Perhaps you can give us some information."

"Saturday? But she just called me yesterday—or maybe the day before. No, it was Monday, first thing in the morning. She called to ask about my brother—her father—and said she was fine."

"That's wonderful news, Mrs. Harrington." News that got fist pumps and thumbs up from the other three listening to the amplified conversation. "Did she call your home number or your cell phone?"

"It was … uh, I think it was my cell phone. I had it charging right here on my bed table."

"Would you please look for the caller and tell me the number she used?"

"Let me get my glasses. I cain't hardly see without them." Clunking noises came through the speaker.

Richard fisted his free hand so hard his knuckles hurt. He squeezed his eyes closed and prayed the woman wouldn't break the connection, and that she could manipulate her cell phone well.

"Okay, I punched 'Recents,' and there's this whole list. Let's see, if it was Tuesday, maybe this one …"

"You should be able to see the date and time. Is there a little 'i' beside the calls? You can touch that and—"

"I think I got it. It's got a lot of numbers, so maybe it's foreign. Definitely not from around these parts." She read the number, stumbled, and read it again.

"Thank you, Mrs. Harrington. Thank you so much. Oh, and how is Mr. Cooper?"

"He's gonna be fine. I was just hoping she'd be able to come home and take care of him. I reckon not, if she's got herself kidnapped and all."

"Not at this time, but hopefully before long. Now Mrs. Harrington, please don't mention to anyone who calls you that you've spoken to us. Not even if Kendra calls back, because she's not in a safe place."

"You tell her to call me when you find her, please. I won't tell her father, because that would just worry him, and he don't need to worry."

Richard closed the call politely, then whooped and jumped. Klaas slapped him on the back and Bader and Hahn bumped fists. When Richard came down off the high, he clasped both hands, looked to the ceiling, and said, "Thank you, God."

For several days Kendra had assumed the small, white mechanical thing high on the wall in the front corner of her studio surveilled her words and actions. She rested her brush and turned the easel so the completed van Gogh copy faced the camera. "There. It's finished. What do you think?"

In a quirk of mischief, she signed "Vincent van Gogh" in black, low in the right corner. Van Gogh only signed paintings which he expected to sell or give to friends, and then with just his first name. If Alex knew that, she'd have to withstand his fiery anger again.

He knocked, unlocked the door, and entered while she cleaned the brushes and palette. Striding toward the painting, he studied it and compared it to the illustration on her computer. "Good job." He stepped back and then turned it toward the window. "Very good."

"It's still wet, of course. I wouldn't recommend you even move it to another room until it has time to firm up. Here, I'll just lean it up against the blank wall." Gripping it by the upper back stretcher, she walked it out of harm's way.

When she turned around, he stood close with his arms open. "Compliance is so much easier, isn't it?"

She dodged his arms and busied herself with paint rags and the solvent without acknowledging his comment. "It will take quite a bit of study to shift toward a Monet pastiche. That's no small task."

"I have complete faith in your abilities, my love." He stood with arms folded over his chest, and his grin showed pride in a proprietary manner.

"May I use your laptop for research? It would help to see as many of Monet's works as possible, and then download photos of several similar ones to come up with the ideas for a new creation." She stared out the window, her chin in one hand with the forefinger absent-mindedly tapping. "Or I could use my own computer, if you'd rather I stay out of yours." She added this last with a one-shoulder shrug as if it didn't matter to her.

But his eyebrows rose, and he lost the grin. "Yours, but in my attendance."

"Fine. I'll use my new one. It's so much faster. Just tap in the Wi-Fi code, and I'll get started."

"Let's have lunch first."

He led her downstairs to the patio, her brief opportunity for unfiltered sunlight and fresh air. She inhaled deeply and rested her eyes on the looming Alps. Matilda brought platters of cut fruits and cheeses, shallow crystal bowls of various pickles, and a basket of fresh rolls.

Kendra had learned to keep her hands in her lap when not actively doing something with them. Otherwise, Alex considered them available. An inner scream traveled through her innards when he touched her. Right now, she concentrated on appearing calm while the wheels of her mind whirled on leaving him and his castle far behind.

She bowed her head in prayer for God to rescue her. Surely Richard was pushing Interpol to search for her. She thought a special connection had developed with him, though he'd backed off after the first kiss.

She sighed, realizing how much her mind wandered toward him when her intention was to offer thanks for the food. Opening her eyes, she caught a smirk on Alex's face.

"A charming little habit you have, dear Kendra, praying before eating." Then he reached for his white wine, one eyebrow arched. "But don't you think you should thank me? It is I who provide your food, your studio, and the chance to make a fortune painting."

His ego stretched as wide and high as the Alps in the distance. She'd better pander to his conceit.

"I do thank you, Alex." She speared a juicy slice of mango, probably imported from South America. "But you've made me a prisoner in your elegant castle. I'm not a friend you've invited as a guest. You have yet to allow me to walk outside."

His eyes squinted black ice. "I must be able to trust you first."

"What's not to trust? Haven't I done everything you requested? And now I want to begin study on your next request." She tore off a bite of a multigrain roll and placed on it a piece of Swiss, redolent with the aroma of nuts. "I want to know your intentions. Do you have a list of chores for me, after which you'll discard me like day-old bread?"

"I have no desire to discard you. Not now, not ever. It's my fondest hope that you will choose to work with me. Together we can make millions." He covered her hand with his despite the food she held.

"Then why didn't you simply propose that instead of bringing me here under anesthetic?" She glared at him, and her voice dripped with anger.

"I'm sorry about that, but I had to stop your evaluation of the art found in the cave. Besides, you have plans to leave Saturday. Kendra, you must not go. There's nothing for you in Texas like what I can give you in Austria—all of Europe, for that matter."

"I *had* plans to leave Saturday, and Dr. Reed still must return to teach at Emory. But the Kimbell has granted me a sabbatical. No one is expecting me back in Texas except my father and Aunt Marilyn. By your leave, I could fly over for a few days to take care of him and be back next week."

First his eyes went wide, then he relaxed against his chair. "I don't think so. Not yet."

"See? You're still treating me like your slave." She spit the words out. "My rooms are locked day and night, despite my claustrophobia." The word rolled off her tongue as if it were true.

"Claustrophobia? Since when?"

She sipped her iced sparking water, buying time. "It's developed since I was a child. I was badly burned when my bedroom gas heater caused a fire. I don't have severe claustrophobia, but when I'm closed in, I have an irrational fear that a fire will start and I won't be able to escape."

"I had no idea."

Did he believe her? She couldn't tell by his wrinkled brow.

"You've installed cameras in my rooms, and an armed guard stands in the hallway. Bars keep me from even leaning out the windows to feel a breeze. Is it really necessary to lock my doors, too?"

He watched her every move as she tried to control her

emotions and continue eating. Sensing she might be getting somewhere in this plea, she persisted. "And that man in the hall. He's there all night. I can hear him every time he walks or coughs. You don't know how afraid of him I am." She shivered.

Feeling tears come to her eyes, she raised her head to make sure he saw them. "Alex, I can't stand him."

"But you know I will never allow him to hurt you."

"That's not good enough. I want him gone."

She pushed back her chair and fled inside.

The guard stepped out of the kitchen and blocked her path. Alex, following her, had to have seen him grab her. He barked a command in German, and the man dropped his iron-hard arms. She ran up the two long flights of stairs making crying sounds, entered her studio, and slammed the door.

Alex knocked a moment later and entered. "Let's talk, Kendra. I didn't understand how you felt … about any of this."

She went to the window, hiding her face and rubbing her eyes to increase their redness. What a drama queen she was becoming.

"Don't cry, Kendra. Believe me, he'll never touch you again. I'll have someone else take his post … just to protect you, of course. As for the computer, I must use my own. So much to do this week. But I can bring it here and work on it while you research Monet with your laptop." He cleared the paint rags off her work table. "I'll type in the Wi-Fi code, and we'll sit side by side. Does that suit you?"

She turned around and sniffed again. "Yes, that will be fine."

Chapter 30

"Dr. Reed! I have something for you."

Richard's head snapped up when Hahn, the geek, spoke with excitement. That just didn't usually happen. "What is it?" He stood and crossed the distance between them in three strides.

"Miss Cooper's computer is on. I got her e-mail address and password from when she used your computer to download her master's dissertation. Then later, since she sent you files from her new computer, I captured that IP address. With this information, I set up an alarm for any time she might log on. The bell just rang. Her computer is online right now."

Richard's pulse raced as if he were running an obstacle course. "Can you see what she's looking at? Or what she's sending?"

"If we assume she's the person on her computer … She's connected to a museum website, on a Monet page."

"Yes!" Richard did a fist pump. "Monet is her favorite artist. Can we make contact with her?"

Hahn looked up, wearing a frown. "I can send her an email, but that might be risky. First, we don't for sure know it is she. Remember, her computer has been in the hands of whoever cleaned out her hotel room. And second, she may be watched."

"Can you track the Wi-Fi she's linked through?"

"Let me try … working with the DHCP," Hahn muttered.

"The what?"

"Dynamic host control protocol." If the monitor could absorb his brain, Hahn must be close to passing through it about now. "First I need to find the domain name server …You see, the IP is made up of four octets separated by periods, and there are sixty-five thousand, five hundred thirty-five possible combinations on the entire Internet. If she were to send a message from her email, I could ping on the port for email …"

Richard considered himself functionally capable of using a computer and other data-generating devices, but the techno-babble went over his head. "Do what you can."

"She doesn't have the laptop locator selected. If she would just take a picture on her cell phone and send it to us, we could find her. That is, if her phone settings allowed that info to travel with the photo. Do you happen to know if she has something like 'Find my Phone' downloaded and activated?"

"Haven't a clue." Truth was, he'd met this woman almost three weeks ago. In that span, she'd moved from suspected felon to honest student of art to art expert for Interpol. He'd been with her every day, some days all day long. He'd introduced her to his parents. In this short time, she'd made him glad he never married Taylor. So soon after feeling wounded and numb, he was still rejoicing to be single when they met.

He well remembered the night he prayed for God's direction, sensing that his engagement led him down a torturous path with a difficult, self-centered, but knock-down gorgeous woman. He had to endure her tears, his father's stern reprimand, and her parents' ostracizing social maneuvers. This last had everything to do with his decision to leave the country for the summer. And that led to Kendra. Looking back, he could laugh at the link of events … if he only had Kendra here, safe.

෨∾ඇ

Kendra surveyed the lifetime works of Claude Monet as represented on many museum web sites and other sites dedicated to the history and appreciation of his paintings. She loved them all …Well, not so much the haystack series.

How did he do the shimmering water and sky? She tried to imagine looking through the paintings to see how he'd started the background and how many layers he patiently dotted on the way to the foreground.

"Are you about finished?" Alex's motions had grown more restless. She counted on his becoming bored and running out of things to do on his computer. If he would just leave her alone for one moment. Go to the bathroom or step out in the hall to speak to the guard. Anything.

She tried to look surprised. "No, I'm just getting to the good stuff. Now I need to print up some articles on his technique. Can I print from here?"

"I think so. I've never tried. But if you've got a strong enough Wi-Fi signal, it ought to work."

"Okay. There's paper in the printer? This dissertation is rather long."

But he didn't offer to get it from the office. "I have important things to do today. I can't stay here all afternoon. You'll have to shut down for now."

She pouted. "If we're going to work together, you'll have to trust me. This dog leash you have on my neck is choking the life out of me."

He stood and pulled her up against his body, his arms drifting below her waist in back. He nuzzled her ear, moving aside her long hair. "Come to my room tonight. We'll talk about our partnership."

Pushing firmly against him, she wriggled away. "You're

married, remember? That dog won't hunt."

He laughed so hard he had difficulty breathing. "I love your Texas expressions. That's one for the books."

"But you clearly understand it, don't you? I'm not your 'love' or your 'dear.' We may have a working partnership, but we will never have an affair."

He lifted a tendril of hair that had fallen forward on her shoulder. "We'll see. 'Never' is a long time."

He removed the Wi-Fi password from her computer and strode from the room.

She'd never seen anything but asterisks and didn't even know how many digits made it up. Nevertheless, she poked around and tried any idea that came to mind.

Please, God, give me a link for just a few seconds.

"It's gone. Her computer's offline." Hahn slumped. "That IP address never sent an email, so we don't know for sure if it is she. Like, even then it could be someone else using her email account."

Richard rubbed his face with both hands. He had to think. "Okay, let's go back to his cell phone number. What do we know so far?"

"It was registered in Amsterdam, and it belongs to Alexander Holt. Wait. He's using it again." Hahn lurched for the land line phone and punched three digits. "Track that number I gave you. It's on now." His demand didn't slow down for niceties.

During the next couple of hours Holt's phone connected several times, and each time the Interpol trackers inched through the networks of two countries. Finally they knew the call originated in Austria but not in the city of Vienna.

When Klaas breezed through to check on their progress, Richard argued for launching a strike on Holt's castle.

"We don't have solid evidence that Holt kidnapped her. We have *no* evidence she's in his family residence. For all the wizardry Hahn has pulled off, we'd still have to have a search warrant to enter and find her, and that has to come from the jurisdiction of the residence, not Vienna."

"But ..." Richard sputtered out, the nerve-jangling frustration getting the best of him. He couldn't argue that he knew she was there because he'd seen her in his dream, calling to him from a green mountain.

"We're working on it. Don't worry. If she's researching Monet, she's still okay."

"I'm going for a walk. I've got to get out of here for a few minutes. I can't ..." He scratched his head, knowing his curly hair looked terrible and had grown much too long. "I can't think anymore. I need some air."

He prayed in circles as he walked. *Please, God, keep her safe. Lead us to her.* He turned a corner and chanted more prayer phrases in his mind. In the States, cops resolved situations like this in fifty-five minutes including commercials. Why was it taking so long?

He had to be on the plane home on Saturday, but he couldn't leave until Interpol found her. An assistant professor who didn't show up for the semester would lose this job and no other decent college would touch him.

He had to go.

He couldn't go.

Exhaustion fell over Kendra like a heavy blanket. She didn't know anything else to try. The scripture said God was strong in her weakness. Well, she'd never been so weak before. This would be a good time for him to kick in.

She wandered to her bedroom awash in despair. Holt wanted full control of her. Foolishly, she thought she could manipulate the master manipulator. He'd made it clear he intended to dominate her sexually as well, and that nauseated her.

Was that an idea she could use? Pretend to be sick, have him call a doctor or take her to one. All educated Europeans spoke English. She could tell the doctor she was being held against her will. Did she have the courage to actually make herself sick?

She collapsed on her knees near the window, looking up toward the Alps. *From whence does my help come? Please, God, save me.*

The tap on Kendra's door came gently. She sensed it wasn't Holt. The lock rattled and Matilda entered.

Kendra stirred from her silent pleading and wiped tears on her sleeve.

Matilda gave her a look of sympathy as she put laundered clothes in the wardrobe. Then she went toward the bathroom with a clean towel.

Kendra thought she made a head motion, as if encouraging her to follow. With hesitating step, she did.

The pretty young maid said nothing, but reached her arm high when she adjusted the shower curtain, allowing her long sleeve to fall back.

Kendra gasped to see Matilda's blue arm. The maid gave her a nod, the cloud of gravity in her eyes.

Was she showing brutality by Holt? Kendra gently took her arm in both hands and said one of the few German phrases she knew, *"Es tut mir leid,"* which she'd been told roughly translated to "I'm sorry."

With sudden inspiration, Kendra put her hand to her ear in the universal telephone signal.

Matilda's eyes opened wide, and her mouth dropped.

Then Kendra acted out holding a cell phone in one hand and tapping numbers with the other.

The maid shook her head slowly, fear written in every line.

Kendra folded her hands in pleading. Then she pointed away from the room and whispered, "Phone, Herr Holt." It would do little good to be given her own phone without a connection to the outside world.

Matilda pushed her aside and rushed from the bathroom and out the door. A moment later someone locked Kendra in.

The moment of sisterhood with another abused woman had passed. She'd missed her chance.

She gathered her courage and knocked on the door.

A much smaller man in khaki uniform called out to her in German, then unlocked the door and cracked it open. After looking up and down, seeing only her showing her empty hands, he widened the gap.

He asked a question which she didn't understand. "Herr Holt," she replied.

The guard nodded, locked the door again, and left.

Ten or fifteen minutes passed as Kendra paced and prayed. Footsteps approached in the hall, stopped at her door, and Alex unlocked and entered. "I'm very busy. What do you want?"

"I want to call my father. It's morning in the US. Please let me at least hear his voice."

Alex's stormy glare pierced her. He huffed.

"I'm his only child. And what if he dies, and I've never even called him?"

"That won't happen. Your aunt said he would recover."

"What did you expect her to say? Please, just a one-minute call."

"All right. Come to my office." He spoke to the guard, who followed them. Then Holt motioned him to wait outside. "Give me the number," Holt snapped.

"It's on my cell. I don't have it memorized. I gave the numbers to you, remember? Would you prefer that I use my own phone?"

He swore. "I didn't keep that scrap of paper after you called from my phone." Fuming, he stirred papers on his desk. "There's no service out here without the modem connection, and I'm not giving you that password." As he handed her his cell, it rang, and she gave it back.

He checked the ID. "I've got to take this." First he greeted the caller, then excused himself and tossed her phone to her. "Get the number. Wait outside." He shoved a pen and paper at her and motioned her toward the door.

She turned on her phone, which took an agonizing length of time to come up. Then she wrote down the numbers for her father and Aunt Marilyn. With a sudden leap of hope, she touched Richard's number, but of course the call didn't go through. With an exasperated sigh and a shrug, she motioned to the guard.

He nodded and put out his hand, and she gave him her cell. With all the commands in English, he couldn't navigate it. She crowded next to him and navigated to its settings. The guard then touched in the password, "alpenheim," and returned it with a smile.

"*Danke*," she said, slipping a finger over the silent button. She stepped near the door in order to hear Alex's footsteps should he approach. Trying to act calm, she controlled the tremble of her fingers to bring up the camera, snap a photo of her face and send it to Richard.

Alex's steps strode to the door. Punching and holding the key hard, she turned the phone off completely. When he opened the door, she held up her notes. "Got the numbers."

ᔯᣆᣇ

Hahn burst into the room where Richard discussed possibilities with Van Der Veen. He waved a piece of paper. "We've got it!" The glee on his face lit the working space. "We have the coordinates for Alexander Holt's cell phone, and it's about ninety kilometers southwest of here. And that's where his family's country home is located."

Richard jumped off his chair, his heart pounding with pure hope. "Let's go get her."

Klaas stood also, but his mouth clamped down and eyes squinted. He took the paper from Hahn. "Okay, we know where Holt is. But we don't know Kendra is there, and still don't have proof he kidnapped her."

Richard's helium balloon slipped from his fingers. He wanted to hop in a car now and blaze a trail toward the Alps to rescue Kendra. He didn't care about proper police procedure.

"Be calm. We're getting close," said Klaas. "If we go politely knocking on his door now, it only tips him off."

The ding of a clear bell sounded from Richard's pocket, and he lifted his phone. "Kendra! It's from … I've got a message … A photo of … It's her!"

Hahn sprang from his computer. "Give it to me." Within five minutes, he had the exact location from which the photo had been sent. "It's Holt's castle. She's there."

Klaas sprang into action, punching numbers on the department line. "Now we get the search warrant."

Chapter 31

Kendra fought to remain calm as Alex poured white wine into her glass.

"I think you'll enjoy this," he said. "It's light, crisp, with just a touch of fruit."

She lifted the cool liquid to her lips, hoping it would relax the trembling of her hands. Its taste, drier than she cared for, perked up her tongue. "Thank you for letting me call Dad."

He huffed a breath. "You knew he would be fine."

She'd learned already that even the slightest disagreement might ignite his anger, so she didn't protest. "Yes, he does have good care. I just needed for him to know I was thinking of him."

He sliced a cherry tomato in halves with a serrated knife and speared a piece on his fork. "Your cell doesn't show a history of calls to your father. You'd only called him twice since being in Europe this summer."

She savored the creamy blue cheese dressing on her salad while stalling. "Voice calls from Europe to Texas are expensive. I kept costs down."

"Did you e-mail him?"

He'd had her computer and probably knew the answer. "My relationship with my father is … difficult. He doesn't respect my career choice."

He gave a sardonic, one-sided grin she'd never seen before. "You defied him?"

"He didn't say I couldn't study art, but he wouldn't pay for it. His choice, nursing, held no interest for me."

Matilda took away their salad plates and brought small grilled steaks with asparagus. Her eyes avoided Kendra's ... and Alex's as well.

"I'm surprised you want to fly to his side now. What has he done for you lately?"

Kendra took a moment to slice into her steak then took a bite, chewing thoughtfully. "He's my father." She shrugged. "I love him. I want to be there to help him." And she did. Despite the tension between them, he was the father God gave her. The only family she had, and she expected that someday they would be closer.

"And you're the only child?"

"I had a brother, but he died as a teenager."

He questioned her about that, and she outlined the facts. She would never tell him the secret she shared with Richard, though. He'd twist it like a knife into her back. She tried to turn the tables and learn more about Alex, but he shut her out.

Both guards stepped onto the patio, alarm on their faces. They said something with a word sounding like "police" and the German word for "four."

Alex bounded up, shouting a command. The big guard she feared so much jerked her out of the chair and dragged her into the kitchen. From there he hauled her past the servants, barking commands to Matilda and Inge. The large woman opened a door to steps leading down into the dark.

No amount of screaming and twisting allowed her to escape. After pulling her onto the stairwell and closing the door, he stuffed a handkerchief in her mouth and held her backwards against his body, one hand keeping the gag in place. She thought surely she would either suffocate or vomit against the muzzle and die. Helpless tears stung her eyes. *Please, God, don't let it end like this.*

ლოიდ

Richard wore a bullet-proof shield and a radio, but wasn't allowed to come to the door with Klaas and the Interpol police force. He had no gun with him. Klaas may have been afraid he'd shoot Holt on sight. Standing by the car, he thought he heard a loud, high-pitched noise, but it stopped. The country place probably had goats, maybe chickens.

Exasperated, he watched some of the men go inside and others circle the castle right and left. Fifteen minutes went by while Klaas and the others spoke brief messages back and forth by radio. Richard wandered away from the car, ambling around the right corner of the castle. Behind stood several buildings of various sizes, some with aged stone walls. What if Kendra had been kept out there?

He radioed Klaas, but was told their search warrant was limited to the main building unless they were given a very specific reason to search the out-buildings. Daring himself to keep walking, he cleared the side of the home and saw the back patio with its wide, striped canvas top. One table there had two chairs. He came closer. On the table were two dinner plates, napkins, and glasses. Food on the plate indicated dinner had been interrupted. He radioed Klaas.

"Where are you, Richard? I told you to stay in the car."

"I'm just walking around outside. I'm not in the house."

"Our men already saw the table. Alex said he'd invited one of the armed guards to dine with him. We aren't buying it."

A minute passed before Klaas spoke again. "There's a bedroom on the second floor—third the way you count it—connected to an artist's setup. One of the team will come down and bring you up. See if you can identify any of the clothing."

He ran ahead of the guide, taking the old stairway at jogging speed. Klaas met him at the bedroom, where he found Kendra's denim bag. In the studio the old computer gaped with its lid up. "She's here. There's no doubt."

Klaas and Richard descended, leaving police to poke into every wardrobe and bathroom and open every door. They found Mr. Holt under guard in the ground floor sitting room. "Handcuff him." Holt stood from his comfortable parlor chair, but the officer pulled his arms behind him and cuffed and searched him despite his protests.

"Let me explain. Ms. Cooper has been here, but she's off for the day in one of the villages. I don't know which one. I loaned her my car, gave her a stack of bills, and told her to have fun. I have too much business to attend to here and couldn't go with her."

"She was dining with you until we arrived." Van Der Veen's voice drilled the air with accusation. "Your steaks were still warm. Her DNA on the utensils will prove her identity, so your lies are needless."

Holt gave a sly grin. "The lady is a guest in my home. She came at my invitation. A gentleman is expected to lie in a situation like this, isn't he?"

Richard's blood boiled at the insinuation that Kendra had a willing relationship going with this slime ball. "I saw a man grab her off the sidewalk and push her into the car. It was not a polite invitation."

"What you saw was an arranged meeting. My bodyguard and the woman who manages this home met Ms. Cooper at an appointed time and place. I repeat, she is my guest."

Van Der Veen shot a look at Richard, brows raised.

"He's lying. I left her in front of the Shönebrunn Palace because her new shoes were uncomfortable after the tour. If she's off on a shopping trip, we'll wait until her return."

"Did she take her cell with her?" Van Der Veen kept a more controlled tone in his question.

Holt's eyes darted about. "Actually, no, it seems she left it. By accident, I'm sure." He maintained as smooth a presentation as possible, considering his cuffed hands behind him.

"Then may we see it?"

"I believe it's in my office. Shall we go up?"

Instead, Van Der Veen radioed for one of the team to bring it down. "He says it's white, on the edge of his desk."

When it arrived, Richard accepted it and quickly found the photo she sent, noting that it was connected to a modem. He didn't give that away, but gave Klaas a nod. "She's here. We have to keep hunting."

Leaving a guard with Holt, Klaas motioned Richard into the hallway to put their heads together. "These old manors have hidden passages and fortified rooms. The team could search all day without finding a door. But there was almost always a way for the lady of the house to get to the kitchen without being seen by guests, or for servants to go to her room. Let's interview the woman he said assisted in the pickup of his guest."

They made their way to the scullery area, picking up a couple of officers along the way.

Finding a stout and strongly built woman, a young, attractive one, and an elderly man there, Van Der Veen began his questions with the woman, who gave her name as Inge. She seemed to be in charge.

As the interview proceeded in German, Richard poked around the area. The bakery and an entire room with glassed cabinets on all sides up to the ceiling boasted every type of cooking utensil, crockery, and china. The shelves resisted his attempts to move them, however. Returning to the kitchen, he observed how the young woman fidgeted. Her white face framed her dark eyes, which darted about the galley. Then she looked directly at him and back to a rack stacked with pans. Twice. Was this a signal? Her eyebrows raised and lips puckered toward the rack. He'd heard of people pointing with their lips. Was that her intent?

He meandered toward that wall and found a thin wood facing around the shelf. Scratched on the floor was the curved sign of a swinging door and the slightest bit of dust, unlike the rest of the spotless facility. "Klaas, I've found it." He gripped the rack and pulled. It moved, but not easily.

An officer pulled with him, and a door opened to a dark passageway. Flipping on a strong flashlight, the officer preceded him into the musty brick corridor. Richard took a deep breath and dashed behind him. The sound of feet scraping against brick came from deeper into the darkness. Then a sudden *ooof* and scuffling.

The officer jogged forward, causing the light to bounce. They turned a sharp corner, revealing Kendra on a stairway, mouth bound in silver duct tape, and a man in khaki uniform scrambling a few steps below her.

"Mm-mm-mm-mm!" She nodded to the man, who pulled up a gun.

The officer spoke in heavy warning tones. The posture of the man in khaki faltered, then he lowered the gun and allowed the officer to take it. A stream of German passed between them, but Richard paid no attention.

Kendra ran to him and fell into his arms. All his fears melted as he held her. Then she backed up and turned around, showing him that her hands were also bound in tape. The officer, having cuffed the guard, unfolded a knife and cut her loose.

As gently as possible, Richard removed the tape from her

mouth.

"Ouch. It's pulling the skin." He'd barely loosened it when her muffled words escaped.

"I'm sorry. Do you want to rip it off?"

"Let me just work it a bit at the time." When she'd balled up the tape, she ran a hand over her reddened face. "My lips hurt." She looked up to him as if he could make them better.

"Let me kiss them well." He bent, placing his lips as lightly as possible on hers.

They followed the officer and guard back to the kitchen, until she paused at the open door and turned to him. "Thank you, Richard. Thank you for coming for me."

Her open arms invited his embrace, and he held her for a long, delicious moment before stepping into the light.

Kendra dashed to her rooms and threw everything into her two suitcases with Matilda's help, under the watch of an Interpol policeman.

"Do you speak English?" she asked the officer.

"A bit."

"Please translate something for me."

Kendra turned to the young maid. "Richard told me how you showed him the door in the kitchen. Thank you so much."

He translated the words, and then she added, "Please tell the Interpol police everything, especially about Holt's cruelty to you." She raised the sleeve of Matilda's blouse and showed the officer. "I will speak on your behalf."

With tears forming in her eyes, Matilda nodded.

As the officer left with her bags, Kendra hugged Matilda goodbye. "*Danke.*"

Entering the Interpol car's back seat with Richard at her

side, she looked back at the estate. "I never even toured the place. You've seen more of it than I have. But I don't want to come back."

Van Der Veen took the right front seat with an Interpol policeman driving. "Please go with us to Interpol headquarters. We need to debrief you immediately."

"Oh. I neglected to thank all those men ..." She twisted to look behind and saw the handcuffed Holt inserted into a police car. The two guards and Inge, also handcuffed, headed toward other cars.

"You don't have to. Saving fair ladies is part of the job."

She leaned forward to speak as the car entered the country road. "Mr. Van Der Veen, how was Holt able to track my movements from city to city? We were so careful to check for bugs."

"Your phone gave you away. You should check all your settings."

"But doesn't that require rather sophisticated equipment?"

Mr. Van Der Veen harrumphed and uttered something under his breath. "Unfortunately, Holt had bought access to police equipment. Several heads will roll in the police force."

"How about Werner? Was he connected to the frauds from the cave?"

"There are no charges against Detective Werner at this time, though he may have been influenced. I will say no more during the investigation, except that the crate and muslin samples you two collected test to be of this decade. Good detective work for people who are not detectives." He smiled in that way of his that never erased trouble from the lines of his face.

During the hour and a half return to Vienna, she never let go of Richard's hand. He had not been alone in saving her from the clutches of Alexander Holt, but she'd employed thoughts of him to chase away her fears of Holt's advances. After the hours when her skin crawled with repulsion for Holt's attempts to "reason" with her, she passed her time alone conjuring up images of Richard. Memories of his kindness and gentlemanly manners warmed her, and she dreamed of resting in his arms.

"I have to leave tomorrow." His brow gathered rows of stress lines. "My job and reputation will be shot if I don't start classes on time."

"I understand. And I really must go to be with my father for a few days. After that, I'm not sure ..." She had a temporary contract with Interpol, but right now, she just wanted to be safe, at home, and see her dad.

"Do you want to come back and keep working with Interpol?"

She tipped her head toward Van Der Veen in the front seat. "We'll talk. It was exciting, and I felt we made a valuable contribution to the art world, but I'm not sure if I want a career in stopping forgers." As they left the foothills of the Alps, the road straightened and became smoother. "But I have thought about getting a doctorate," she added with a bright smile. "I could do my thesis on methods of fraud detection. A doctorate would open a lot of doors, even university teaching. Don't you think?"

"I do. Anything is possible."

Chapter 32

Richard waited for Kendra through hours of debriefing. Finally she was allowed to leave. "Would you like to go to dinner at a certain fine restaurant my parents visit on every trip to Vienna? It's my last evening in town, and I'd like to spend it with you."

"I'm so sorry I missed our dinner and symphony evening with your parents and their friends."

"They had to go back. Dad couldn't help here, and he had a board meeting to attend in the US. But there will be other times ..."

"Do you think?" Her gentle smile and raised eyebrows caused him to consider exciting possibilities.

"I'm sure, if you're willing."

The elevator in the police building was always busy at this time of day, so they entered the stairwell. Taking advantage of the privacy, he stopped and held her close on the landing. "I told my parents we had become 'special friends,' and I intended to continue seeing you. We did something very unusual Saturday night, up in their guestroom. We prayed together for your safety."

She smiled up at him. "I'm glad to hear it. I prayed the same prayer."

He hadn't been allowed into Kendra's debriefing room. So much he didn't know yet. "Holt didn't ... hurt you?"

"No. He made a lot of advances and suggestions of how

we could have a long and prosperous relationship, but I kept him at a distance most of the time. If Interpol—and you—hadn't come when you did, though, I don't know what would have happened." She shivered and stepped back into his embrace.

When she lifted her face to his, he kissed her with a promise to himself to carefully explore this new relationship. If they could transition from here into the real world, which he defined for now as living and working in the States, he had most likely found the woman who would be his partner for life.

An Interpol armed officer drove them through the late afternoon traffic to their hotel while they clasped hands in the back seat. Kendra would check in for one more night in Vienna.

"Mr. Van Der Veen is arranging my tickets to Texas tomorrow, then I'll probably return for a month or so. It depends on so much which is all beyond my control." She leaned against him as the driver took a sharp corner. "Is the restaurant quiet, sort of private?"

"Of course. I'll ask for a table out of the way." A tip to the right person would suffice.

"I'm going to miss you," she murmured. "We've worked together so closely."

He brushed her forehead with a kiss. "Those days I tried to evaluate the paintings when you'd been kidnapped … They were awful. I've never felt so alone." He would return to Atlanta tomorrow. A world without Kendra. "Perhaps you could visit me. You could stay with my parents," he quickly added. She had to agree to keep the relationship growing.

"Or you could come to Texas. The Kimbell is a fantastic museum, and we have others as well. The Modern is just a few steps away. Then there's the Amon Carter, and a very small private western art museum in the middle of downtown, the Sid

Richardson—"

"Or I might just come to see you. Meet your father. Tell him I'm interested in his daughter."

Her cheeks flushed pink, and he felt a slight tremble in her hand.

The driver pulled up in front of the hotel and assisted with her bags. She checked in, and Richard escorted her to her new room. "See you at seven. We'll get there ahead of the crowd."

He stepped inside to kiss her, careful not to provide a scene if anyone should pass by. He found it excruciatingly difficult to turn and leave.

৩৵৵

Kendra took her eyes off Richard long enough to appreciate her elegant surroundings. Just as Richard had promised, they had a private table. In a nook, actually, with gossamer fabric pulled to each side. She sighed again, exhaling the terror of the previous days.

After a delightful dinner—scallops for her and steak for him—he took her hand. "Is a month long enough to know if you're in love with someone?"

A thrill traveled down her middle. "It's at least enough to know if you want to pursue a relationship." She toyed with her glass. "But Richard, we're from such different socio-economic levels. Would your family ever accept me?" She felt heat rise to her face. She'd overstepped the direction of his question.

"I've moved into an apartment near the campus, you know. I don't play the high society game. In some ways, it's similar to your self-determination in choosing an education and career in arts. People are no longer obligated to remain in the family business."

She laughed. "Right. I can just see me in coveralls under someone's sink."

He smiled, crinkling his eyes. "I've been with you in several social situations, and you have sophistication which will serve you well in all social circles."

Despite living in distant cities, she wanted to hold onto this man and never let go. Wisdom told her, though, they should move with caution.

His hand trembled as much as hers. He captured both of her hands and gave a gentle squeeze. "At least tell me you feel as I do, that we might have found that perfect choice for the rest of our lives. That when we part tomorrow, it will only be temporary."

She looked into his clear blue eyes from mere inches away. "You're everything I hoped for and more than I dared to dream about. I'd come to believe that any man who met all my qualifications would be too good for me."

He chuckled, and then after glancing about, gave her a little kiss. "We'll have to work on your self-confidence factor. You're an amazing woman. You'll give me a lot to live up to."

Early the following morning, he stole a few private moments with Kendra in the executive lounge at the airport before walking her to her flight to Dallas/Fort Worth. "I *will* come to see you, whether in Texas or Europe. We'll stay in touch and make plans."

He hoped it would be in Texas, because a jet-lagged weekend in Europe amounted to lots of flight time for a precious few minutes together.

Drinking in her hazel eyes, touching her smooth skin once more, he ached at their parting in a way he'd never experienced before. "Call me when you get home. I'll land in Atlanta an hour after you land in Texas." He hugged her close once more. When she walked to the check-in line, the loss left him feeling like an empty shell. The woman who had become his friend, his partner, took her heart with him.

ঔ৹৻ঽ

Dry heat hit Kendra as she flagged down the airport shuttle. The Texas August oven drew the moisture out of her skin. She'd left her car at the shuttle parking in downtown Fort Worth, and drove from there straight to her dad's house. The home in which she'd grown up.

Within an hour she pulled into the driveway and let herself in with a key. "Dad? I'm home."

The TV played a daytime game show back in the den. She followed the noise, calling out so she wouldn't startle him. That wouldn't do, especially since he kept a handgun and hunting rifles.

"Come here, girl." He muted the TV and reached out to her without rising from his easy chair. "How's my sweetie?"

The surprise was all hers. He hadn't called her that since she was a small child.

She hugged her dad. "How are you doing, Dad?"

"I reckon I'll be okay. Doctor said I can go back to the office in another week, but I have to do therapy." A cloud passed over his jovial expression. "So what's this I hear about you being kidnapped?"

"That's right. But Interpol got right on the case and had me back in a few days." It seemed like an eternity when she didn't know if they would ever find her, or if she'd live through the experience. So much had happened in so little time. The long flight and arriving here the same morning she'd left

Vienna had her head in a fog. Her body clock said it was night.

"Is Aunt Marilyn here?"

"She had some ladies' meeting to go to at her church, but she cooked before she left. You want some chicken?"

She really, seriously didn't want any of her aunt's greasy fried chicken. "Thanks, but I ate a little on the plane. Maybe later."

"Sit down and tell me what you've been doing over there. I thought you said you were just going to Holland to paint some pictures."

"That's the truth, Dad, but the craziest thing happened." She gave him the condensed version of the past three and a half weeks. "So now I'm on a sabbatical from the Kimbell and have a contract with Interpol as an Art Expert to help them identify the fakes. They want me to come back for a little while to wrap up this case, and then I'll come home."

"An Art Expert for Interpol? Well, I'll be golly. Who'da ever thunk it?" Laughing, he tapped his fist to her arm. "I guess this art thing is gonna lead to a good job after all."

She held her tongue, not mentioning she'd been supporting herself working at the Kimbell for three years already.

"Yes, and I'm thinking about using art fraud as a subject for a doctoral thesis." Alexander Holt had been charged with multiple crimes, including kidnapping. She'd need to return for his trial in a year or so, but he'd be locked up tight for a long time. Meanwhile, she'd have an inside track on the investigation of art fraud which could lead to a PhD and an unusual toe-hold in her career.

"Aw, honey, do you have to go back to school?"

"I don't have to. I want to. This is what I do, Dad, and I'm good at it."

"I never doubted that."

He'd always doubted that, but she wouldn't argue. "And I think I've found myself a feller, Dr. Richard Reed."

"A doctor?" His smile lit up.

"PhD, Dad, assistant professor of art at Emory University in Atlanta."

His delight dimmed about seventy-five watts. "Well, if that's what you're gonna be doing …"

"It is, and I'm very happy doing it." Where had she gotten such determination? It seemed as if she were re-introducing herself to her father. "We'll invite him for a visit some time when everything settles down a bit. When I'm back for good and you're strong and working again."

Her father seemed a bit dazed by all this as if he had an overload of things to ponder. "I was kinda hoping …"

"That I'd marry a plumber? Not in this lifetime. But don't worry. You'll find someone to pass your business on to."

ം❧ം

Almost a year later, Richard stood at the front of a Texas church looking into those same hazel eyes. Nearly as tall as her stocky father, she floated down the aisle like an angel in candlelight silk and lace. His mother, quietly dabbing her tears on the front row, had helped her choose the dress.

The two months Kendra had spent in Europe before returning to the Kimbell and beginning her doctorate collapsed into this moment. She'd refused to move to Atlanta until they were married, so their lives together began today. All the separation, the pre-nuptial counseling, the long what-if discussions came to this.

He took the hand of his bride and promised to care for her forever.

The pastor turned to her, and she spoke her vows from

memory, her lilting voice assuring him of her undying love. After the prayer and yet more music, she lifted her face to his kiss.

They turned to the overflowing congregation as the pastor rested a hand on each of their shoulders. "I'm pleased to present to you Dr. and Mrs. Reed."

The End

Acknowledgements

I am indebted to my husband Darrel, with whom I traveled to the European cities mentioned in this book and dozens more. I am able to write because of his generous support, which includes plot brainstorming and patient manuscript reading.

Enormous thanks go to my critique partners Autumn, Christy, and Ginger. Far past grammar and syntax, you saw into my characters and how they would move through their challenges.

Exploration of Amsterdam, Budapest, Vienna, and other bastions of fine art kindled the desire to share their flavor, their excitement, and their intrigue.

Writers write for their readers. I invite you to walk the cobblestone streets of Europe with me. May you find your own happily ever after.

Author Biography

Lee Carver, unable to fully retire to a quiet life in Fort Worth, sets her novels in a few of the forty-five countries she has experienced. When at home with her husband of forty-eight years, she volunteers as a Stephen Minister, alto in the choir, and pianist. She crochets with the Prayer Shawl Ministry and works with United Methodist Women and the local chapter of American Christian Fiction Writers, fondly known as "Ready Writers." This vast resource of common support and education is essential to the solitary effort of writing.

The Carvers have two adult children and five grandchildren.

Recent Publications by Lee Carver

The end of her disastrous marriage and her grandmother's illness bring high school teacher Ashley back to Shelter Creek. She reunites with an old acquaintance, now a roofer with resilience through the Texas heat and life's hard spots. To her surprise, the family guard-pig and an out-of-her-comfort-zone job teaching first grade put her on the path toward overcoming bitterness.

As a wife betrayed and dumped by her husband, she can either lock herself away from further hurt or forgive and start over. But is there a man alive who's worth the investment?

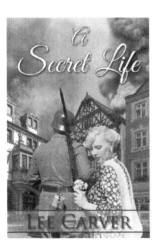

The German Army of World War II rips KARL VON STEUBEN from his family and privileged life, forcing him to conceal his American sympathies and Jewish heritage. Stripped of every tie to his home country, he determines to escape. As he crawls to the Siegfried Line, only he knows the hiding place of gold ingots melted from the jewelry of prisoners. Wounded after assuming the identity of a fallen American soldier, Karl briefly deceives even himself.

Discharged and shipped to America, he discovers God's unmerited favor in a beautiful Atlanta nurse. But he must return to Germany or relinquish his family fortune and rear children under the name of another man. Will Grace forgive his duplicity and accept him as an American?

Volunteering in Brazil to escape a broken heart, American RN Camille Ringold serves two weeks with missionaries in the Amazon jungle. She re-examines her life's direction as she confronts hijackers, malaria, and her attraction to a certain blue-eyed missionary pilot.

Pilot Luke Strong longs for a wife and family to share his life and mission. Suffering past rejections due to the rigors of life in the Amazon, he hardly dares to hope a short-term nurse with fear of flying could catch the dream and stay. Priorities change as experiences of faith mount. Where is the intersection of God's will and their personal desires?

Watch for *A Sweet Noel* novella set, to be published in November, 2016. Seven authors contribute inspirational romance novellas with a Christmas theme, including *A Cordial Christmas* by Lee Carver.

Made in the USA
Charleston, SC
16 November 2016